GUILTY SILENCE

FREYA BARKER

GUILTY SILENCE

Copyright © 2025 Freya Barker

All rights reserved.

No part of this publication may be reproduced, distributed, or transmitted in any form or by any means, including photocopying, recording, or by other electronic or mechanical methods, without the prior written permission of the author or publisher, except in the case of brief quotations embodied in used critical reviews and certain other non-commercial uses as permitted by copyright law. For permission requests, write to the author, mentioning in the subject line: "Reproduction Request" at the following address:

freyabarker.writes@gmail.com

This book is a work of fiction and any resemblance to any place, person or persons, living or dead, any event, occurrence, or incident is purely coincidental. The characters, places, and story lines are created and thought up from the author's imagination or are used fictitiously.

9781998529216

Cover Design: Freya Barker
Editing: Karen Hrdlicka
Proofing: Joanne Thompson

Bess Choi is proud of what she's accomplished. Owner of Strange Brew, a popular coffee shop in Silence, she's worked hard and has overcome many obstacles to build the life she has. It's a good life, one that includes work she loves, an apartment to call her own, and plenty of good friends.

But an unexpected phone call comes as a brutal reminder of a time she thought she'd left far behind. Suddenly, she's faced with the choice to turn her back on the beautiful life she created, or break her guilty silence.

Chief Deputy Hugo Alexander isn't sure when exactly he started seeing the quiet coffee shop owner as more than simply a good friend. It's hard to pinpoint the moment when she went from a supportive friend to him and his teenage son, to the woman who features in his dreams and fantasies.

Unfortunately, Bess Choi seems to have him firmly locked in the friend zone, and it's not until worrisome things start happening around her, she cautiously starts lowering the barriers.

But when he discovers she might be in far more danger than she's been willing to let on, he's done tiptoeing around.

CHAPTER 1

B*ess*

I BITE off a curse and immediately cover a second yawn with the back of my hand.

Another early morning after yet another sleepless night.

One of these days, one of my employees is going to come in and find me passed out on the kitchen floor. Unless Chance Tanek finds me first. He's the town drunk and I swear he watches this place, waiting to see the light go on in my apartment upstairs.

He is usually already at the back door by the time I make my way downstairs in the morning. I normally have a paper bag with the prior day's leftovers ready for him. He's such a lost soul, not a particularly friendly one, but I feel for him nonetheless. I figure there's no harm in giving him some day-old baked goods to soak up all the alcohol he consumed in the previous twenty-four hours. Plus, everyone deserves at least one friendly interaction a day. I'd like to think of it as doing a public service, although a couple of people in my circle of friends may not agree with me.

This morning, I was too tired to even spare him a basic greeting, almost tossing the paper bag at him before slamming the door shut and shuffling into the kitchen. This is getting ridiculous; I can count the hours of sleep I've managed to cobble together over the past week on one hand. I'm going to have to ask Dana if there is anything she can prescribe because this is not sustainable.

I have a business to run, bills and employees to pay, and I can't afford to fall down on the job, but that's exactly what I've been doing since that damn phone call last week.

So far this morning, I already overproofed my Chelsea buns, burned a batch of cookies, and now the apple streusel muffins I just pulled from the oven are collapsing. I can't seem to do anything right, and it's only a little after 6:00 a.m.

Something's got to give.

As I quickly slide the muffins back in the oven—hoping I can salvage the batch—I hear the back door open. Lola, my only full-time employee, pokes her head into the kitchen. She takes one look at the lackluster Chelsea buns, and the discarded tray with my cookies' charred remains before turning to me with a sympathetic look on her face.

"Let me put my stuff away and I'll come give you a hand."

I open my mouth to tell her not to bother—she shouldn't have to pick up my slack like she's been doing all week—but she's already disappeared down the hall. Letting my eyes drift around the kitchen, I do some damage assessment. At least the date squares and the bacon and cheese scones came out fine. The Chelsea buns will have to do, and hopefully the muffins will turn out, but I'll have to redo the cookies and should probably whip up a batch of lemon-poppyseed muffins as well, just in case.

Lola grabs an apron off the hook as she walks into the kitchen and ties it on.

"What's next?" she asks, and I swallow against the sudden flood of emotions.

Damn, who'd have thought when I took a chance on the rail-thin girl who answered the help-wanted sign in my window six years ago, she'd become the rock I lean on these days. As it turned out, hiring her was not only the best thing that could've happened to her, but me as well. She has become invaluable to me and Strange Brew.

Lola has shared only bits and pieces of her history with me over the years, but it was enough information for me to realize my own sordid past pales in comparison. The woman has a core of steel though, and has completely reinvented herself. The pretty, well-put-together woman in front of me is a far cry from the skinny kid who first walked in here.

"Lemon-poppyseed muffins and pecan chocolate-chip cookies."

"On it," she states, checking the wall for the recipes.

Every time I add a new item to our weekly rotation, I tack a laminated copy to our recipe wall. I don't have any secrets, at least not with respect to my baked goods.

"Why don't you take a break, go make yourself a coffee," Lola suggests, glancing at me over her shoulder. "You look like you could use it."

Ugh. I purposely avoided looking in the mirror this morning. I figured it wouldn't be an improvement on the pale, haggard reflection staring back at me last night. Guess I was right.

I don't bother arguing; I could use a boost of caffeine if I'm going to make it through today.

"Oh, and I'll take Carson under my wing when he gets here," she adds when I start out the door.

Shoot, Carson. I'd forgotten about him; the kid is supposed to start today.

I overheard him talking to his girlfriend, Tatum, when they dropped in after school last week. He'd been complaining he had a hard time finding an after-school job. It just so happened one of my weekend part-timers gave me two-weeks' notice a few days prior, and I hadn't started looking yet. I ended up offering him the job, provided his father approved. I'm sure working at the local coffee shop wasn't Carson's first choice, but the promise of free baked goods had been enough of an enticement for him to accept.

I'd all but forgotten he's supposed to start today.

"I need him to fill in a few forms for me first, but after that, yes. If he could shadow you for a bit during the rush, that would be great."

The rush is usually between seven—when we open—and nine. After that things slow down a bit until noon, when it picks up again for the lunch crowd. Our menu isn't big, since we're supposed to be a coffee shop and not a restaurant but, especially on the weekends, people have a tendency to pop in here for a quick bite while they run their errands. We offer sandwiches and a daily soup or stew during the winter months, but it's all pretty basic.

When I get here at around four in the morning, baking is the first thing I tackle. Usually by the time the doors open, most of the pastries are done, and I start prepping for lunch.

When I started, I was very ambitious and baked all my own breads as well, but that proved to be too labor intensive. I ended up ordering in from Crumbs, a local, artisan bakery with whom I was able to negotiate a great deal. It leaves me more time to spend on salads for the sandwiches and whatever special I am serving that day.

Then after lunch, I normally do my ordering and administration, and when I close the doors at five, I'm dead on my feet.

I haven't had much of a life since I opened Strange Brew eight years ago, working thirteen- or fourteen-hour days, but it has been a labor of love building this place into what it is now. At least these days, with Lola running things so I can take a day, sometimes two, off every week, I have some downtime.

Tomorrow is Sunday, my standard day off. Normally, I'd be looking forward to the break, but at the moment I'd rather be busy. Less time to think and worry.

I've barely booted up the computer in my office when I hear the back door fall shut. It sounds like Lola is intercepting whoever walked in, but a few moments later I hear footsteps coming down the hall.

"Hey."

Hugo Alexander, Carson's dad, pokes his head in the door.

"Hi."

I'm annoyed I sound breathless whenever I talk to him. It's ridiculous. Sure, the man looks more like a reincarnated Viking the older he gets, but I've known him forever, and he's not the only handsome man in town. He just appears to be the only one who affects my vocal cords. It's aggravating.

"Are you sure about this?" he asks, obviously referring to his offspring working here.

"Positive. He's a good kid, Hugo, he'll do fine."

He runs a hand through his unruly, straw-colored hair laced with a decent amount of silver.

"I know, it's just...we're friends, and I'd hate to see him fuck up and—"

"And what?" I interrupt sharply, for some reason extra annoyed by the friend label I'm slapped with. "You really think I'd be so petty; I'd take that out on you? Please, you should know me better."

He looks appropriately sheepish and maybe a little surprised at the edge in my voice.

"No, I just meant..." He stalls before continuing with, "I don't want things awkward."

I snort before getting up from my chair so I'm not looking up at him. Well, I guess I'm still looking up at him, since he's a towering six foot three to my modest five two, but standing makes me feel taller.

"Things would only be awkward if you make them so," I return pointedly.

He narrows his eyes on me, scanning my body down and up again.

"Are you okay?"

Instantly self-conscious at his question, I run my hands down my flour-dusted apron.

"I'm fine, why?"

"You don't look fine."

∽

Hugo

Smooth.

Her sharp, "Thanks for sharing that observation. Now if you don't mind, I have work to do," served as an effective dismissal.

Apparently, I'd already put both my feet in my mouth and I figured my safest bet would be to make myself scarce and try again another time.

I don't know why, but I seem to be making an art out of saying the wrong thing to her lately. To my recollection, this was never an issue before, but the past several months I can't seem to say the right thing.

After a quick goodbye for my son with a warning to behave, I walk out to my cruiser, frustrated and brooding. Funny, because I was in the best of moods when I pulled in here five minutes ago. I'd planned to beat the crowd and score a couple of coffees and some pastries to take to the station, but I'm empty-handed when I slide behind the wheel. I highly doubt Bess would be willing to serve me early after I pissed her off.

"Who the hell pissed in your Wheaties this early?" Brenda Silvari, our office manager, asks as I walk into the small office kitchen, looking for a hit of caffeine.

"Don't know what you're talking about," I grumble, reaching for the pot of black tar Brenda manages to brew every morning.

I swear, she adds engine oil to the coffee grinds to create the dark sludge she serves us, but it does the trick when in need of caffeine, and right now, I need that jolt to my system.

"Let's just say, you don't look particularly cheerful this morning," she responds.

"And this conversation is not helping," I point out.

But that doesn't deter Brenda, who is more like a den mother than an office manager some days. She puts a hand on my arm.

"That boy giving you trouble?"

She's referring to Carson, who hit a rough patch there

for a while after his mom died and got himself into some trouble. Having two teenage boys herself, I found myself sometimes confiding my struggles with him to Brenda.

"No, it's not Carson. He's fine, he starts his part-time job at Strange Brew today. I just dropped him off."

"Ahhhh." She nods with a smirk. "You didn't run into Bess by chance, did you?"

I have no idea how she manages to zoom in on the sore spot every time. Like I said; den mother.

"Bess?" I feign ignorance, an effort I know is wasted anyway. "Barely. I was in and out of there in minutes."

"Hmmm," she hums, making it clear she's not buying what I'm trying to sell.

I quickly toss a few spoonfuls of sugar in my coffee in hopes of killing the bitter taste, and dart out the door before she has a chance to dig her claws in deeper. The woman is a terrier.

Once at my desk, I can't help but replay my conversation with Bess to try and figure out where I may have messed up. Even under her usual ivory complexion, she'd looked pale, almost gaunt, with dark circles under her eyes. She'd also noticeably lost weight. Even being a small woman, she's always been sturdy. This morning, she looked like a stiff wind could blow her over. There's definitely something wrong with her, but in my attempt to get to the bottom of it, maybe I was a bit too blunt.

The radio on my desk crackles with an incoming message, interrupting my trailing thoughts.

"Dispatch to all units, structure fire reported at 104 Main Street. It's Main Street Mechanics, risk for explosion. All units, acknowledge."

Jesus, that's Clem Tanek's auto shop. I just drove past it on my way here and didn't notice a thing.

I snatch up my radio and check for my keys in my pocket as I respond.

"Unit 42 acknowledges. En route."

I rush down the hall and out the doors to my cruiser, as more calls come through from the fire department and two of our sheriff's units.

Engine one of Silence's Fire Department is already on scene when I pull up in front of the building. Smoke is pouring from one of the partially opened bay doors and an orange glow can be seen from within the shop. I don't interfere with the work of the fire department, which is well in the hands of fire chief Randy Nichols, who is already barking out orders at his crew.

"Is anyone inside?" I ask him quickly.

"Not as far as I know; the place doesn't open until eight."

I leave him to it and turn to the crowd forming on the sidewalk and street. Crowd control is my main concern, and I need to get these people back and out of the way. Tons of hazardous and potentially explosive materials inside could go off at any time.

"Hey!" I holler, trying to draw attention as I wave my arms. "I need everyone to back the hell up!"

A few listen and move out of the way, but there are still some folks trying to get closer, getting in the way of firefighters doing their job. But as I try to block their path, I'm knocked to the ground by a massive blast from behind.

My ears ring and I'm disoriented, my vision is obscured by a thick cloud of dust and smoke, as debris rains down around me.

A hand lands on my shoulder and when I look back, I see Deputy KC Kingma standing over me. His mouth is moving, but I can't hear a damn thing. He grabs me under my arms and hauls me to my feet.

"You okay?" he mouths.

Other than that damn ringing in my ears and a slight stinging at the back of my head, I seem to be in one piece.

"I'm fine."

Then I look around me to find chaos. Some of the people I was trying to push back are lying or sitting down, appearing injured by debris from the blast. When I look back at the auto shop, almost the entire front of the building is gone.

CHAPTER 2

B*ess*

I carry another tray of sandwiches into the coffee shop which, at the moment, looks more like a field hospital than a business.

Not the type of morning rush we were expecting.

I was in my office when I heard the first sirens right outside Strange Brew. Emmet, another of my employees, was just walking up to the shop when I stepped out to investigate. He was able to tell me it appeared Clem's auto shop was on fire, and when I poked my head out the front door, I could see vehicles and people congregating down the street.

The explosion came just as I turned to tell Emmet we should open a bit early. The blast rattled the large front windows in their frames, and shook me in my boots.

The first walking wounded—mostly minor cuts from flying debris—showed up moments later. While Emmet—

with Carson's help—started working on coffee for everyone, I hauled out my first aid kit and began cleaning wounds and applying bandages.

It's been almost an hour and I'm still not sure what happened out there, but I know it wasn't good. Almost the entire street is now blocked off by emergency vehicles, and the acrid smell of smoke is thick in the air.

Dana—who is a nurse practitioner—showed up a while ago and jumped into action taking over medical aid, which left my hands free to slip into the kitchen and get some sandwiches made for folks coming in from the chaos outside.

"Hey, you. What's happening out there?" I ask Savvy, our sheriff and my good friend, when she walks in the door.

"It's a mess. Clem's place is a total loss, and the fire department is busting ass to keep the fire from spreading to neighboring buildings. We've got two firefighters injured in the blast, who were transported to the hospital, so they had to call in assistance from neighboring towns. Hell, my own second-in-command got caught in the blast, so I've had to get extra staff out there myself. They're redirecting traffic and making sure the public stays safe, but it's nuts out there."

I barely hear anything after she mentions Hugo and grab her arm.

"He got hurt?"

She shoots me a sympathetic look.

"Hugo's fine. Or, he will be if he'd stop being so dang stubborn and gets himself checked out. He's walking and talking," she clarifies. "And I've got KC keeping an eye on him." Then she adds, "Don't worry."

"I'm not worried, I was curious, that's all."

My quickly uttered excuse doesn't appear to impress Savvy, who flashes a quick smile.

"Sure thing," she mutters under her breath, before continuing in a normal tone of voice, "I popped in to see if I could grab some coffee for my guys. Most of us got called straight out of bed and didn't have a chance to pick something up before getting to the scene."

"Of course. I've got some cardboard carafes. I'll put something together and will get someone to help me carry it over. Where do you want it?"

"My cruiser. I'm parked in front of the real estate office. I'll leave the gate open, just leave it in there."

I give her a thumbs-up and watch as she stalks back outside. All business, even with one hand covering her small, burgeoning baby bump protectively as she rushes back to the scene.

I'm happy for her—I am. She deserves it all; her full-circle love story with Nate, the surprise pregnancy. My friend has had enough hardship in her life, and it's about time things turn around for her. I don't begrudge her any of it.

Still, every so often, I feel an unwelcome pang of jealousy. It's not pretty, I don't like what it says about me and shove the feeling down the moment it rears its ugly head, but it's hard to snuff out completely. It's usually followed with the bitter realization a happy ending like that is simply not in the cards for me. Fate already took that out of my hands a long time ago.

Ten minutes later, I get Emmet to help me carry two large cardboard containers with coffee, a box of extra sandwiches, and a basket with cups, sugar, and creamers.

The first person I see, sitting on the curb behind Savvy's cruiser, is Hugo Alexander, his head in his hands. When I get closer, I notice a dark stain on his collar and down the back of his shirt.

"Jesus, Hugo!" I burst out, setting down the box and basket I'm holding before rushing to his side. "You're bleeding."

He lifts his head and turns to me.

"I'm fine," he says immediately.

"You don't look fine," I return, throwing back the line he used on me just a few hours ago as I carefully probe the back of his head. "You have a cut."

"I know." He gently removes my hand from his head and pulls me in front of him. "It stopped bleeding a while ago. It looks worse than it is. It's just a small cut."

I narrow my eyes as I look down on his face, taking in the deep set of his eyes and the tension around his mouth.

"Then how come you look like you're in pain?"

He keeps hold of my hand as he gets to his feet. Then he lets go and reaches for the side of his head.

"A headache, that's all."

"That's all? You could have a concussion," I point out. "You probably do. You need Dana to have a look at you. She's at Strange Brew."

Without hesitation, I grab his wrist and start pulling him down the sidewalk.

"Emmet! You've got this? I'm heading back."

"Sure thing, boss."

Halfway back to the coffee shop, Hugo suddenly stops moving. When I turn to look at him, he's wearing a little smirk on his face.

"How about a deal?"

Confused, I shake my head. "What are you talking about?"

"Tit for tat. Since I didn't blow you off when you

inquired about my health, and am even letting you drag me down the street, I was thinking you owe me an honest answer to the similar question about your well-being I asked this morning."

Dammit. Of course he'd pick up on the parallel.

Realizing he could easily pull free, head the other way, and there'd be nothing I could do about it, I decide to give him something.

"I haven't been sleeping well," I mutter, as I start moving again, pulling on his arm.

"Are you sick?" He wants to know.

"I'm fine."

I push open the door to the coffee shop, shove Hugo down in the first chair I see, and immediately call for Dana, who rushes over. When I explain to her he was hurt in the blast, she immediately starts examining him.

As I walk away, leaving him in her capable care, he calls after me.

"Hey, Bess...our conversation isn't done yet."

Oh yes, it is.

H*UGO*

T*WO* *HOURS* later I walk out of our small hospital, where Dana insisted I have that new doctor check me out.

Rohan Sharma. I still haven't decided whether I like the guy or not.

He did take good care of Carson after he was attacked last year, but I'm not a fan of him hanging around Strange Brew and chatting up Bess.

No concussion, which I'm glad for, but I did rupture my right eardrum, which is why, according to Sharma, the entire right side of my head is hurting.

He gave me some antibiotics and suggested warm compresses or over the counter pain relief. I was instructed to keep the ear dry until I see him again next week. Not sure how the fuck I'm supposed to wash my hair if I can't stick my head under the shower, but I'll figure it out. I was also told I should take it easy, probably sleep on my back for the time being, and to call him if anything changes.

I'm just glad he's letting me get out of here, but since Dana dropped me off this morning, I'll have to walk back to the station. The sound of a car horn has me scan the parking lot where I spot a sheriff's unit just pulling around. Randal Donahue—a retired deputy who still volunteers occasionally—pokes his head out the window.

"I was told to swing by and pick you up. Y'all right?"

I get in the passenger seat.

"I'm fine. But I got released like five minutes ago and haven't talked to anyone. How'd you know?"

The old man shrugs as he chuckles. "This is Silence; news travels."

I'd hardly think my visit to the ER constitutes news, but he makes a point. I guess someone let either Savvy or Brenda, back at the office, know, and they must've kept tabs on me.

But when I walk into the station, Brenda looks surprised to see me.

"What the hell are you doing here? I just talked to Savvy, she's still out there up to her eyeballs, and she said you were in the hospital."

"Just to check me out, but I'm fine." I turn to Randal, a little confused. "Then who the hell sent you?"

"Didn't I tell ya? That gal at the coffee shop. Bess. Popped in there to grab a quick cuppa and she pulled me aside. Seemed like everyone was congregating there. Busy as all hell. Saw your boy too, slinging coffees like a pro. Anyway, she asked if I had time to fetch ya, and seeing as I was on break..." He shrugs before continuing, "Guess I should be heading back out there now though. Break's over."

With that, he turns and heads toward the exit, slightly stooped with the arthritis I know is plaguing him.

"Appreciate it, Randall," I call after him.

He lifts a hand over his shoulder in response as he pushes through the door.

So...Bess, huh? Interesting.

"Don't look so damn happy," Brenda snaps. "The shit's hit the fan today. The latests are a fender bender on Lincoln at Elm, a report of vandals spray-painting the bleachers at the ball park, and to top that off; Jack Fender's bull escaped and is running wild in Mountainview Park. I've got no units left to send out, so, unless you are incapacitated—in which case, what the hell are you doing here—I'm gonna need you to put on a clean shirt and get your ass out there. We're drowning in calls today."

Anyone but Brenda taking that tone with me would get their ass handed to them. However, for her to break out in a rant like that, things must really be bad. I give her a thumbs-up and go in search of a clean shirt.

Three hours later we have the bull cornered and caught by the public washrooms at the park entrance, the vandals intercepted and cited, their paraphernalia seized, and the fender bender had already been resolved without my help. In the meantime, I've also taken a report from the gas station attendant at the Texaco, who had a fill-and-flee incident, and was waved down by Mrs. Dixon, our old librarian, who wasn't able to get her garbage bin down to the curb for tomorrow's pickup.

All in all, it was a busy afternoon, but none of it related to this morning's fire and I feel out of the loop, despite the constant radio chatter on the subject. So, when I return to the station and notice Savvy's cruiser parked out in front, I immediately go in search of her to get an update.

She's in her office, her head down on her crossed arms on the desk when I walk in.

"You all right?"

She looks up and winces. "I should be asking you that. Brenda tells me you got the all clear. I'm sorry I didn't follow up with you, but this day just—"

"Got out of hand, I know." I wave her off. "Fill me in on the fire at Clem's place. I noticed we still have a part of Main Street blocked off."

"Yeah." She gestures for me to take a seat. "Wasn't easy to get that fire down with all the flammable materials in the shop, and the fire department had a hard time making sure the neighboring buildings weren't a total loss as well. As it is, they sustained a lot of damage. Nichols is still at the scene, waiting for the regional fire marshal to get there. He called them in, suspecting arson."

"Seriously?" I'm surprised, and add, "I can't imagine anyone having a beef with Clem, he runs a fair business and is generally well-liked."

Arson would imply he or his shop were targeted and I'm finding that hard to believe.

"I know. I talked to Clem, who is understandably broken up about the whole thing; his great grandfather bought that building and started the business after WWII. He says he can't think of anyone who might want to hurt it or him.

Claims his bills were paid up, and he had no unhappy customers he could think of."

"Simply a firebug then?" I wonder out loud.

Savvy shrugs. "I guess it's always possible, although those usually start with smaller fires—dumpsters, sheds, maybe abandoned houses—building their way up, but we haven't had any of those in years."

"What about Chance Tanek?" I suggest. "I mean, Clem may not have any enemies, but his brother has made plenty over the years. You just said this was a family business. You and I know Chance no longer has any stake in Main Street Mechanics, but that's not necessarily common knowledge."

Four or five years ago, Chance Tanek was arrested after he lost control of the truck he was driving, hitting three parked vehicles in front of the Methodist church on a Sunday morning. Not only was he drunk out of his skull, and already lost his license as a result of multiple prior DUIs, but he *borrowed* the truck he was driving from the shop. It belonged to a customer who was scheduled to pick it up Monday morning.

Clem about lost his shit when we notified him. He took a huge hit and ended up paying damages out of pocket to save his business; there was no way insurance would cover any of it. Then he turned around and had his brother sign over his share of Main Street Mechanics as repayment.

She nods in agreement. "Althof is already on that. I put him in charge of the investigation, and he's trying to track Chance down for a word."

Rick Althof is the Edwards County Sheriff's Office newest addition. A transplant from Coeur d'Alene where he was a detective for the police department, he now fills the newly commission-approved role of sheriff's investigator.

The guy is a bit of a loner, keeps to himself most of the time, but seems decent enough.

"Now...about you," Savvy redirects the conversation. "What did the doctor say?"

"No concussion. Just a scratch on my scalp and my right ear is a bit messed up, but—"

"Messed up, how?"

"Ruptured eardrum but it should heal on its own."

"I bet he told you to take it easy, and yet, here you are," she says pointedly, gesturing at me.

"But I'm heading home now to do just that," I quickly announce, getting to my feet.

"Is there any point in me telling you not to show your face tomorrow?" she asks when I'm halfway out the door.

I shoot her a grin over my shoulder.

"Probably not."

CHAPTER 3

B*ess*

"Do you have a minute?"

Dana lifts her eyes from the chart she's reading and registers surprise, seeing me at the clinic. She immediately gets to her feet.

"Bess? Sure. Everything all right? What are you doing here?"

She fires off questions as she ushers me into the nearest treatment room.

"I'm fine. I was passing by on my way to Sacha Levy's place to pick up some eggs and thought I'd pop in."

Dana looks at me expectantly, knowing full well I wouldn't just drop in at the clinic unless there was a good reason.

"And..." I continue. "I figured I could ask you about a sleep issue I've been having."

"As in...what kind of issue are we talking about?" she prompts

"As in, I can't get any. Sleep, that is."

"That explains a lot." She nods.

"Like what?"

She shrugs. "You've seemed a bit...absent. Not all there. And, I'm sorry to say it because I love you, but you look like a dish rag. Wrung out with that slightly gray tinge." She pinches her thumb and index finger together. "I was this close to pulling you aside the morning of the fire, but it wasn't the right moment for a concerned friend talk."

She gestures for me to sit on the edge of the bed while she pulls a rolling stool from under the small desk and sits down right in front of me.

"What are we talking about? Can't fall asleep? Can't stay asleep?"

"Neither. It takes me hours to finally doze off and then I sleep maybe half an hour, at best, before I wake up again."

"More frequent bathroom breaks?"

I shrug. "I go a lot more, not because I have to, but because it's something to do in the middle of the night."

"Any complaints other than sleeping? Any pains or ailments? Irregular periods?"

I bark out a laugh before realizing it isn't really funny.

"Did you forget my uterus is long gone?"

She winces. "Jesus, I'm sorry. Of course."

She's one of the very few who know I was diagnosed with endometrial cancer at twenty-three years old which cost me my uterus, but that left me alive and cancer-free.

I was living in Seattle at the time. My mother had moved us there when I was fourteen because of better job opportunities for her. I didn't want to move, but I had no choice;

being a single mother, Mom was the only parent, the only one providing for us, so she made the call.

"What about mood swings? Hot flashes?"

"You think I'm menopausal? I'm not even forty," I protest.

"You will be in three months and it's not unheard of, women who have a hysterectomy but still have their ovaries can enter perimenopause earlier than average."

I scoff. I might as well have *official spinster* tattooed on my forehead.

"No new pains or ailments. I haven't noticed any hot flashes, unless you count pulling my muffins out of the oven, and the only mood swings I have are a direct result of not sleeping," I grumble, already regretting my impromptu visit.

Dana grins and lifts her hands in capitulation.

"Fair enough, but I think it's been a while since you've had your blood work done, so why don't we do that and make sure there's nothing else going on."

I quietly concede with a nod, and Dana opens a drawer to pull out a couple of collection tubes, a syringe, alcohol wipes, and a tourniquet.

"It was the phone call," I blurt out when I feel the needle slide under my skin.

Dana, who is focused on her work, lifts her gaze.

"Phone call?" she prompts.

"Yeah. Remember Ken?"

She looks shocked. "Your half brother? I thought you lost touch with him."

I nod. More like I banned him from my life, but lost touch with him sounds much friendlier.

"I was surprised too."

I'd actually been too shocked to speak which, as it turned out, wasn't necessary anyway. He did all the talking.

"Seeing as you think it had something to do with your inability to sleep, I gather the call didn't go well?" she probes gently as she slips the needle from my arm.

"Fair statement. He was just stirring up old family drama."

It had been a lot more than that, but there's no way I can talk about it.

Hell, other than Savvy, I haven't even told anyone Ken was in jail. He'd been seventeen when we moved to Seattle and quickly got himself tangled up with a street gang, The Lotus Squad. That was not a great time. Mom did her best to pull him out of that world, but he brushed her off. He dropped out of school and barely came home anymore.

By the time he was twenty-one, he was in jail, convicted of a list of violent, gang-related crimes—including an aggravated robbery—earning him a twenty-five-year sentence. I only saw him once while he was incarcerated. Let's just say that was an experience I didn't wish to repeat, and I actively erased him from my life out of self-preservation.

Until he called me, I hadn't spoken to him in twenty years.

"Family drama is the worst," Dana commiserates.

She tapes down the cotton ball she's had pressed against the puncture wound.

"There. I'll send these off to the lab. In the meantime, let's see if we can't help you sleep a little better, because you look like it won't take much before you hit a wall."

"Gee, thanks," I mutter, as she pulls a prescription pad from a drawer.

She tosses me a sympathetic smile. "It actually pisses me off a little that even looking like a dish rag, you are still this beautiful."

"Nice try," I return.

She signs the prescription and tears the note off the pad, handing it to me with a flourish.

"I only speak the truth," she insists, before getting back to business. "Ambien; take five milligrams once a day, right before bedtime. Let's see what that does, we can always go up. Keep in mind though, this a short-term fix and not recommended for continued use, but it should get you some decent sleep."

"Thanks. I appreciate it."

"I'll call you when I get the results of your blood work back, and we'll go from there."

I thank her again, and with my prescription clutched in my hand, I walk out the door, only to smack into a solid form.

"Whoa, imagine bumping into you."

I lift my head to find warm brown eyes in a handsome, friendly face looking down at me.

"Dr. Sharma. Sorry, I didn't look where I was going."

"It's Rohan, and the fault is all mine. What brings you here?"

Feeling a bit put on the spot, I shove the prescription Dana wrote me into my coat pocket. That's when I notice a pair of perfectly blue eyes watching me from behind Rohan.

The sight of Hugo flusters me a little, and I'm suddenly in a hurry to get out of here.

"Just popped in to see Dana," I skirt around the truth. "But I'm afraid I have to run. See you around, Doc."

I turn on my heel and bolt for the exit, ignoring the hospital pharmacy in the lobby. I'll hit up the pharmacy downtown after I close the shop, it's only a block or two away.

I'm almost at my little white Toyota Prius when my name is called. I turn to see Hugo is easily gaining on me.

"How long are you going to keep lying to me?"

Hugo

Once again, as soon as the words leave my mouth, I realize they probably weren't the most diplomatic ones to invite answers.

The instant anger flushing Bess's face confirms it. She turns her back on me and unlocks the doors of that little white dinky toy she drives.

I brace my hand against the door in an effort to prevent her from getting in and taking off, before I have a chance to make things right.

"Can I try that again?" I plead in a soft voice, adding, "Please?"

Her head remains low, so I can't see her expression, but from the set of her shoulders I deduce I'm not her favorite person right now.

"Bess, come on, we're friends. We've been friends forever. Being concerned about each other's well-being is normal. Why is it you get pissed off at me when I'm just worried about you?"

When she doesn't respond, I push on, "Are you ill? Is that why you were seeing Dana in the clinic?"

Thinking I have her attention, I let go of her door, but she immediately pulls it open and gets behind the wheel.

Not about to give up, I shove my head inside the car before she can slam the door shut on me. With my face suddenly inches from hers, I notice her eyes swimming with tears.

"Hey..."

I lift a hand to brush her bangs out of her face, but she quickly jerks her head out of the way and lifts a hand.

"Don't..."

Realizing I'm getting in her space, I crouch down in the door opening beside her car to give her some room.

"Look, I'm here for you. I may not always be good with words, but—"

She snorts loudly and interjects with a healthy dose of humor, "Now there's an understatement."

"But..." I repeat. "I am a decent listener, and I'm your friend. I care."

Funny how every time I use the term *friend*, it feels progressively wrong. I've known Bess forever. Only by sight when she was a kid, before her family moved away, but I've gotten to know her in person since she returned to Silence. Especially since she opened Strange Brew and it became an almost daily stop.

She proved a good friend during Emily's battle with the aggressive cancer that took my wife's life way too soon. While we were spending most of our time in Spokane for treatments, Bess offered Carson a safe and caring place to come after school. She made sure he ate a decent meal when we'd run late. On top of that, she organized a support tree of friends and neighbors who helped with basic things like laundry, cleaning, groceries, and cooking. Especially during that last month, when my singular focus was looking after my wife. If not for the quiet support at my back, I don't think either my son or I would've come through.

But at some point in these past months something changed. A slow realization Bess is different from others I'd consider friends. *More.*

After losing a loved one—and even though Emily's and

my marriage was far from ideal, I did love her—sometimes you need to raise a protective shield in order to be able to put one foot in front of the other. There was little I let myself care about, especially that first year after her death. Numb was my preferred state of being, getting through everyday life from muscle memory. It was easier that way.

Then I almost lost my son last year. A wake-up call of epic proportions that ripped the protective layer right off my soul, leaving me raw. Bess was there, in the aftermath. Always unassuming, but also unmistakable, to the point where I felt it when she was not around.

I've always thought her beautiful; the black hair framing her delicate features, and her generous mouth that would easily split into a wide, ready smile. There's a lightness to Bess. Something happy and uncomplicated and nurturing.

But right now, that lightness is gone, and that's what worries me.

I'm rewarded with the hint of a smile when she looks at me.

"Insomnia. I haven't been sleeping and it's taking its toll," she finally explains.

"How come?" I probe gently, keeping a lid on the instant flood of creative ways I can imagine myself helping her get to sleep.

She scoffs and her eyes slide out the front window.

"Who knows. Old age?" she jokes with a humorless chuckle.

"You? Hardly. If you're old, what does that make me? I've got quite a few years on you."

Seven to be exact, but who's counting?

"Yeah, but guys get better with age; a little silver, more rugged, slightly seasoned. Women...well, we get sagging boobs, cankles, and menopause. It's not fair."

I almost choke trying to keep from busting out laughing. I have a feeling that would not be a good move.

"I'm not sure what cankles are and I'm guessing menopause is still some years off, but I am positive your boobs are perfect right where they are."

I'm glad my only slightly off-color comments put an instant blush on her cheeks and have her slapping a hand over her mouth to contain a surprised snicker. I was hoping to lighten the mood a little, and maybe drop the hint I see her as more than just a friend.

Encouraged, I decide to push that envelope a bit.

"I have an idea. Why don't I pick you up at six, and we'll go grab some dinner and have a few glasses of wine. I've been wanting to try out that new place, Fusion. I was told it's good. And who knows?" I add. "Maybe a good meal and a few drinks will help get you to sleep."

And if that doesn't work, there are a few other tricks I might have up my sleeve.

"I don't know. It's been a crazy week. I probably should—"

I'm not surprised she's trying to blow me off. That seems to be her default, but I'm not going to let that stop me.

"You've gotta eat anyway. Might as well be a fabulous meal at a nice restaurant in good company."

"Oh, Carson will be there?" she jokes, laughing at my expense.

"As awesome as my son is, that was cruel and unnecessary," I scold her. "I'm afraid you'll have to content yourself with me."

I stand up, needing to stretch the cramped muscles in my legs.

"I guess I can manage a meal with you for company," she

teases, and I'm glad to see a bit of a sparkle back in her expressive eyes. "As you said, a girl has to eat."

"Good. Six, be ready."

She throws me a mock salute and starts her car. I close her door and step back, as she pulls out of the parking spot and drives off.

When I get behind the wheel of my truck a few moments later, I catch a glimpse of myself in the rearview mirror.

I'm smiling.

CHAPTER 4

B*ess*

A QUICK GLANCE at the clock shows it's too late for me to cancel now.

I'd planned to, even as I drove away after saying yes to dinner with Hugo. I wasn't going to go through with it, but Strange Brew was packed when I walked in after filling my prescription in town. I was busy all afternoon and I didn't lock the doors until a few minutes before five. Then I had the kitchen to clean up and get ready for tomorrow morning, and I only just now got up to my apartment.

It's twenty to six. I barely have time to rinse off and throw on some clean clothes. Dry shampoo will have to fix my hair, washing it will have to wait for tomorrow night.

I keep telling myself it's just dinner; he reminded me often enough we're just friends, and it's not like we've never shared a meal before. So then, why does the thought of sitting across from him at the swanky new restaurant in town have butterflies swarming my stomach?

It feels like a date, that's why. I'm pretty sure it was the comment about my boobs that put that thought in my head. I'm probably reading way more into that than I should. Hugo's a guy, guys joke about boobs, it's genetically imprinted, like scratching their balls when they think no one is looking, or sniff-testing their clothes to determine their cleanliness. Some may come off a little more polished than others, but ultimately, they are all the same underneath.

Still...

I rip the shower cap off my head and quickly towel dry my body, before I duck into my closet for clothes to wear. One perk of having only three minutes left is there is no time to agonize over what to wear. I grab the first thing I see, which is the cobalt-blue wraparound sweater Savvy gave me for Christmas that I haven't had a chance to wear yet. I hope it'll look okay with my go-to pair of black wide-legged pants I wear any time my jeans aren't fancy enough.

I get dressed, going on faith alone, since there's no time to check my reflection. Then I give my hair a quick upside-down spray of dry shampoo to fluff it up. The knock on my outside door comes as I'm blindly wiping some gloss on my lips.

Instantly panic sets in.

What the hell was I thinking?

This is not a good idea and it won't end well.

For me.

A few weeks ago, I felt in full control of my life. Everything was where it belonged—either buried deep or kept at a safe distance—and I knew my place in this world.

Somehow, between then and now, the wheels have come

off and my life is spinning off course in every which direction. And right now, I stand to lose more than just my control.

This time the knock on my door is a bit firmer, and I briefly wonder if I can pretend I'm not here, but then I hear Hugo's voice.

"I know you're in there, Bess. Open the door."

Busted.

"Hold your horses," I snap defensively. "I'll be right there."

I slip my small cross-body bag over my head and stuff in my phone. Then I grab my duffel coat and my keys, and open the door.

Dammit.

He looks good. Dark jeans, a cream-colored sweater with a few buttons at the neck, and a black car coat. His hair looks rumpled, like it usually does, but his angular jaw is clean-shaven. That's where my eyes linger until his voice draws my attention.

"That's a fantastic color on you."

Automatically, one of my hands smooths down the front of my sweater, making sure my Buddha pouch is well hidden.

"It was a gift from Savvy."

"She has good taste. It looks great on you."

Weirdly enough, I appreciate the fact he chooses to compliment something I'm wearing versus me. It takes some of the pressure off.

"You clean up well yourself," I feel comfortable sharing.

"Yeah, well, I'll have you know that took a lot of effort," he jokes, taking my coat from me and holding it open for me to slip my arms into.

Then he turns me around and starts closing a few toggles on my coat.

"It's chilly out there," he explains, as I hold my breath when his fingers brush close to my chest. "I hope you're hungry, because I'm starving, and I had a quick glimpse at their menu."

Then he grabs my hand and leads me from the apartment, taking my keys to lock up behind me, before guiding me down the outside fire escape.

My apartment is accessible from the stairs in the rear of the coffee shop, but my official front door is at the top of the fire escape at the back of the building. I only use those stairs when I take my car, which is parked in one of the two parking spaces in the back alley. Tonight, Hugo's truck is parked in the second spot. It feels almost intimate, seeing it towering next to my little Toyota.

I'm grateful for the running board, trying to get into the passenger seat of his truck, although I wouldn't have put it past Hugo to lift me in if I hadn't managed on my own.

"So where is Carson tonight?" I ask in an effort to fill the silence in the truck.

"Having dinner at Tate's. Savvy invited him over," he shares, briefly taking his eyes off the road to glance over at me.

Since Nate returned to Silence with his daughter last spring, it didn't take long for him and Savvy to rekindle the connection they lost well over a decade ago. That makes Savannah Tatum's stepmother, especially now she's pregnant with Tate's little brother or sister too.

The girl was hungry for some motherly nurturing after losing her mother. That's also what first connected Tate and Carson; the loss of their respective mothers. The girl's father hadn't been too keen on the idea, especially given the age difference between the two, but everyone can see how protective and smitten with her Carson is.

"I guess Nate is getting used to the idea of his fifteen-year-old daughter dating," I observe.

"I don't think there is ever a time a father gets used to his daughter dating. In truth, I'm not sure I could handle it, I'm relieved I have a son, it's certainly a little easier. I told Carson in no uncertain terms if he screws up with this girl, if he is anything but an absolute gentleman around her, he's not only going to get his butt kicked by yours truly, but I'll invite Tate's father *and* her stepmother to have a go at him." He chuckles at himself. "You should've seen his face. I'm pretty sure he was more afraid of what Savvy might do to him than her dad or me."

I smile. "That only confirms he's a smart kid, because there isn't a doubt in my mind Savvy would do damage."

The easy conversation serves to alleviate some of my anxiety, and by the time Hugo pulls his truck up to the quaint new restaurant just south of town, my stomach is no longer in knots and I'm actually a little hungry.

The Fusion is housed in an old warehouse. They maintained the original industrial feel with the old brick and exposed ductwork, but juxtaposed it with large windows, sleek glass tables, rich, jewel-toned fabrics on the luxurious chairs and banquettes, and a gorgeous, gleaming marble floor. At the center of each table is a simple, but modern, copper standing lamp, creating little warm islands of privacy in each booth.

"Wow," I express under my breath as the server leads us through the restaurant.

Hugo's hand at my elbow gives me a little squeeze in confirmation.

"Chair or bench?" he asks me when we arrive at our table.

"Bench," I opt.

"You can just tap the base of the lamp to dim or brighten the light," the girl, who introduced herself as Rachel, indicates. She hands us each a menu. "Can I start you off with something to drink?"

"Would you care for some wine?" Hugo prompts when I hesitate.

I'm not supposed to drink alcohol with the pills Dana prescribed, but it seems like a waste to just nurse a glass of water in a restaurant like this. Beautiful as it is, it's a little intimidating, and I can't help feeling a little out of place. Still, at least I can pretend to belong by sipping a glass of wine. I can always start the medication tomorrow.

"I would love some. Do you have a pinot grigio?"

"In fact, we do. We have an Italian Santa Margherita pinot grigio, or a Church and State sparkling pinot gris from British Columbia."

"Oh, I'll try the BC sparkling one."

I have no idea of the brand names. I'm not really a wine aficionado, I just know what I like. The odd time I buy a bottle, I look for pinot grigio and then let myself be guided by the price tag and appealing label. A sparkling wine sounds festive.

"Sir?" the server addresses Hugo.

"I'll have what she's having."

"Excellent. Let me get those for you, and I'll give you some time to study the menu. You can find today's specials on the blackboard on the wall behind you."

When she walks out of earshot, Hugo leans over the table and stage whispers, "I have no idea what I just ordered, but please tell me it doesn't come with an umbrella."

An unexpected, hearty laugh bubbles up all the way from my toes. Hugo's eyes sparkle as he sits back in his chair, a pleased smile on his handsome mouth.

Then my phone rings in my tiny purse, interrupting the moment.

"I'm so sorry. Let me turn it off."

I fumble to free my phone, and quickly turn off the ringer.

But not before I recognize the number on the screen.

Hugo

"Everything okay?"

I'm not sure what happened, but it felt like the air got sucked out of the restaurant just now.

She plasters on a smile and nods. "Yes, fine. I meant to turn off the sound before and forgot."

She places the phone face down on the table beside her glass.

"Please don't on my account. I have mine on vibrate, but I want to be reachable for emergencies." I narrow my eyes on her face which has gone pale. "I hope that wasn't one."

At the questioning look on her face, I clarify, "An emergency, I hope that call wasn't one."

"Oh, no. Wrong number."

Odd. How would she know it was a wrong number if she didn't answer the call?

Bess looks relieved when the server comes back with our

drinks, and I'm grateful to see my order isn't some fruity cocktail.

"Do you need a few more minutes with the menu?"

"We do, actually," I tell her, picking up my, as yet untouched, leather binder and opening it.

Bess does the same, and seems to be a little preoccupied, her eyes only drifting over the menu.

"What are you in the mood for?" I prompt her, scanning the blackboard on the wall behind her. "One of the specials is smash-burger tacos with mango salsa, which sound really good. I might get those."

"That does sound tasty. Maybe I'll order that as well."

She lowers her menu decisively and slides it to the edge of the table. A move noticed by Rachel, who promptly appears at our side. With a nod from Bess, I order for both of us.

As soon as the young woman collects the menus and disappears, Bess's phone starts vibrating on the table. She quickly grabs it and drops it on the bench beside her.

"Do you need to…?"

"No." She shakes her head, but doesn't elaborate.

A slightly awkward silence settles over the table, and I quickly lift my glass for a toast.

"Cheers, hoping the food is as good as it promises to be."

"Well, well, well…"

I turn around to find the voice belongs to Buck Wilson, our local veterinarian. To my surprise I spy Bonnie Sadlowski, who owns a hair salon in town, behind him. That's a matchup I would not have guessed. Bonnie looks a little flustered as she raises a hand in greeting.

"I could say the same, Buck."

Ignoring me, he turns to my companion.

"Bessie, darlin'. Fancy seeing you here...and with this big lug."

He claps me on the shoulder and squeezes it with some force. For an old guy, he's got a strong grip.

"You, I've been meaning to have a word with," he directs at me. "Someone dropped a box at the clinic last Sunday. Three, maybe four-month-old pup inside. Little guy was malnourished, but otherwise healthy."

I raise my hands to cut him off. We've had these discussions before. Emily was allergic, so it was a non-issue then, but ever since she passed away, Buck's been on my case.

"Told you before, Buck, not getting a dog. It wouldn't be fair to the animal with my hours."

"Ahh, bull hickey," he dismisses my point. "You've got a kid, and every kid needs a dog."

I shake my head in exasperation. "Yeah, except my kid is graduating next year and will be going off to college, so where does that leave the dog then?"

"Aghh, cute little thing too," he grumbles, before turning hopeful eyes on Bess. "What about you? He's not overly big, smart as a whip, and would make for a great companion. You could keep him with you in the coffee shop. He wouldn't be any bother."

To save Bess from being put on the spot like that, I quickly intervene.

"Another time, Buck? It's our first date."

"Well, shit—pardon my French—why didn't you say something in the first place? Letting me gab on." He flashes a toothy grin and two thumbs-up. "Go on then...as you were."

As fast as he appeared, he's gone, being hustled to a table clear on the other side of the restaurant by Bonnie.

"I thought this was just a friendly dinner," Bess notes when I turn my attention back to her.

"Yeah, well. I lied," I confess. "But in all fairness, you must've known it wasn't when I first suggested this place." I run a hand over my clean-shaven chin. "And I don't shave for just anyone."

She avoids my eyes but a smile pulls at the corner of her mouth. Then she floors me with a question that tells me more about her than she's looking to have answered by me.

"Why?"

She doesn't elaborate. Not *why now*, or *why me*, but simply *why*. It betrays curiosity, interest, insecurity, and uncertainty. Which means answering is going to be a trip through a minefield for someone who has a history of blundering like a bull in a china shop.

I lean my elbows on the table and look her in the eye, even though hers are still focused on a spot somewhere beyond my shoulder.

"Because any time the subject of dating or relationships comes up in any conversation with anyone, the first person I think of is you. Because I like being with you, talking with you about anything and everything. Because when I have a crap day, one of those smiles of yours flashed my way when I walk into the coffee shop washes it all away. Because I've wondered for a long time what your lips taste like. And because I know I'm ready to take this step and hoped you were too."

Somewhere halfway through my declaration, her eyes slid back to lock on mine.

She's quiet for a moment, and I'm half prepared for her to give me the old heave-ho, when she suddenly tilts her head to the side, a slight glimmer in her eyes and a half-smirk on her face.

"For someone who self-proclaims he's not good with words, that was pretty impressive."

I grin back at her. "Yeah? That good?"

She rolls her eyes. "Don't get carried away, now."

"Damn, I was hoping for a reward."

I love the way her face is so quick to betray emotions. The blush is cute.

"Oh look," she quickly diverts attention. "That must be our food."

As loaded as both her question and my answer were, the rest of dinner was as easy as you'd expect between two people who've been friends for a long time. Conversation was light and comfortable, topics spanning from the merits of pet ownership, via the start of the turkey hunt, to next Friday's pastry of the day at Strange Brew.

But just as I've asked for our bill, Bess's attention is once again drawn to her phone as it has several times during our dinner. The difference is, this time she looks up at me.

"I should probably take this."

"Of course."

I have no choice but watch her go as I wait for the bill, even though my instinct is to follow her outside. She didn't even bother with a coat. Whoever it is who has been blowing up her phone, it's crystal-clear Bess does not really want to talk to them.

That does not sit well with me.

Grateful I have enough cash on hand when the girl brings me the bill, I peel off enough bills to include a generous tip and slap them on the table. Then I grab both our coats on my way out the door.

At first, I can't find Bess. Shoving down a flash of panic, I scan the parking lot before walking around the side of the building where I catch a flash of the vibrant blue of her sweater.

She's leaning against the wall halfway down the alley, her back turned to me and a slump in her shoulders I don't like seeing. I slowly walk toward her, straining to hear at least some of her side of the conversation. I'm a cop, I can't help myself.

I only pick up a few words before she catches on to my approach and swings around.

"I can't, Ken. I can't."

Her eyes are wide when she sees me, and she immediately ends the call.

"Who is Ken, Bess?"

CHAPTER 5

Bess

I TRY to take a deep breath in, but my lungs don't seem to want to expand.

Peeking at Hugo's rather formidable profile as he focuses on the road, I notice the tension in his jaw. I worry he didn't buy into my spiel.

I reminded him Ken was my half-brother—which he recalled—and explained we'd only recently reconnected, but things were still a little tense and awkward. It was kind of weak, but not exactly a lie, even though that brief conversation was a lot more than just awkward.

It was downright scary.

Underneath all the anger and the vitriol my stepbrother was spewing at me, I could hear the fear in his voice. Part of me had hoped it was just a feeble attempt by him to get money out of me after his release, but I'm starting to believe some, if not all, of what he said was true.

And if that is the case, I could be in real trouble.

Oh, how I wish I could confide in Hugo, but I can't. Especially after he opened up to me tonight, it wouldn't be fair. Last thing I want is to put him in a difficult position, he's had enough to deal with in his life, he doesn't need me to complicate things once again.

That's why, whatever tonight promised to be the start of simply cannot happen.

It's too messy. *I'm* too messy, and he has no idea.

"Are you sure you're okay?" he asks, pulling into the parking slot beside my Prius.

Plastering a smile on my face, I turn to him.

"Absolutely. Thank you for tonight, that was lovely. Delicious."

I already have my hand on the door handle, ready to bolt as soon as the wheels stop rolling.

"Yeah, I had a good time." He gives my knee a quick squeeze before adding, "Sit tight, let me get your door."

Before I have a chance to stop him, he's out the door and rounding the front of his truck. He stops right outside my door and pulls his phone from his pocket, putting it to his ear. He appears to listen and nods as he pulls open my door.

"...and I'll be right there." He tucks away his phone and holds out his hand, explaining, "That was work."

Hugo is revealing himself to be quite the gentleman. Unexpected and, unfortunately, it does nothing to dull his appeal.

No, quite the opposite, I'm afraid.

When he starts walking me up the stairs to my door, I turn and stop him.

"Really, don't let me keep you if you have to go; I can find my own way up."

With Hugo standing two steps lower, I find myself at almost nose to nose with him, his blue eyes even prettier this close up. The darker ring only emphasizing the clear, ice-blue irises, but they are far from cold, instead radiating a heat I can feel down to my toes.

"Work will have to wait. I picked you up at your door, I'll drop you off at your door," he states in a low voice that has goosebumps break out on my skin.

I'm in so much trouble.

Resuming my trek up the stairs, I start digging my keys from my purse, but they're quickly taken from my hand when we reach the top. Hugo steps up beside me and unlocks my door, opening it an inch before handing me back my keys.

"Well, thanks again," I mutter, stepping inside and turning back to face him, my hand on the door, ready to close it.

But Hugo has different ideas, his hand shooting out to cup the back of my head as he leans in.

"If I had time, I'd dig for the reason you've been withdrawing from me since we left the restaurant. As it is, it'll have to wait for a later time, but I'm not going to walk away without giving you something to think about."

No sooner have the words left his mouth, when his lips hit mine.

His kiss is like that first sip of cold water when a hot day has you so parched you're lightheaded.

For all my determination not to allow things to progress this far, I'm ashamed to admit, my free hand finds purchase on his chest, fingers curling into the front of his sweater. It's instant capitulation, and my knees feel weak.

He's thorough, his tongue testing as he slightly shifts and changes the angle to reach every inch of my mouth, and I'm a slave to his explorations.

"*Fuck*," he curses when he tears himself from the kiss, his head resting against mine.

I don't have the breath to say anything. Not even when he presses his lips to my forehead, and whispers, "I'll call you later."

I'm in so, *so* much trouble.

∼

Hugo

Holy shit.

That was...unexpected.

I'd anticipated chemistry and I was prepared for it to be enjoyable, but that kiss was explosive. From zero to a hundred in a heartbeat, creating an instant addiction.

Then why does it feel I just opened Pandora's box?

I didn't believe Bess for even a second when she gave me that story about the reconnection with her long-lost brother, Ken. Don't get me wrong, I believe she was talking to him, but she looked way too spooked for it to have been simply an awkward conversation. Something is going on she is not ready, or willing, to share.

I'm not going to push her, but I'm also not going to wait around for her to be ready to share. I don't like her scared if I can help it, so I sure as hell am going to do a little digging on my own.

As I approach the location Warren indicated in his call, I see several first responder vehicles already parked in front. I pull in behind a cruiser and turn off the engine, reaching over to retrieve my badge and sidearm from my locked glove compartment. Then I grab my sheriff's department windbreaker to put on over my sweater, and get out to join the small group about fifty feet down the sidewalk. Deputy Warren Burns, Deputy Lloyd McCormick, and one of the new recruits, Deputy Heather Solingate.

"Sorry," Warren says when he sees me approach. "I know it's your day off, but Sheriff Colter had a medical emergency, so she wasn't available."

Immediately concerned, I look for clarification.

"Why? What's going on with Savvy?"

Warren shrugs. "All I know is what her husband told me when I called her cell and he answered."

God, I hope she hasn't been overdoing it. Some of us have tried to get her to slow down, now she's getting a little further along in her pregnancy, but the stubborn woman simply won't. I can't help but worry, even though it's possible this has nothing to do with her pregnancy—or even Savvy herself—but either way, there's nothing I can do about it.

Shoving down my concerns, I focus on the reason we're here.

"So...get me up to speed," I suggest.

Ever since the morning of the fire at Clem's garage, we've been trying to locate his brother, Chance. A drunk, his movements in town are generally either predictable or obvious. Everybody knows him and frequently sees him around.

Not so this past week. He hasn't shown up at his usual watering holes, hasn't been seen around town, and after Clem let us into his brother's small apartment, it was clear he hadn't been there in a while either.

Of course we considered the possibility he might have been inside the auto shop when it burned down, but no human remains had been found. Even with the fire burning as hot as it did, you'd expect some evidence to be left behind.

But as it turns out, he'd been right under our noses the whole time.

"Mrs. Dixon put a call in to 911 to report an intruder in her shed. She was in the middle of explaining to dispatch what happened, when a loud crash could be heard, followed by screaming. Then suddenly the line went dead," Warren shares.

"Solingate and I got here first," McCormick continues. "Circled the house and found the back door kicked in. When I approached, I got a glimpse inside the kitchen through the open door, and saw Chance with Mrs. Dixon. He's sitting on the floor with his back against the cupboards holding her in front of him with a large knife pressed against her neck."

"Lloyd says the guy is completely wigged out, and was asking for his brother, so I sent KC to pick up Clem," Warren finishes up.

I nod. "Good. Is anyone keeping an eye on things?"

"DiVecchio is back there."

Good call, Sal DiVecchio is a veteran with the sheriff's office, and as calm and solid as they come. He's dealt with Chance Tanek on plenty of occasions and knows how to handle him.

"EMTs?"

"Yep, en route," Warren confirms, and adds, "No sirens," anticipating what would've been my next request.

You don't want to chance anything—like the sound of sirens—triggering an already tweaked individual.

Burns obviously had that point covered so I move on.

"And has anybody talked to the neighbors yet?"

"Heather and I were about to," Lloyd responds.

"Good. Do that." Then I turn to Warren. "Would you mind waiting for KC to get here with Clem and make sure he's calm before you bring him around back?"

He acknowledges with a nod, and as I start walking around the side of Connie Dixon's bungalow, I keep my hand on the butt of my sidearm, just in case.

"Sal..." I announce myself calmly as I walk up to the deputy, crouched at the base of the set of steps leading up to the small covered porch.

I take stock of the splintered doorframe and the broken glass in the door opening. In between the shards of glass, I notice what might be drops of blood trailing in to the kitchen.

He may be injured.

"Hey, Chance," I greet the wide-eyed, pale-faced man, as I crouch down right outside the door, making myself as small as possible.

Last thing I want is to panic or scare him even more than he already is.

Then I seek out Connie Dixon, whose eyes are clear and surprisingly steady as she calmly stares back at me.

"How are you doing, Connie?" I ask, noting blood on the front of her clothing.

It looks like it's dripping down from a nasty cut on Chance's forearm which is curved around his hostage, the knife in his hand. I also notice some blood on the floor by his hip, but that may have come from the same injury.

"We're doing okay, here. Aren't we, Chance?"

Age-stooped to five-foot nothing, looking very fragile with her spindly legs sticking out from the blood-stained housedress and her white hair in disarray—not to mention the knifepoint trembling against her throat—but Connie

Dixon most definitely is not helpless. The woman is composed, steady, and smartly trying to diffuse the very dangerous situation she finds herself in.

"That's good," I use the same gentle tone Connie used. "As long as everyone is good, we're just going to wait for Clem to get here. You wanted to talk to your brother, right, Chance?"

I'm trying to get a casual dialogue going, find a way to get him to release Mrs. Dixon. Maybe get him to tell me what got us to this point.

"Clem...is he...he's coming?" he stammers.

"Yup. He's on his way. Hey...did you know you hurt yourself? You've got a cut on your arm."

Chance pokes his head over Connie Dixon's shoulder to look at his arm. "It's fine," he mutters as his eyes come back to me.

"Okay, if you're sure. But it seems to be bleeding quite a bit. Maybe we can wrap it in a tea towel until you can get that looked at."

"I said it's fine."

The old woman suddenly tenses up and I can see the paper-thin skin of her neck pucker as he presses the knife tip deeper.

"I already offered," she courageously intervenes. "Chance would rather wait until Clem gets here, isn't that right, Chance?"

He acknowledges with a grunt.

"Then we'll wait," I confirm.

It doesn't look too likely he'll be letting his hostage go voluntarily, and I don't want to risk agitating him any further, so I take a moment to reassess.

I've barely had a chance to consider my options when I

hear movement over my shoulder. I hope to fuck it's Clem. Stretching a hand behind me, I hold off whoever is there.

"Let me just go see if your brother is here yet, is that okay?"

"Yeah." He nods, stretching his neck, trying to look beyond me.

"I'll be right back."

I back away slowly and move out of sight of the kitchen before I turn around. Clem is off to the side with Warren holding on to his arm. I approach them.

"Did he hurt her?" Clem hisses when I get close.

"It doesn't look like it," I try to reassure him. "The blood on her clothes is from a cut on his arm I think he got breaking in the back door."

"Jesus Christ. What the hell is he doing?"

"Hey, I don't know, but I'm hoping he'll talk to you. Stay by the door, and I'm gonna need you to keep your cool. He's pressing that knife tip pretty hard in Mrs. Dixon's neck."

Clem hisses and drops his head down, pressing the heels of his hands in his eyes for a moment. Then he straightens up, takes in a deep breath, and nods sharply.

"I'm good."

Just as I'm about to step aside to let him by, I hear the woman's wobbly voice behind me.

"Hugo?"

When I turn around, she's standing in the doorway in her blood-stained dress, backlit by the kitchen lights, looking like she stepped clear out of a horror movie.

"Something is wrong with Chance."

CHAPTER 6

B*ess*

"One daily special and a decaf vanilla latte for table four."

Today's special is a hearty black bean, chorizo, and vegetable soup with cheese and jalapeño cornbread. I'm almost out of both already.

Lola is off today, so it's just Emmet and me handling the lunch crowd. It's busy, so Emmet is doing all the serving and the coffee machine, while I prep and plate food. At this point, I'm running on automatic pilot, but I did notice Buck Wilson at the small table by the window. I've been rehashing last night ever since he sat down.

Sadly, the glass of wine I had with dinner did nothing to help me sleep, nor did the memorable kiss at my door. Unfortunately, I think after Ken's call my sleepless night was already a given. This time he didn't even bother with fake pleasantries and dove straight into the threats.

When he initially called, it was a shock he made an effort to seek me out, but even more so that he'd apparently been paroled last month. I don't even know how he got my number; I meant it when I said I distanced myself from him all those years ago. I wanted nothing to do with him or anybody associated with him, and that included his defense lawyer. There was no one to notify me he'd even went up before the parole board.

But the biggest shock came when he stopped pretending he called to make sure I was okay, and shared the real reason he chased me down.

Money.

When our mother died, almost ten years ago now, I was surprised to find she'd left me some money. Well, according to her will, it was technically money my father had left in trust for me. I never knew my father and didn't know anything about the money, she'd never mentioned it. She didn't leave much herself, a few thousand in a savings account, and some family heirlooms she'd divided between Ken and myself. But my father's money had grown to a little over a hundred thousand over the years.

At the time, I had been fairly recently declared cancer-free, and I was still trying to figure out what I was going to do with the rest of my life. The money gave me the opportunity to fulfill a dream I'd had of starting my own small business, which I finally did eight years ago when I opened Strange Brew.

And that is precisely what is at stake now; my coffee shop.

My brother's lawyer must've received a copy of our mother's will with his share of her estate to keep in trust, that's why Ken knew about the money my father left me when he called. It's what he was after.

He told me he needed to disappear, get out of the country. Apparently, his former gang, the Lotus Squad, had it out for him. He asked if I forgot that I owed him.

The kicker is, I do owe him. Even when he was up to his eyeballs into Lotus Squad business, he still managed to be protective over his little sister. I still have nightmares to this day, so no, I'll never forget what he did for me. I pay with my guilty silence.

But, like I told him that first time, I don't have the money anymore; it's invested in my coffee shop.

I knew it was too much to hope for he'd let it go, so last night he turned the pressure up. This time he tried to blackmail me, threatening to throw me under the bus with the gang. He suggested they probably already know where I am, and all he'd have to do is enlighten them of my involvement. I tell you; it scared the shit out of me. I know all too well how ruthless they can be, it's what got me in this predicament in the first place.

But I can't see myself selling Strange Brew, which is what Ken suggested. When Hugo caught me on the phone, I was just trying to tell my brother as much. The phone calls didn't let up all night after I'd hung up on him, so I finally blocked the number he'd been calling me from.

It was a lot quieter but, unfortunately, it didn't help me sleep. I spent most of the night trying to think of other ways I might be able to raise some money for him, but there's no way to do that without involving Strange Brew. Of course, should he decide to point the Lotus Squad in my direction, it'll all be moot anyway.

I was so tempted to confide in Hugo last night, to just lay it all out in the open and let the cards fall where they may, but I couldn't. I can't. There's no way I could do that to him, lay that kind of burden on him. I'd sooner sell the shop and disappear myself.

I'll treasure that kiss last night, but I'm afraid it can't happen again.

No, I'm going to somehow have to resolve this on my own and be careful not to involve anyone else. It's a terribly lonely feeling.

"Is that for table four?" Emmet asks.

On a whim, I slip around him with the black bean soup and cornbread on a tray.

"I've got this."

I shoot a smile at him before making my way to Buck's table. He's reading something on his phone when I walk up.

"Bessie... how did you like the new restaurant? Sorry again for interrupting last night."

"Don't worry about it," I assure him before answering. "Yeah, nice, and the food was really good."

"Sure is," he confirms, dipping his spoon in the soup. "As is yours, my dear."

"It's just soup," I remind him, with a self-deprecating chuckle. "No culinary handstands here."

"Nothing wrong with wholesome grub, don't sell yourself short."

I shrug, never quite sure what to do with a compliment, and quickly change topics.

"You mentioned a dog last night..."

Buck drops his spoon and completely twists around.

"You want him?"

I lift my hands defensively. "Not so fast. I'd...I think maybe I'd like to meet him though."

"Absolutely. This afternoon?"

"Well...umm...I guess. It would have to be after I close up here."

The moment I set foot in the door, I'm almost bowled over by a mostly blond, knee-high, hairy whirlwind, trying to jump up on me.

"Easy, boy," Buck walks up, scolding the dog as he grabs him by the collar.

The dog's pink tongue is lolling from his mouth as he seems to be smiling up at me, his big paws clawing at the air in his attempts to get to me.

"He's already taken a shine to you," Buck points out.

"Wait…"

This is the puppy he was talking about? If he's this big now, what kind of giant will he turn into?

I'm pretty sure when Buck mentioned the pup last night, he said something about it not being too big. He also mentioned the animal being underfed. I beg to differ on both accounts. I'm willing to bet this dog never missed a meal in his life.

"This is him? The malnourished puppy you were referring to?"

Buck at least has the grace to look a bit sheepish.

"Well, he was mighty hungry when I got him out of that box."

"Must've been a refrigerator box," I mumble, but I can't resist holding out my hand, which immediately is bathed in puppy love.

I have to admit, he seems like a sweet boy.

"He's only three months old?"

The older man shrugs. "Maybe a month or two older."

Obviously Buck is not averse to tweaking the facts a little to get his foot in the door. It clearly worked on me. I was expecting a little fluffy thing.

"He's got a lot of fur."

The dog shifts slightly to sit on my feet and lean against my legs, as I scratch him behind the ears. In my head I'm already trying to fit him into my life.

"It's hair, actually. He doesn't shed," Buck explains. "I'm pretty sure he's some kind of doodle; part poodle, part whatever else. Hypoallergenic, most of them."

That would certainly be helpful. Wouldn't want to be covered in dog fur when you spend a lot of time in the kitchen.

I'm feeling myself getting sucked in more and more. No one to blame but me, I set myself up for this, even though I live in an apartment over a coffee and food establishment with no backyard. What was I thinking?

Of course, that doesn't stop me from asking, "What's his name?"

"Doesn't have one. You can name him yourself."

Half an hour later, when I drive home with my trunk filled with a bed, some toys, and a massive bag of food, I glance in my rearview mirror at Ragnar, the giant blond puppy, and wonder once again what the hell I was thinking?

To be honest, I'm not sure there was a lot of thinking involved, just an impulsive need to have something warm, something alive and happy to see me. Something for me to hold on to when I feel I'm teetering on the precipice of my carefully crafted life collapsing.

I must be nuts.

~

Hugo

. . .

I LOOK UP and close my laptop when Savvy stops by my desk.

"Hey, I didn't expect you in. How are you doing?" I ask her.

"I'm fine, baby is fine." She sits down heavily in the visitor's chair across from me. "It's embarrassing, really. Had some cramping last night, which turned out to be nothing, but when they took my blood pressure at the hospital it was a bit high. Because of my advanced maternal age..." She uses air quotes, highlighting the term. "They gave me something and kept me overnight for monitoring. Numbers were fine this morning, so I was sent home but was told I'd have to take it easy."

I raise a mocking eyebrow and glance at my watch, which shows it's coming up on three o'clock. "And you lasted 'til now?"

"Don't you start. Nate had me lie on the couch and was hovering over me most of the day. Thank God, he had a meeting about a new job this afternoon."

"And I bet the moment he was gone; you were off that couch and heading for the door yourself."

She shrugs. "Yeah, well...turns out he knows me well. Apparently, he called Brenda to keep an eye out for me. She was waiting for me and already gave me an earful about being careful, but it's not like I'll be chasing bad guys. Sounds like you guys caught some excitement yesterday though. I saw Althof when I was leaving the hospital this morning and he filled me in."

I lean back and stretch, folding my arms behind my head. Rick Althof, who'd been put in charge of the investigation, had been out of town for a couple of days dealing with some stuff in Coeur d'Alene. He hadn't been briefed until he came in this morning and immediately left for the hospital to check on Chance Tanek's condition.

"Yeah. That was a crazy scene. I've dealt with Chance since I started here as a rookie, but I've never seen anything like what happened last night. You should've seen Mrs. Dixon, she was cool and collected, and handled that situation like a pro."

"Rick says he was injured worse than you guys thought?"

"Yeah. Clem just got there; we'd been waiting for him. Then suddenly Mrs. Dixon alerts us Chance collapsed. Apparently, when he'd crashed through her kitchen door, he'd not only cut his arm—which we could see—but a large shard of glass was embedded in his side. He was hopped up on adrenaline and probably booze, and had been quietly bleeding out as he sat there, holding Mrs. Dixon hostage."

"Rick mentioned he was hoping to talk with him this morning. Have you heard anything?"

"No luck, so far," I fill her in. "He's conscious, but alcohol withdrawal is apparently complicating things. Last I heard he had started hallucinating and they were medicating him. Doesn't look like we'll get information from him any time soon."

Savvy leans forward in her chair. "Think he's responsible?"

"For setting the fire? I mean, it's possible. He might feel he got cheated out of his share of the business, and we know things have been strained between him and his brother," I point out, although that explanation doesn't feel right.

Even less so after running it over and over again in my head all day long.

It appears Savvy agrees, as she shakes her head. "That was six years ago, why on earth would he lose it now?"

I wouldn't know, but then again, I have no idea what

would drive a man to sacrifice his life to alcohol either. I guess anything is possible.

"Beats me."

She slaps her hands on her knees before getting to her feet.

"Anything else brewing?" she wants to know.

"The lights on Main and Severance were out again, so I have Solingate out there directing traffic until Public Works shows up. It's been over three hours," I grumble.

Public Works is probably too big a title for a department that, over the past three years, has been whittled down to four employees. It's frustrating, because the money saved by those budget cuts our esteemed mayor deemed necessary now come out of our department's slim county budget, seeing as we have to pay one of the deputies to handle traffic for half a day.

"Why don't you let me handle City Hall?" Savvy offers.

"Gladly."

She definitely has more patience than I do dealing with Mayor Don Merrick or any of his pencil pushers, so I'm happy to hand off that job.

She starts to walk away when she suddenly stops and turns, fixing a pointed look on the laptop in front of me.

"What were you working on when I walked in?"

Caught off guard, it takes me a moment to react.

"Just looking over some old cases."

She lifts her eyes to mine and for a moment I wonder if she's going to push for more, but she finally nods and continues to her office.

Technically, I'm not lying, but it's still a severe misrepresentation of the truth, which makes me feel uncomfortable. Especially since Savvy already appears to have that disappointed-mother look down pat.

But Savvy and Bess are the best of friends, and if Savvy knew I was digging up Bess's family history, she might feel compelled to share that fact with Bess, and I'd prefer for her not to know. At least not yet.

For now, all I was looking for was some background information to better understand what might have put the fear in her eyes after she spoke to her brother. What I got was far more than I bargained for.

Kenneth Choi was just released on parole from a twenty-year stint in prison for an assortment of crimes ranging from drug smuggling, to assault, to robberies, and the list goes on. And those were just the crimes he'd been convicted of. The guy was a known member of the Lotus Squad and, from what I can tell, was suspected to have had involvement in much more than those charges.

The fact that a known gangbanger—brother or not—is blowing up Bess's phone does not exactly fill me with the warm and fuzzies. It can mean nothing good. But I'm afraid if I confront her straight up, she'll simply shut me out and push me away, which would make it much harder to keep an eye on her.

I'd much prefer for her to volunteer the information, and that will require diplomacy; an attribute I wasn't exactly blessed with.

CHAPTER 7

H*ugo*

"Homework?"

Carson stops at the door and looks back at me.

"Dad, I've got all weekend."

"You mean you have Sunday. You work tomorrow, remember? Are you really going to want to spend the only full day off you have worrying about homework?"

He rolls his eyes up to the ceiling and sighs dramatically.

"Come on, Dad. I haven't seen Tate at all today. First school, and my shift at Strange Brew started right after, then when I got home, I even got dinner started. I promised Tate I'd come by for a bit after dinner. I swear I'll be home by nine to do my homework."

That's right too, he'd mentioned he got called in to help out at the coffee shop for a few hours. I bite off a grin, looking at those big, innocent, blue eyes he's trying to ply me with.

"Fine," I concede, and he's halfway out the door before I call him back. "Hey, what was going on at the coffee shop they needed you for?"

He throws me a grin over his shoulder.

"Clean up. Ragnar demolished the pantry."

I'm puzzled, not sure what the heck he's talking about, but it doesn't sound good.

Ragnar? Who the fuck is Ragnar?

I manage to grab the front door before it latches and step outside to try and catch Carson, but he's already hopping into my old pickup. I don't bother waving him down, and instead head back inside to grab my coat and my keys.

Guess I'll just have to go find out for myself.

"No! Bad boy. That's enough out of you."

The loud barking as soon as I started climbing the stairs had been a firm clue as to the elusive Ragnar's identity, so when the door opens and I see Bess struggling to control a dog, it's not a surprise. What *is* a bit of a shock, is the size of the animal.

"I'm in over my head," Bess blurts out by way of greeting.

Hard to hear her over the incessant barking of the dog, but my eyes were already fixed on her mouth, remembering the last time I was standing on her doorstep.

"Ragnar! Quiet!" my voice booms.

To my amazement, the dog promptly shuts up and sits down in front of me, his tongue lolling from his mouth. I reach out to scratch his head and notice Bess has one hand still on the door, and is clutching the dog's collar with the other.

"How did you—" she starts, when I interrupt her.

"Can I come in?"

My question appears to catch her by surprise, but she rallies and releases her hold on the door.

"Yes, of course."

It's not until I step through the door, I realize I've never been inside her apartment. It smells like her, with hints of cinnamon and citrus. But at the moment the scent of wet dog is almost overwhelming everything else.

Towels are draped over every piece of furniture, and I see the remnants of what I'm guessing were once the guts of a pillow strewn across the floor.

"I had to give him a bath, but he won't stay off my furniture," Bess explains, her voice wobbly.

I get the sense she's on the verge of a meltdown.

A sharp whistle coming from the kitchen area triggers the dog again. He starts barking furiously and struggles against the hold Bess still has on him.

"Let the dog go, I'll handle him," I tell her. "You take care of whatever that is." I nudge my head to the kitchen.

I manage to snag the pup before he bolts after Bess and drag him to me as I sit down on the towel-covered sofa. The ear-piercing whistle, I'm guessing was a water kettle, stops abruptly.

"Ragnar, quiet," I repeat my earlier command, hoping for the same result.

Whether he was following direction or stopped because the noise did, I'm not sure, but the result is the same. Peaceful quiet. At least, until the dog decides to climb on my lap to show me some love.

"Hey, you mutt," I grumble, dodging the large pink

tongue trying to lick the stubble off my face. "We don't know each other that well."

I shove him off my lap and he immediately curls up beside me, his body pressed up against my thigh. Almost instantly his eyes close. That's when I hear the sound of someone blowing their nose.

The dog doesn't budge when I get up and walk over to the kitchen, where I find Bess wiping her nose with a tissue. She looks like she's been crying.

"Like I said, I'm in over my head," she says by way of explanation.

I could ask her what she was thinking, taking on a dog who is more like a teenage version of a puppy, and not little or even average by any stretch of the imagination. I could admonish her for letting Buck con her into adopting the animal—since there's no doubt in my mind the single-minded vet is behind this. But I'm pretty sure she doesn't need that from me.

"Nah, it'll all work out," I assure her, tucking a stray hair behind her ear. "I remember when we first brought Carson home from the hospital. Shit, I couldn't even recognize our house. Diapers, laundry, dirty dishes, I mean, the house was in a constant state of chaos, as were we, trying to fit a kid into an existing routine. It took a while, but a new routine evolved that included him. I'm guessing adopting a pup wouldn't be that much different. Except it looks like it might be more like adopting a three-year-old than a newborn," I joke to lighten the mood.

With some success, since her pretty mouth spreads in a smile.

"The difference is, we were kinda stuck with Carson, but you always have the option of finding him a new home."

She shakes her head adamantly. "No, I couldn't do that. I couldn't give him away."

"Understandable."

I knew she wouldn't, but I wanted to make clear there was that option.

"My point is; give it time, you'll figure it out," I conclude, adding, "And in the meantime, there are plenty of people who can help."

She shakes her head. "This was my choice, my decision, my responsibility. I couldn't burden others with it."

"Who says that's a burden? When you looked out for my son after school, or brought food to the hospital when Emily was sick, or when Carson was attacked, did that feel like a burden to you?"

"Of course not," she blusters, clearly annoyed by my question. "But I enjoy helping, I like being useful."

All I have to do is raise an eyebrow for her to huff a reluctant concession.

"Maybe give others a chance to do the same for you. No, scratch that," I correct myself, folding her in my arms. "Give *me* a chance."

BESS

"DID you know I slept last night for the first time in weeks?"

Hugo shakes his head and grabs a seat in my mother's old wing chair across from the couch, where I'm sitting.

I'm not sure what moved me to share that information, except that Ragnar is once again pressed up against me like a warm, living, weighted blanket. Much like he was last night, when he jumped uninvited into my bed and burrowed under my covers with me.

I slept. Boy, did I sleep.

After way too many mornings watching the clock creep slowly toward the time my alarm would go off, I almost slept through the familiar ring this morning. I might have, if not for Ragnar loudly signaling his need to answer the call of nature.

That's when things started going downhill.

Thank goodness no one is living in the neighboring building, because they would've gotten an earful this morning when I tried to leave the dog in my apartment. I had to get downstairs to start baking and had planned to leave him upstairs, but he wasn't having any of it, barking and howling, so I ended up taking him with me.

It was fine for a while, he kept busy for a bit chewing the marrow from a bone I'd intended to use to make stock. When Lola came in, they made fast friends, and he ended up tagging after her while she got the place ready for customers.

But I couldn't have him roaming around the coffee shop when we opened the doors at seven, so I tried to keep him contained in the kitchen, which was no mean feat. He would cry and scratch at the door every time I stepped into the shop. The one time I didn't close the door properly behind me, he got out, excitedly barging into the coffee shop. Fortunately, there were only a few customers, none of whom seemed particularly upset a rambunctious dog jumped up on them in greeting. Still, I apologized profusely while I chased after Ragnar, who wasn't about to give up his newfound freedom.

My biggest mistake was locking him in the walk-in pantry during the worst of the lunch rush. Most of the supplies in there are either sealed in storage bins or up on shelves. Fridays are always busier than the rest of the week, in part because that's the day I test out new recipes. Except, with the dog taking up a good chunk of my morning, I never got around to it today.

I thought I'd found the solution, especially when Ragnar stopped whining and scratching after a few minutes. Hopeful he'd curled up and crashed from the morning's activities, I focused on filling lunch orders. I didn't discover the silent carnage he wielded inside until we ran out of lids for the take-out cups, and I poked my head in to grab a new box.

As it turns out, the heavy-duty plastic bins are no match for a puppy's sharp teeth. The entire inside of the closet was covered in flour, rolled oats, and remnants of the almonds he'd managed to get down from the second shelf.

I'd barely even been aware of my audience of one as I relived the events of the day, until Hugo started chuckling. When I look over, I notice his blue eyes sparkling with humor. In hindsight, I guess it is kind of funny, and I find myself cracking a smile, even though the whole experience had me in near tears a little bit ago.

"You always hear parents say you should start worrying when the kids are too quiet. Nobody told me it's true for dog owners as well," I observe.

"Learned that the hard way myself," Hugo commiserates before adding, "Carson mentioned something about someone going nuts in your pantry, but I wasn't sure who or what until I saw the dog."

Maybe that's why he showed up at my door unexpected.

"Is that why you stopped by?"

He jerks his shoulders, a self-conscious grin on his

handsome face. "Well, yeah. The kid never clarified the culprit was a dog."

Once again Hugo came to my rescue, and once again I find my resolve to keep my distance weakening. At the moment I'm so overwhelmed by everything, feel so out of control and scared, I can't bring myself to resist him. Things don't seem quite as dire when he's around.

"So, obviously, Buck managed to convince you."

I snort at his assumption. "You'd think, wouldn't you? But no, this one is all on me. I had the misguided idea getting a dog would give me some dependability and predictability in my life. Guess the joke is on me, but at least he makes for a good sleep aid."

"Predictability would need some work, but dependability is my middle name, and I would've been more than happy to help you get to sleep. I'm right here."

Hugo leans forward, resting one forearm on his knee, while reaching out with the other hand. When he looks at me, his eyebrows pull up and his forehead creases. I don't know why, but I love those creases. So many times, over the years, I've wanted to reach out and smooth my fingertips over them. Same with the crow's feet at the corners of his eyes. Lines that map the story of his life. A life in which I was a mere spectator on the sidelines.

But that's no longer the case; the invitation is clear in his eyes.

It would be the easiest thing in the world just to give in. To grab his hand and give myself over to a reality that only existed in my imagination before. However, it wouldn't be fair to him. I know what I'm getting, but he has no idea.

"There are things you don't know."

"Sure," he responds easily, keeping his hand out and

open. "But what I do know is enough, and everything else I can learn."

I close my eyes and shake my head. "Not all of it is pretty."

"Mistakes are what shape us," he counters.

My eyes snap open.

"Do you have an answer for everything?"

He laughs in my face. "No, but I know whatever it is you want to throw at me, we can figure it out."

His hand is still there, hanging in midair, and I finally reach out and touch my fingers to his. He immediately grabs hold and leans in to press a kiss to the inside of my wrist, lingering his lips against my rapid pulse. He lightly tugs on my arm and I slip off the couch with the intent to crawl on his lap.

Unfortunately, despite my efforts not to disrupt Ragnar, he wakes up and immediately hops off, ready for action.

"I need to take him for a walk," I point out when the dog heads for the front door.

In hindsight, a backyard would've been handy, but as it is, I need to take him out many times a day to do his business. I learned that lesson very quickly last night when, in the span of a few hours, he'd had two accidents on my floor. Thank God for the vinyl planks I had installed a couple of years ago, because cleanup was a breeze, but discovering a puddle of pee when padding around in your socks is not a fun experience.

"I'll come," Hugo offers, giving my fingers a squeeze before releasing my hand.

As soon as we hit the bottom of the back stairs, he takes Ragnar's leash from me, grabbing it in his left hand as he folds mine in his right. On previous walks, the dog almost pulled the leash from my hand, but the first time he tries with Hugo, he's scolded in an extra deep rumble. The damn dog instantly eases up on the leash.

"Figures," I grumble. "Of course, I'd pick a dog who won't listen to a woman, but instantly submits to two words uttered by a man."

Hugo doesn't bother hiding his amusement.

"Has little to do with gender; it's tone of voice and clear commands most animals respond to. You're trying to have a conversation with him, it doesn't work."

"How do you even know this? You don't have a dog," I point out.

"I grew up with dogs," he explains as we pass by what is left of Clem's garage, which isn't much. "The idea is to get their attention by calling their name, and when you know you have it, give them a one or two word command in a firm tone. Anything more and they stop listening, and he may not understand words, but he'll recognize intent."

As he goes on to tell me about his childhood pets, we walk to the small park up the street where Ragnar does his business.

"I should've timed this better, instead of getting him right before the busiest days of the week," I confess, when we start walking back. "At least I'll be off the day after tomorrow."

When we get to my front door, Hugo turns to me.

"Get Carson to help you with Ragnar tomorrow. He won't mind. In fact, I'm sure he'll get a kick out of it. Should the dog get out of hand, call me. I'm working, but he can always ride in the back of the cruiser, and I'm sure nobody will mind if he sleeps under my desk at the office."

"I couldn't ask you to do that," I protest, shaking my head.

"You're not asking, I'm offering."

I roll my eyes at him when he does that thing with his eyebrows, challenging me.

"We'll see how it goes."

"Fair enough."

Once again, he takes my keys and unlocks the door for me. Then he ushers Ragnar inside before pulling it shut again, leaving the two of us standing on the small landing.

"Thank you for talking me off the ledge," I offer.

He slips one arm around my waist, and cups my face with his free hand.

"Any time."

Then he kisses me, and I let him.

CHAPTER 8

H*ugo*

"Stop drooling on me."

I shove Ragnar back over my shoulder while I try to navigate the streets of Silence. Because my seat is shoved so far back to accommodate my legs, the dog is able to reach the backrest with his front legs from the rear of the cruiser. Apparently, he enjoys looking out the front window and shows his enthusiasm by panting in my ear.

I was surprised when Bess called me a couple of hours ago. She'd managed to get through the breakfast crowd with Ragnar quiet in her apartment upstairs, which was already an improvement on what happened yesterday, but after taking him for a quick pee break, he indicated he'd had enough alone time and was ready for some action. She said she'd put him in her office with his bed and a few toys, but he wouldn't stop howling unless someone was with him.

I was ready for another coffee anyway, and swung by the coffee shop to pick him—and a decent cuppa—up, stealing a quick kiss in the privacy of Bess's tiny office. I took advantage of the fact she'd been too flustered to protest. She made it clear again last night she is definitely not opposed to kissing me. By indulging every chance I get, I'm hoping she won't have a chance to convince herself she doesn't want what is happening between us.

Ironically, it's distracting me as well. I'd hoped to maybe probe her a little about her brother's call, and never got around to it last night. I wasn't going to broach the subject when I swung by Strange Brew, she seemed rattled enough as it was, but perhaps I'll get an opportunity tonight when I return the dog.

I drive past the hospital, making my way back to the station, when I notice someone sitting at the picnic table in the small park across the street. I recognize the parka.

"Hey, buddy, wanna get some fresh air?"

Ragnar is virtually vibrating when I clip on his leash and lift him down from the back seat. He could probably jump, but since he's still growing, I don't want him to hurt himself. His nose hits the ground the moment his paws do, frantically sniffing all the scents, as I start walking toward the seated man.

Hearing our approach, Clem lifts his head. Ragnar, who probably thought that still figure was part of the scenery, starts barking at the sudden movement.

"Ragnar, quiet."

A hint of a smile briefly softens the strain on the man's face.

"Let me guess...a Buck Wilson special?" he teases, holding out his hand for the dog to sniff.

Ragnar takes it as an invitation to jump up on him to get better acquainted.

"Yes, but he's not mine," I clarify. "This unruly creature belongs to Bess."

Clem chuckles. "Bess? Who'd have thought? Bet she's got her hands full with this one."

"That's putting it mildly," I confirm, sitting down across from him. "Which is why he's with me during her Saturday rush."

"Ahh."

He nods slowly, a glint of speculation in his expression I choose to ignore. Not that I feel the need to keep what's developing between Bess and me a secret, but I also don't owe anyone an explanation. Except perhaps Carson, which is something I should probably tackle before people start yapping.

I jerk my head at the hospital across the street. "How's Chance?"

The response takes a while in coming as a myriad of emotions flit over the man's face.

"He's...a mess. I mean, his wounds will heal, but fuck, man, he's a mess. Withdrawal is taking a toll. Whenever his sedation wears off, he starts hallucinating and gets violent, so they have to strap him down to administer more. It's pretty hard to watch."

I bet. I feel for Clem, who has no family other than his alcoholic brother.

"I'm sorry, man," I commiserate.

I'd secretly hoped perhaps we'd be able to get some information from Chance, but that's clearly not in the cards at this time.

"Yeah, well, I guess if he comes out the other end clean, all this will have been worth it."

Except it's rare that addicts of any kind stay off the juice or the drugs when sobriety was forced on them. From what I understand—and I'm sure Clem knows this as well—the one most important ingredient in successfully kicking addiction is making that choice to get clean.

"Have you been here the whole time?"

He shrugs. "Pretty much. Not like I've got anywhere else to be."

My heart goes out to him, he sounds pretty defeated.

"What's happening with the shop? Did you hear from your insurance company?"

He scoffs, "Yeah, they sent by an adjuster, but nothing will happen in the short term. They already know the fire was arson, per the fire inspector's report, so they'll likely wait for the outcome of the investigation to make sure it wasn't me or my brother setting it."

I was afraid of that. My guess is damages would total well north of a million—there is nothing but an outside shell left—and I bet they're not in a hurry to pay that kind of money. Damn insurance company will likely stall as long as they can.

"That's tough, my friend. Are you looking for a temporary place to set up shop?"

He shakes his head. "Nah. I mean, I could get by for simple jobs with the tools I have at home, but I only have a single garage and I doubt my neighbors would appreciate me trying to run a business from my home."

True. Most folks in Silence would be neighborly enough to overlook the inconvenience of vehicles and noise for a little while, and I'm sure the sheriff's department could ignore the various bylaws it would break for a short period of time, but after a few weeks that collective goodwill would surely run out.

Thinking about it, there aren't that many places in or around town that would suit his needs. I mean, there's the old warehouse heading out of town toward Watts Lake, but it's so run-down, I'm surprised it's still standing. I think the fire department has used it a time or two for exercises since they built their new fire station on the outskirts of town. The old station behind our office was getting too small, with only two bays...

Wait.

"What about the old fire station?" I suggest, the solution suddenly clear in my head. "It's got two massive bays with doors front and back, loads of storage, an entire upstairs level for offices or whatever, bathroom, kitchen. Oh, and a fuck load of parking space."

I see the wheels start turning as his head slowly bobs.

"Doesn't that belong to the town though?"

"It does, but it's been empty for almost a year. I haven't heard of any plans for it, and I'm happy to check into it for you."

"Yeah, for sure."

Glad to see a little more life in his eyes at my suggestion, I get to my feet. Ragnar, who was exploring as far as his leash allowed, is instantly by my side.

"I'll let you know what I find out. Before I go, is there anything I can get you? Maybe something for dinner?"

"Thanks, but I'm good. Bess sent over some food earlier, enough for dinner as well. Only an idiot would pass up on a good woman like that."

He delivers those wise words with a smirk and a raised eyebrow.

I chuckle and shake my head.

"Guess it's a good thing I'm not an idiot."

Bess

What a day.

It wasn't even one o'clock when I ran out of my white chicken chili, I had to bake two extra batches of cornbread, and I just closed the door on my last customer at four forty-five.

I'm not sure what brought everyone out in droves, but it feels like the entire town was coming through Strange Brew today. I even had people sitting outside at the two small tables that make up my little patio.

Maybe it was the weather; it felt like the first day of spring with still a little nip in the air, but the skies were blue and the sun warmed things up nicely. Not that I spent much time outside, other than to carry the occasional trash bag to the dumpster in the alley, but the few minutes with the warm sun on my shoulders felt good.

Silence hits me when I walk into my apartment. I miss the click of nails on the floor and the happy whimpers and pants of Ragnar greeting me. It's amazing how fast you become accustomed to having another living creature around.

I should give Hugo a call to see how my dog is doing. I wouldn't mind taking him for a nice walk along the river while it's still light out. Enjoy what is left of the sunshine. Or maybe I could take him for a hike up in the mountains tomorrow.

Even though Sunday is my day off—the shop is closed—I often still spend time in the kitchen downstairs, trying out new recipes or prepping for the week to come. It's not that I never go out and do something, but not often on my own. But I'm looking forward to being a little more adventurous now I have Ragnar.

A few weeks ago, Emmet was talking about a pretty trail up on Black Mountain that visited a waterfall. I think that's what I'll do tomorrow. Maybe the fresh air and the peace and quiet will give me the mind space I need to figure out what to do about my brother. He hasn't tried to contact me after I blocked that number and, if anything, it makes me even more edgy.

But I don't want to think about that now; dog first.

"I was just about to call you," Hugo says when he picks up my call. "Carson tells me you guys had a busy day."

I've got to give it to the kid, he worked his buns off all day without a single complaint.

"I think spring fever hit Silence. I swear everybody was out and about, and most of them stopped in at some point."

"I noticed. I was outside at a little after four but saw you still had customers, so I went home instead."

"Hope Ragnar is behaving. Was he okay today?"

"He's fine. Currently asleep on my couch."

"Aww. Let me quickly change into clothes that aren't covered in food stains and I'll swing by to pick him up."

"Take your time. I'm only just heating up the grill, so dinner won't be for at least another half hour or more."

"Dinner?" I echo, a little unsure of what he's suggesting, if anything.

"Yeah. Roasted potatoes, chicken breasts, and Carson is throwing together a salad. Sound good?"

"Um..."

Hugo's soft chuckle in my ear gives me goosebumps.

"You've gotta eat, Bess. It's not complicated."

Except it is. For one thing, Carson is there, which

could make things awkward. Also, it feels like this thing between us is steadily moving ahead, even when I'm still struggling to wrap my head around what is happening here.

But I can't come up with a decent enough reason to decline, and I'm not even sure I want to.

"Okay. Give me ten minutes."

It ends up being more like twenty by the time I pull up to the house. Of course, the yoga pants and oversized sweater I'd planned to change into suddenly didn't seem right, plus I had to run back down to the coffee shop to see what I could scrounge up for dessert, because one can't arrive empty-handed.

I grab the half of a cheesecake I'd pulled from the freezer, hoping it'll be defrosted by the time dinner is done, and make my way to the front door of the two-story home.

Funny, I've driven past plenty, walked up this path a couple of times, and even stood on this front porch before, but I have never actually been inside this house. Now, with my finger on the doorbell, I can't help wonder why I always avoided going in. Running a business like mine is all-consuming and doesn't leave much time for a social life, but surely I could've spared half an hour, or even ten minutes, at some point during the past years to come in and have that coffee or drink I was offered.

The excited barks on the other side of the door pull me out of my musings, and when it opens, I try to balance the cheesecake in the air with one hand, while greeting my rambunctious dog with the other.

"He missed you," Hugo's voice sounds somewhere above me as I feel the plate with dessert being plucked from my hand.

"I have to admit, I didn't have much of a chance to miss

him, but my place sure was quiet when I opened the door earlier."

I glance up at him, meeting his warm eyes as I get to my feet. Without hesitation he tags me behind the neck with his free hand and pulls me close, ducking his head for a sweet kiss.

I freeze when I hear a soft giggle behind him that most definitely does not belong to Carson.

"Carson invited Tate over," Hugo explains as he releases my neck. "Come on in."

Most of the main floor of the house is open concept, so the kids—both of whom are sitting at the kitchen counter—had full view of Hugo's welcome. Tatum seems in favor, with a big grin on her face, but Carson is wearing a more serious expression. I wonder what he's thinking?

I wave awkwardly. "Hey, guys."

"Hi," Tate chirps.

But to my surprise, Carson jumps up and, like a proper host, asks, "Can I get you a drink?"

"I popped a bottle of white wine in the freezer, Bud. It should be cold enough," Hugo informs him.

"Wine, Bess?" his son asks.

"Um...sure, please."

When he pulls the bottle from the freezer, I recognize the label. It's the same BC wine we had with dinner at Fusion. One glance at Hugo tells me that's not a coincidence, and something warm unfurls in my chest. The thoughtful gesture makes me feel instantly welcome.

"Come outside with me while I keep an eye on the grill," Hugo suggests. "It's not that cold, have a heater going out there."

The large deck off the kitchen is great, so is the rest of the backyard, but what steals the show is the view of the river and the mountains. This neighborhood is one of the newer subdivisions, with houses spread a fair distance apart, and backing onto the river that cuts through this valley.

"Wow. This is nice."

Ragnar almost bowls me over in his rush to run into the yard.

"We like it."

He casually throws a smile over his shoulder as he opens the lid of an impressive stainless-steel grill.

"You could cook half a cow on that thing," I point out. "It's big enough."

"What can I say?" he returns. "In a household with two active guys, you need a big grill." Then he adds with a wink, "Size matters."

I shake my head at the cheesy joke, and grab the ball Ragnar drops on my feet. Tossing it toward the river, I grin watching the dog lope after it, ears flopping. I tug the edges of my cardigan closed against the definite chill in the air.

"Here," Hugo says, coming over to wrap an arm around my shoulders.

Next, he moves me closer to an outside heater that looks more like a lamppost, and pushes me down on an outdoor couch underneath. The pillows are nice and warm on my butt. To my surprise, he goes down on his haunches in front of me, his hands on my knees as he locks eyes with me.

"If we didn't have an audience, I could think of a thing or two to warm you up," he rumbles in a low voice that causes an immediate physical response from me. "But for now, the heater will have to do."

Then he gets up, drops a kiss on top of my head, and returns to the grill.

My eyes are glued to his fine ass every step.

I *really* like this side of him.

CHAPTER 9

B*ess*

"Oh, come on! You cheat, Dad."

Hugo laughs as his son tosses his remaining cards on the table. Carson is joking, but you can tell he's annoyed his dad just won the third game in a row.

"You can't really cheat in Crazy Eights, Carson," Tate points out, quietly gathering up the pile of cards.

It had been her idea to play a game after dinner. I got the sense Hugo might have had different ideas, and Carson probably would've done anything suggested by Tate, but I was actually excited about the prospect.

It's been so many years since I've last played any game. Mom used to love card games, any card games. Crazy Eights, Canasta, Rummy, you name it, she'd play. I remember many nights after we cleaned up the dinner dishes, we'd sit down at the table with a cup of tea, a plate of cookies, and a deck of cards. Even in my teens, I preferred that over going out and partying with my friends, like my brother used to do. Not that I had a ton of friends to start with. Not back then anyway.

"I bet you if anyone could, it'd be my dad," Carson insists, with a little smirk on his face that seems to be reserved for Tate.

I think it's sweet, those two. I hope they get to keep what they've found so young, but growing up can be an angsty, sometimes messy business, and it's not often these young relationships stand the course of time.

Of course, there are exceptions, like Tate's father and Savvy, but even though their love survived the decades, their relationship was nonexistent for most of those years. Plus, there's a lot they had to overcome to get where they are today.

Then there are some of us who never had much luck in love at all, and almost give up on it completely. Until one day the opportunity is right there, ready to grab, if they can overcome their mistrust.

"You sure are thinking hard on something," Hugo says softly, covering my hand resting on the table with his.

"Never mind me, I'm still trying to figure out how you managed to win three times when it is well known I'm the queen of Crazy Eights," I tease to deflect.

"Could've fooled me," Carson mutters, teasing a snort from me.

"Sorry, Bess, you were pretty brutal," Hugo adds, clearly laughing at me.

"We can always play one more so you can claim your crown," Tatum offers with a grin, already shuffling the deck.

Since I was the one who indicated the third game would be the last because I wanted to get home, the challenge is for me. It is a little after ten, which is already beyond my regular bedtime, but tomorrow is my day off. Besides, this has been such a surprisingly fun and relaxing night—I've barely given any thought to my troubles—I don't really want it to end yet.

"Fine," I concede. "But don't say I didn't warn you; I'm not going to go easy on you this time. Start dealing."

Twenty minutes later, I'm about to get clobbered for the fourth time—this time by Tate—when my phone rings.

I'm instantly apprehensive, and I can feel Hugo's eyes on me when I check the caller.

"It's Lola," I announce, relieved when her name pops up on my call display. "Excuse me for a minute."

I get up and walk across the room to the front window as I answer her call.

"Hey, what's up?"

"Where are you?"

Her question jars me, and I get an uneasy feeling in the pit of my stomach.

"Um...at a friend's place. Why?"

"I'm just driving down Main on my way home from arguably the worst date ever—remind me to tell you about it later—I passed the coffee shop and glanced over, and I could've sworn I saw a flashlight or something inside. I thought maybe the power was out, or the breaker tripped, but it was probably just a reflection of headlights. I can go back and make sure."

That uneasy feeling has grown into sour churning, and I almost jump when a hand lands on my shoulder.

Hugo.

"Everything okay?"

"Yes," I answer him.

"Okay, I'll go check it out," Lola responds in my ear.

"No," I quickly tell her, alarm bells going off in my head. "Don't go in alone. I'm leaving now."

I turn to Hugo as I end the call. I'm probably overreacting—hopefully—but my gut tells me not to try and handle this on my own.

"Are you going to tell me what is going on?" he asks, his jaw set.

"Lola thinks she saw someone inside the coffee shop with a flashlight. She thought it might've been me."

I haven't even finished my sentence when Hugo is already on the move.

"Stay here," he orders, grabbing his phone off the charger in the kitchen and snatching his keys from the table.

"I'm...um...no. Definitely not," I snap, scooping my purse from the couch and going for my coat. "That's my business *and* my home."

He already has his hand on the doorknob, and rolls his eyes to the ceiling, clenching his jaw.

"Fine, but you ride with me. Son, I need you to drive Tate home and make sure to take Ragnar with you."

"Why can't—" I start objecting, when he jabs a finger in my face.

"Do you wanna argue, or do you wanna come?"

I snap my mouth closed and shrug into my coat, bristling when he adds under his breath, "Smart choice."

Hugo gets on the radio as he backs his cruiser out of the driveway.

"All units. Possible burglary in progress. One forty Main Street. Be aware; front entrance, side alley entrance, and fire escape entrance in the rear."

"She said it might've been the reflection of a headlight," I share, worried maybe we're overreacting.

He briefly takes his eyes off the road to look at me. "What does your gut tell you?"

When I don't immediately answer, he adds, "Yeah, mine too."

The moment we turn onto Main Street, I can see a couple of patrol cars already parked in front of Strange Brew. Then I spot Lola's blue Volkswagen Beetle, it's driver's side door wide open.

"Dammit, Lola," I grumble, as we pull up to Strange Brew.

That's when I see the shop's front door wide open, smoke streaming out, and my heart lodges in my throat.

"Stay put," Hugo barks, jumping from the cruiser.

But he shouldn't have bothered; I'm right on his heels when he runs straight into the smoke-filled coffee shop.

Hugo

Even as Lloyd updates me with the fire chief's report, I don't take my eyes off Bess.

Stubborn woman ran in right after me without thinking, sucking in big lungfuls of smoke. Even coughing so hard she couldn't stand up straight, she blundered her way into the kitchen, which apparently was the source of the fire.

Lola had stuck around, keeping an eye on Strange Brew from the street. She didn't see anyone leave—we later discovered they exited through the side door and likely went behind the buildings—but she did notice the smoke filling the coffee shop. That's when she called 911, unlocked the front door, and went in.

KC Kingma arrived on the scene moments later and followed her inside. Between the two of them, they were able to knock down the fire. It had been a simple setup; a couple of kitchen towels liberally doused in cooking oil and left on the industrial-sized range. One burner was left on low, igniting the fire.

Luckily, as per safety regulations, Bess had a couple fire extinguishers. Lola had grabbed the one in the kitchen and directed KC to the second one behind the counter in the shop. When the fire department showed up shortly after Bess and I got there, they doused the area of the fire with the hose, making sure nothing could flare up again.

If Lola hadn't already been keeping an eye on the coffee shop, it's unlikely anyone would've noticed the fire until it was already too late. Other than the occasional second-floor apartment, most of the buildings on this section of Main Street are businesses. It's quiet here at night.

Unfortunately, even as quickly as they got to it, the damage to the kitchen is quite extensive. Only the side of the range and hood was directly affected by the flames, but the smoke and water damage affect the entire kitchen and beyond. At the very least, the range, ovens, and exhaust hood, as well as any and all supplies and staples will have to be replaced.

It's a massive loss, and I can see the impact starting to hit Bess, as she sits on the stretcher in the back of the ambulance, staring out blankly while the medic checks her over. She didn't want to leave her shop, but I forced her to get looked at when the EMTs showed up.

"What the hell is going on, man?" Lloyd asks, staring

down the road. "First Clem's place, and now Strange Brew. Do we have a firebug?"

"Fuck if I know."

Chance sure as hell couldn't have had a hand in this one; he's still in the hospital. Are we dealing with two firebugs? In a town our size that seems a bit of a stretch, to put it mildly. With little evidence to suggest otherwise, Chance's guilt seemed a foregone conclusion, but I'm thinking we might want to reexamine that.

I don't believe in coincidence.

The sound of squealing brakes has me whip around to see Savvy's cruiser come to a stop behind the fire engine blocking most of the road. She comes flying out of the vehicle and starts running toward us, leaving her door wide open.

"Lloyd, can you…"

"Yeah, I'll move it."

I step into Savvy's path, intending to block her. "Bess is fine. She wasn't home at the time."

Savvy strains to look around me, and I know she's caught sight of her friend when she pokes a sharp finger in my chest.

"Then how come she's in the back of a fucking ambulance?"

"The place was filled with smoke when we got here. She's getting checked out as a precaution."

"She shouldn't have been in there in the first place," Savvy points out.

I nod. "Right, you try telling her that."

She grunts in response.

"All I heard from Tate when Carson dropped her off was there was a break-in at Strange Brew. It wasn't until I got behind the wheel and turned on the radio, I heard all the chatter. Get me up to speed."

I do as she asks, filling her in on everything up to the fire chief's preliminary report of suspected arson.

"Well, this sure wasn't Chance," she reacts, echoing my own conclusion. "Two businesses, a little over a block apart on the same side of the street. What the hell is going on here? What are we missing?"

I'm wondering the same thing.

"Can't think of anything an auto shop and a coffee shop might have in common that would generate a common enemy. It doesn't make sense. Could be random, but whatever it is, we need to increase patrols of the downtown."

Savvy groans. "We don't have a hell of a lot of room in the budget for the extra man hours, we hardly have enough bodies, and given my earlier phone call with Don Merrick, I'm pretty sure a supplement to our budget is not in the cards."

Our mayor is a fucking tool, more interested in optics than safety or efficiency or anything other than what makes him look better.

"What about a neighborhood watch?" I throw out there.

I bet we could have at least a handful of volunteers who'd be willing to help monitor Main Street.

"Last thing we need is a bunch of vigilantes running around wild in town," Savvy grumbles.

"I was thinking more along the lines of concerned citizens," I suggest cautiously. "And by organizing them, they wouldn't have to be running around wild."

She sighs. "Well, I'm not sure where you think you'll find the time, because it won't be me doing the organizing. Nate already threatened to shackle me to the bed if I don't follow doctor's orders."

Good luck to him, trying to manage Savvy.

"I don't," I admit. "But I'm thinking the retired Sheriff Colter might be able and willing to take it on."

"Dad?" She's quiet for a moment, a faint smile spreading on her face. "That might actually not be a bad idea. I'll give him a call, but let me check in with Nichols and our guys first." She looks over my shoulder and jerks her chin. "You can drop her off at my place or you can take her home, but Bess can't stay here tonight. Either way, she won't want to listen and fight you, but I'm trusting you to take care of her. Handcuff her if you must."

I bite off a grin. I don't think Savvy will appreciate the irony of her suggestion.

When she goes in search of the fire chief, I turn around to see Bess being assisted down from the ambulance.

"All good?" I ask, turning to Jim Turcotte, one of our veteran paramedics, when I get elbowed in my side. "Ouch."

"I'm right here," Bess snaps. "And I can talk for myself. Yes, I've been checked out and I'm fine, thank you very much."

Jim grins as he quietly retreats to the ambulance. *Wise man.*

I, however, appear to have blundered into it with my size thirteens once again. Rather than making excuses and risking secondary offenses, I go straight for the apology.

"I'm sorry, you're right."

Simple and straightforward—without any justifications—appears to be the way to go.

After a moment she merely nods and moves on.

"Have you seen Lola?"

"Yes, after she was checked out, she chose to go back to the station with KC to give her statement, while everything is still fresh in her mind."

"Okay, good. I'm gonna need to start making some phone calls; let Emmet know what's going on, call my suppliers with urgent orders to replenish my inventory. Then I have to figure out how I'm gonna clean up this mess before we open on Monday," she rambles, suddenly full of energy.

"Slow down and breathe," I urge her, placing my hands on her shoulders. "It's late, you'll be calling people out of bed. All that will have to wait until tomorrow. This is a crime scene, and you won't be able to do anything until we've gone over the coffee shop with a fine-tooth comb," I explain gently.

She looks deflated. "Oh..."

"Look, Savvy just arrived and she's got things here. You and me are going back to my place, where Carson is waiting with your dog. We'll take Ragnar for a walk and then we should try to get some sleep. We'll have a better idea tomorrow of everything that needs to get done, I'll help you."

I wait to see if she needs more convincing, but to my surprise she easily concedes. Almost too easily.

"Okay."

On the way to my cruiser, I call out to Lloyd we're heading out. I'm sure he'll let Savvy know.

We're just pulling away from the curb when Bess pipes up.

"Can we stop at the convenience store on the corner?"

"You need something? Want me to run in for you?"

She shakes her head. "No, I just need a few necessities."

I resist the urge to argue, realizing she may not feel comfortable having me pick up toiletries or personal items for her. Instead, I park right out front so I can keep an eye on her as she gets what she needs.

But I can't keep quiet when I see what she has in her hands as she gets back in the cruiser.

"Seriously?"

"What?" she counters innocently.

I gesture at the familiar box she's holding on her lap.

"Necessities? Twinkies?"

She shrugs.

"Essential comfort food."

CHAPTER 10

B^{ess}

I REFUSE to open my eyes.

I've been lying here, listening to the unfamiliar life of this house, but I know as soon as I open my eyes I'm going to have to face the day, and I don't want to.

I'm not sure what time my body finally gave in to sleep, but it was a little after four the last time I checked my phone. My systems were on overload, unable to process the chaos of events of the evening. Starting with the unexpected invitation to dinner and what turned out to be an amazingly fun time until it shifted into a nightmare. The whole night just kept playing in my head like disjointed movie scenes pasted together. Anytime I would attempt to sort my thoughts in some order, try and zoom in on one thing so I could determine what my next step should be, another wave of random flashes would knock me off my focus.

The fact I ended up in Hugo's massive bed, wearing his T-shirt, didn't help matters.

I blame it on shock; last night I didn't have the wherewithal to assert myself in any way. Too numb to care, I simply tapped out. When Hugo showed me to his bedroom and offered me its use, I didn't object. In fact, I don't think I would've said a word, even if he had crawled into bed with me and the box of comfort food I was clutching. He didn't stay, but he gave me one of his shirts to wear.

Where he ended up, I don't know, but now I can hear him downstairs talking to Carson, putzing around the house, and I'm too much of a chicken to crawl out of my cocoon.

I must've fallen back asleep because the next thing I know, I feel someone sit down on the edge of the bed, pulling the covers off my face. I squint at the bright light of day, and am able to make out Hugo's smiling eyes.

He reaches over and peels off a plastic wrapper stuck to my cheek.

Wonderful.

I should be embarrassed I stuffed my face with Twinkies in his bed last night, but at this point it almost doesn't matter. It's not like he hasn't had a front-row seat to the absolute disaster my life turned into in these last twenty-four hours.

"It's noon," he shares. "I've held off the troops as long as I could, but Savvy was already here once this morning with a few things from your apartment, and she said she'd be back to talk to you."

He points to the bag by the bathroom door, and I silently thank my bestie for thinking ahead.

"Also, Lola and Emmet called, and I told them you'd call them back."

I reach over to the nightstand to grab my phone, but all my fingers find are more wrappers.

"I took it," Hugo explains.

"What? Why would you do that?"

"Because when I checked in on you this morning and saw you'd finally dozed off, I wanted you to get some sleep and took it with me. It was almost out of juice too, so it's charging in the kitchen."

I hold my breath when he leans over and brushes my lips with his, and don't release it again until he gets to his feet and moves to the door.

"I put some towels on the counter in the bathroom. Go grab a shower and get cleaned up before Savvy comes back, and I'll go put on a fresh pot of coffee."

The moment the door closes, I'm out of bed and heading for the bathroom, grabbing the bag with my stuff on the way. One glimpse in the mirror has me groan out loud. Between the giant bags under my eyes, one side of my hair sticking up, and the dried smear of pastry filling across my cheek, I'm not exactly looking my best.

Not smelling my best either; a combination of smoke, restless night, and morning breath. I can't believe he voluntarily put his lips on me. I'm disgusting.

I strip in two seconds flat and step into the walk-in shower.

Twenty minutes later, I walk down the stairs feeling—and smelling—a hundred times better. Savvy is already sitting at the large kitchen island, a bottle of water in front of her.

"Good afternoon, Rip Van Winkle," she says in greeting.

"Hey," I return, taking a seat beside her.

Hugo immediately sets a cup of coffee in front of me. I don't clue in until I take my first sip it was already doctored to perfection; generous on the cream with just a hint of sweet.

"Mmm. This is delicious. Just what I needed," I mention, rewarding him with a smile.

"Don't rub it in," Savvy grumbles beside me. "I'm going to be stuck inhaling the fumes while drinking water and herbal tea for the foreseeable future."

I should probably feel more sympathetic than I do, but if I am to deal with this day, I deserve this coffee.

"Where did Carson go?" I ask when I notice he's not around.

"At my house," Savvy answers, "helping Tatum paint the nursery."

I smile at her. "You've got colors picked out?"

"Not me," she scoffs. "That's Nate's project. He's got a vision and I'm not about to mess with it. He wants it to be a surprise."

She feigns annoyance, but I can tell she secretly loves it.

But talking about painting reminds me I probably have a bit of a project of my own to tackle.

"When can I get back into the building?" I ask her.

"Rick Althof is there now with the fire inspector, so give them another hour or two." She reaches over to put a hand on my arm. "Brace yourself though. It looks pretty dismal in daylight."

I nod, swallowing hard. The only way to the other side is to barge through this, so I'm going to have to toughen up.

"I'll see if Lola and Emmet can meet me there and help me take inventory of what needs to be done. See if we can do clean up ourselves, or—"

"That may be a little premature. Besides, you're gonna need professional cleaners for that. That smoke gets into everything," Savvy suggests.

"I think before anything else," Hugo weighs in, "maybe let's take a notepad over, make a list of all the things that need to happen, and then prioritize before you call in the troops. You're going to have to call your insurance company, they'll want to send someone out."

"Yes," Savvy jumps in. "And Nate already offered to walk through with you to give you an idea of repairs that will need to be done. But get the adjustor in there, you'll want to leave things as they are."

The heavy feeling returns when I realize it means my plans to get busy and gain some control over this glitch in my universe will not start today, or possibly even tomorrow. In fact, I have no idea how long it'll take to get an insurance adjuster in, so I can get to work restoring my life.

"What about my apartment?" I ask her.

She smiles sympathetically. "It's smoky up there. I ended up washing your things at home before I brought them here this morning. It's gonna stick to walls, furniture, fabric, and it can be pretty toxic. You don't want to breathe that in, which is another reason to bring in the cleaning pros, they wear protection."

The tentative tally I've started in my head of the things that are going to cost money is growing.

Hugo seems to sense where my mind is traveling and reaches across the island to give my hand a squeeze.

"That's why you have insurance, and should put in a claim before you do anything else."

I nod, at least that's something I can do. I'm not good at sitting idle—I tend to get in my head if my hands aren't busy—and the prospect of waiting around, twiddling my thumbs, is a scary proposition.

Then suddenly a thought pops in my head, and flies from my mouth unchecked.

"Where am I gonna stay?"

Hugo

"Here."

My response is drowned out by Ragnar who starts barking. The next moment the doorbell rings.

Rick Althof is standing on my doorstep.

"I was told I could find Bess here, and I wanted a word. The boss is here too?"

"They both are. Come in."

I immediately notice the strain on Bess's face as she watches Althof approach.

"Grab yourself a coffee," I offer, opting to move in behind Bess.

I slide my hand under her hair and curl my fingers around the back of her neck, feeling her lean into my hold slightly.

"The fire inspector is done," Rick starts. "He confirms arson, and we should have his report by tomorrow morning."

"I'll make sure you get a copy," Savvy offers her friend. "You're going to need that for the insurance company."

Bess nods. "Okay."

"We figure the suspect came in through the side door by the kitchen. We know it wasn't random. This guy came prepared, because he had tools to cut out the small pane of glass so he could reach the deadlock. It doesn't look like this was a random robbery or a straightforward arson. It's obvious he was looking for something specific, because your office was a point of focus, as was your apartment upstairs. We noticed a charging cable for a laptop in your office."

I feel her back go rigid.

"Just the cable? What about my laptop?"

"I was wondering about that too," Rick mentions. "I'd hoped perhaps you'd brought it with you."

She shakes her head. "It rarely leaves the office. Are you saying it's gone? What would anyone want with my laptop? It's an older model, it's not like it's worth anything. I keep my recipes on there, run a bookkeeping program and do payroll, but that's an encrypted software and I have two step verification through my phone. Other than that, I check emails, place orders, and maybe run the occasional internet search, but I do most of that on my phone. Same with banking."

"The suspect clearly believes there is something important on there, or he wouldn't have taken it and left the money in the cash register," Althof points out. "Do you have any idea what he might've been looking for?"

"No. Nothing," Bess responds, but I can hear the slight hitch in her voice.

Rick does too and narrows his eyes on her. "No documents, photos, letters, emails, contacts that might be of interest to someone?" he probes.

I clench my jaw at his tone. I understand better than most he's doing his job, but I don't like him pushing Bess, who is starting to tremble under my touch.

I have questions of my own I'd like to be asking her—I've had plenty of time to think about the fire last night and this morning—but I'm not about to badger her. Not after watching her tap out last night, traumatized. Fuck, I had to listen to my bed creak upstairs as she rolled around restlessly most of the night. I was on the couch in the living room, wide awake too.

"No," she repeats in a shaking voice. "I can't think of anything."

It's Savvy who steps in to smooth over the sudden tension in the room, leaning forward to pat Bess's wringing hands in her lap.

"Don't worry, we'll figure it out. Do you think you might be up to doing a walk-through of the coffee shop and your apartment to see if maybe anything else is missing?"

"Yeah. Okay."

Despite her affirmative answer, I get the sense she'd rather crawl back into that cocoon she turned my bedsheets into and hide.

"Why don't you guys go ahead and give us a few minutes, okay?" I suggest, directing my focus on Savvy.

She nods, understanding I want to give Bess a moment to process. Getting up, she addresses Rick.

"Let's go, Althof."

The moment the door closes behind them I swing Bess around and fold her in my arms, resting my cheek on the top of her head. She's stiff as a board.

"It's going to be okay," I whisper against her hair. "I'm not going to let anything happen to you."

It's like a spring releases as she suddenly slumps against me, her fingers digging into my back. We stand like that for a while, silently, even though a lot is being conveyed in body language. I'm glad she's at a point where she feels she can lean on me, quite literally at the moment. Maybe the next step will be opening up to me. I hope so; I'd really like to find out more about that brother of hers.

"I hate to be a bother."

I take a step back and catch her eyes. They're dry, but haunted.

"You couldn't be a bother if you tried," I assure her before adding jokingly, "but we should get going before they send out a search party."

That seems to snap her into action and she darts for the stairs.

"I'm just going to splash some water on my face," she clarifies as she heads up.

While waiting, I collect the coffee mugs and load them in the dishwasher. Then I remember Bess hasn't had anything to eat yet, and quickly slap a peanut butter and jelly sandwich together. I'm sure it's not up to her standards, but it's a kick of protein and something in her stomach.

Since she's still not back down when I'm done, I yell up the stairs.

"Hey! Let's go, Twinkie!"

Two seconds later she appears at the top of the stairs. I can see she put a little makeup on, a little mask of protection, I imagine.

"Twinkie?" she returns as she comes down the steps, her eyes twinkling.

I shrug.

"Seems fitting, since that's all you've eaten since dinner last night," I point out, helping her into her coat and handing her the sandwich I made before I finish my thought.

"That, and, like you, it packs a lot of goodness in a small package."

She smiles softly as I usher her out the door. Once inside my vehicle, she takes a healthy bite of her sandwich and, with a mouthful, turns to me.

"You're getting pretty good at saying the right thing."

CHAPTER 11

B*ess*

"I'm calling Roy Battaglia."

Hugo is already pulling his phone from his pocket as we approach his cruiser, but I quickly block his path, holding up my hand.

"Wait. Why do you need to call Roy?"

I desperately want some control back. I feel like I'm a bit character in a convoluted plot and someone forgot to give me the script. It feels like I'm the only one struggling to keep up.

Roy Battaglia runs a security company that mostly entails the installation and monitoring of security systems regionally, but he also runs a trained team of protection officers providing a variety of security services almost anywhere in the country. I'd rather not have him sic his guys on me, watching my every move.

Hugo forcefully blows out a breath before inhaling audibly through his nose, visibly calming himself.

"Because as much as I'd love to shackle myself to your side twenty-four seven, I can't. We are short-staffed, Savvy is already doing more than she should be in her condition, and we need all the manpower we can pull together to get to the bottom of what the hell is going on here."

He drops his hands on my shoulders.

"And until then, you're not safe."

He gives me a little shake when I open my mouth to object.

"Someone clearly thinks you have something they need; information of some kind. They waited for a time when you weren't around—which means you were being watched—broke in like pros, went through your apartment and your business, grabbed what they thought was pertinent, and casually proceeded to burn it down. At least try to." I get another little shake before he adds, "Tell me you realize you are not safe."

Better than anyone, but that doesn't mean I want anyone else at risk. I don't want more people dragged into my family's mess. Because I have a serious suspicion, even if it perhaps wasn't my brother doing the actual breaking and entering, he's definitely at the root of it. Although it doesn't make sense to take my laptop and some bills, and leave the almost three hundred dollars in the till or anything else that might have value.

Not sure what he was thinking; maybe that he could hit me up for any insurance money? Given how long they may take to pay out, that wouldn't have been the smartest of plans, even for Ken, who has a history of less than smart decisions.

The truth is, I have no real idea who my brother is. I

know nothing about him, except that he's desperate and I don't blame him. If, as he claims, the Lotus Squad is after him, he's in big trouble, and I could well be too.

But as much as I dread involving more people, Hugo does make some compelling points, not the least of which is the stress this situation is putting on others.

So this is what catch-22 feels like. Stuck between guilt over the potential harm I'm bringing into people's lives on one side, and on the other the kind of guilt that has forced my lips sealed for two decades.

"I realize that, but I can be careful." I try to negotiate in a last-ditch effort. "Besides, if anyone would've wanted to harm me, why would they have waited until I was gone?"

"And what if they don't find what they're obviously looking for?" he counters sharply. "They may come back to ask you in person, and I seriously doubt they'll be polite about it. Or maybe they decide you're a loose end of some sort they need to eliminate. All that assuming we're dealing with someone of sound mind, because if not, all bets are off," he ends in a raised voice.

His obvious anger rattles me. Although he's usually calm and laid-back, I've seen him upset, sad, and even happy, but I've never seen him angry like this.

Still, at the risk of angering him even further, his comments spur me on to make one final point. Something I'd tried to highlight before but which fell on deaf ears. That's when we were packing up a few more things for me and Ragnar, and Hugo wouldn't take no for an answer when he made it clear he expected me to stay at his place.

"Why then insist I stay with you? Wouldn't I be putting you, or even worse, Carson, in danger?" I indicate.

The mention of his son starts a muscle twitching in his

already clenched jaw. I figured that last point might give him pause.

"Can I propose a compromise?"

The change in his stubborn expression is infinitesimal, but I take it as encouragement.

"I'll check if Doug and Arno can put me up for a few days, if you could look after Ragnar. I don't think dogs are allowed."

Douglas McShire and Arno Nobel are the couple who run The Carriage House, a large turn-of-the-century farmhouse converted into a bed-and-breakfast on the outskirts of town. I could hole up there for a few days, make my phone calls, get my bearings, and figure out what the best move forward is with the least amount of damage.

"Where's the compromise?" he questions before I have a chance to finish.

I give him a pointed look before I continue.

"Doug dropped by Strange Brew about a month ago, mentioning how Roy and his crew were installing a security system at The Carriage House. He got the full package with alarms, cameras inside and out, and twenty-four-hour monitoring," I share.

I observe him as he processes the information and slowly nods.

"That would work, but I still don't like letting you out of my sight," he grumbles.

"Letting me out of your sight?" I echo with a hefty dose of sarcasm. "May I kindly remind you I am an adult and, although I've made my own decisions since I turned eighteen, I'm willing to take your opinions into consideration because I know you care. But don't mistake me for a doormat."

His lips press together, but the fine laugh lines deepen at the corners of his eyes.

"You? A doormat? Never," he grumbles.

Then he slides his hands on either side of my neck and pulls me closer, dropping his forehead to mine.

"I worry," he adds on a whisper.

I curl my hands around his wrists. "I know. I wouldn't be standing here otherwise."

∽

Hugo

"What would anyone want with her phone bills, anyway?" KC mutters beside me.

Exactly my first thought when Bess pointed out she had a file folder containing that information missing from the small filing cabinet in her bedroom. But when we discovered an agenda she kept in her desk drawer downstairs with mostly information on her suppliers, the deliveries, as well as her employees, schedules, and more of that kind of stuff was missing as well, a possible objective emerged.

"Her contacts," I clarify for KC. "They took her laptop, her phone bills, and her agenda. If they're looking for someone they think she's communicating with, it could be in any one of those things."

It made sense and, taking into account who was blowing up Bess's phone just a few nights ago, I'm pretty sure who is up to his neck in this. The timing of all this is such, I'm convinced she knows too, not that she shared that with me.

I was going to bring up her brother when we got back to my place, but instead she ended up at The Carriage House.

Alone. My little dust-up outside the coffee shop yesterday afternoon had her calmly set me straight, resulting in my concession to her alternate plan. She didn't raise her voice, but the message was heard loud and clear.

Boy, did she tell me.

I'd been so busy worrying about Bess, so focused on keeping her safe, I didn't think of the risk it might pose to my son. She reminded me. So even though I wasn't a fan of leaving her at the bed-and-breakfast by herself, after talking to Roy, who reassured me she'd be covered, I felt pretty comfortable she'd be safe there.

Unfortunately, it also means that right now, I feel compelled to share a few things with my colleagues I am fairly certain Bess won't be happy about.

We're in the large meeting room at the sheriff's station, where Savvy called a briefing this morning on the break-in and fire at the coffee shop. Rick Althof is leading, going over all the details of the case.

"That's right," he confirms my comments to KC. "This suspect is looking for someone and hoping to find answers in the stuff he took."

"So why set the fire?" KC persists.

"As a message," I offer. "A taunt, knowing the person they're trying to find has a close enough connection to Bess to draw them out in the open."

Savvy, who is standing on the opposite side, suddenly leans forward and plants her fists on the table. Her narrowed eyes focus on me.

"What are you suggesting?"

"I think we need to look into Bess's brother, Ken."

"Half brother," Savvy corrects me sharply, clearly not happy with me. "And she hasn't seen or spoken with him in decades."

"I wasn't aware she had any relatives," Rick states. "She didn't mention a brother."

"Because he's out of the picture," Savvy insists, before adding with a glare in my direction, "He's in jail."

I meet her angry look straight on. "Not anymore. He was paroled last month."

"What?"

That news obviously comes as a surprise to Savvy, who immediately turns to her laptop, where I assume she is pulling up the Washington State Department of Corrections website to do an inmate data search.

A muffled curse a few moments later tells me she found confirmation.

"Who is this guy? There's gotta be a reason you bring him up," Rick points out.

"I just can't believe she told you and didn't mention anything to me," Savvy grumbles in the background.

"Only reason I know is because I happened to be around when he called her and overheard part of a conversation. She claimed she wasn't really comfortable talking to him." I shrug and add, "I guess I'm just suspicious by nature, and think he's worth looking into. Especially since, three days after, her business was broken into and set on fire. I don't like coincidences."

"I don't either," Rick agrees. "Let's see what we can find on the brother."

Ten minutes later, Savvy follows me out of the meeting room.

"My office, please."

I figured she'd have a thing or two to say to me. Believe me, I'm not happy spilling the beans on Bess's brother either, but I don't regret bringing up his name. If there is even the slightest chance he's involved and poses a threat to her, I'm not about to risk her safety by staying silent. I'll happily take whatever repercussions come my way.

"She's not going to be happy with you," Savvy starts when she's closed her door for privacy. "I'm the only one who knew her brother was incarcerated. When she moved back here from Seattle, she was eager for a fresh start; a life of her own on her terms and without the trappings of her brother's chosen path. I respected her choices and her privacy all these years. You learned about Ken only days ago."

She doesn't spell it out, but the accusation is clear. Rather than getting on the defensive, I ask her a simple question.

"Knowing what you know now, would you still have stayed quiet?"

The long stare tells me enough.

Then she asks, "Did you talk to her first?"

"No, I didn't. She probably would've told me to keep it to myself. She has been evasive on the subject of her brother, brushing off his phone call as inconsequential, even though I could easily see their conversation left her unsettled at best. She also chose to stay at the B&B instead of my place…"

When I notice Savvy bristle at that information, I put up my hand and quickly enlighten her. "The Battaglia Security team is monitoring and I'm the only one who knows where she is. Well, and now you do too. But my point is, I think she's actively trying to avoid any questions I might ask, which tells me she—at the very least—suspects her brother has some knowledge of, or involvement with, what happened at the coffee shop."

"Possibly," Savvy concedes, nodding slightly before she

tilts her head. "What exactly is happening with you and Bess?"

"Right now, I'm focused on keeping her safe," I evade, getting ready to leave her office

"She's my best friend, Hugo," she pushes, "and I'm not an idiot; somewhere along the line things have moved well past friendship between you two."

"Key words there are *between you two*," I point out.

"You're annoying. I'll just go talk to Bess myself, I wanted to have a word with her anyway."

Yeah, I don't think so. At least not before I have a chance to talk to her first. I should tell her myself and use the opportunity to get some more information out of her.

"Get in line," I tell my boss. "I am heading there now to give her a heads-up we are looking into Ken and will undoubtedly take the heat for that, but I hope it'll push her to open up about that call with her brother. If you want to talk to her after, be my guest."

"Oh, all right," she gives in. "And then I'll get her to talk about you and her."

I just shake my head and reach for her office door, but before I step into the hallway, I leave her with a parting thought.

"For someone who claims to respect privacy, you're pretty nosy."

CHAPTER 12

B*ess*

"Feel free to test your experiments on us any time you like."

Arno hums as he licks the sugar off his fingers.

Doug looks after the guests and the rooms, but Arno is the chef. This morning when he served me a simple but delicious breakfast, he noticed my notepad with ideas for new menu items and offered me the use of the kitchen and its pantry.

I wasn't able to take him up on it until I tackled another list in my notebook; the index of dreaded phone calls I compiled last night when I, once again, couldn't sleep. I thought I'd be busy with those all day, but I was lucky and it went pretty fast once I got to it.

With my checklist complete, it didn't take long for my mind to start spinning. I ended up downstairs in Arno's well-equipped kitchen to give my hands something to do.

An inventory of his staples led me to the pumpkin-spiced cruller donuts he and Doug have been snacking on. It's not really the right time of year for pumpkin, but I found a leftover can in the pantry, and was trying to come up with some seasonal pastries.

Earlier, I tried out a spring strawberry and rhubarb crumble muffin, and for summer I came up with a lavender peach custard tart with a shortbread crust. Both of those also received high praise from the couple.

"I appreciate it. It certainly helped me from climbing the walls today," I admit with a self-deprecating smile. "By all means, feed those leftovers to the guests," I suggest, indicating the remaining pastries.

I'd made a dozen of each, so there was plenty left over.

"I'll set them out with afternoon tea at four," Doug offers.

It's one of the charming features The Carriage House offers that seems terribly out of place in the Columbia Mountains but works. It makes perfect sense when you meet Doug McShire, who is a Scot by birth, was raised in the English Cotswolds, fell in love with a Dutchman, and built a life in eastern Washington.

I love how they were able to stay connected to their heritage, while fully embracing and engaging in life in Silence. Their individual and joint histories can be found all over the large and ornate farmhouse.

As I go up the oak stairway to my room, I let my eyes drift over a collection of pictures and art pieces covering the wall; a patchwork of cultures creating a meaningful gallery.

I would love to feel some connection to the Korean part of my ancestry, but it wasn't something my mother valued or even tolerated. She despised the heavy accent she never seemed able to shed, and claimed to have nothing but bad memories of her life before she emigrated here.

The other half of my genetic pool is a bit of a mystery, although my mother tells me my father was Caucasian. That's all I know. I have no idea of his heritage. I've thought about trying one of those DNA test kits that can give you an idea of your ancestral origins. As intriguing as it seems, I'm not so sure I want to find out more about any possible family. The one I had—have—is taxing enough.

This community has more than made up for my lack of family though. Nobody seems to care where or who I came from; I'm accepted here for who I am. But there are still those rare times—mostly when I'm alone—when I miss that sense of belonging only family can bring. A grounding connection from the past to the future.

Instead, I have a half brother, who appears to pose a real threat to the modest life and legacy I've built here in Silence. The more I think about what I stand to lose, the darker my sense of doom returns.

Shaking my head, I try and stop the endless string of thoughts that seems to start up when my hands still, and inevitably sucks the air from the room, leaving me to feel like I'm drowning.

I turn the TV on in hopes it'll dull the noise in my head, and flip through channels to find something that can hold my attention. I've just landed on a home improvement show that looks interesting when someone knocks on my door.

I don't hesitate opening it, expecting one of the guys, but it's Hugo standing in the hallway.

God, how I wish I could give in to the urge to throw myself in his arms, grab the few moments of bliss I know I'd find there. But that wouldn't be fair to him, since I know whatever happens between us has a very limited shelf life.

Not that it wouldn't be good, because it would. In fact, I have no doubt it would be perfect. I've harbored feelings for this man for so many years, it's hard to remember when it started.

"Is it okay if I come in?"

His somewhat amused question snaps me into the here and now, and I quickly step away from the door I realize I've been blocking. He steps inside and pushes the door shut before leaning in for a kiss that tastes bittersweet to me.

"Is everything okay?" I ask, suddenly worried something may have happened to prompt this midafternoon visit.

"Fine," he responds, taking off his coat and folding his large body into one of the dainty-looking Queen Anne chairs across from the love seat where I was sitting. "But there's something I need to talk to you about."

I return to my spot and wrap one of the throw pillows in my arms, bracing for whatever is coming.

"We had a case briefing earlier on the break-in and fire at your place. It's basically a meeting with everyone involved in the investigation, where we go through each piece of evidence and any and all information we've pulled together to see where we're at," he explains. "I want you to know I brought up your brother's name."

Suddenly I'm free-falling, the shaky ground I was trying to balance on abruptly gone.

Part of me knew this was coming, but I spent so many years burying the past, I almost deluded myself into believing it never happened. This is only the first layer, but it will lead to the next one, and the next, until there's nowhere left to hide and I'm completely exposed.

I want to be angry at Hugo, but what would that accomplish? Besides, it isn't like he had any way to understand the ramifications, or could've stopped the truth from coming out. It always finds a way.

So I simply nod, resigned to the fact I no longer control my history.

"I looked him up," he confesses. "I had a sense there was more to the estranged brother. I'm sorry, but you seemed scared after that phone call, and I didn't quite buy in to your story." He shrugs. "It's the investigator in me. But knowing his background, his connection, plus the fact he only recently was paroled, I couldn't sit on that information. Not when you may be in danger."

Of course, he was looking out for me. It's the kind of man he is: kind, caring, protective, dependable, and honest to the core.

God knows I don't deserve him.

∽

Hugo

I'm surprised at how calm she seems.

Not sure what I was expecting, but definitely some level of upset.

Instead, her voice is level as she opens up about her brother. A lot of the factual information she shares I was already able to pull together on my own, but she puts the facts in context, providing me with a more complete, three-dimensional story. I hear the love she still feels for her brother, or at least the brother he used to be. I can tell how painful it was for her to cut his toxicity out of her life, and how conflicted she is now he's trying to force his way back into it.

Listening to her gives me a better understanding of her motivations for keeping all this information hidden, even from me.

"So, he's after money from you so he can skip the country?"

"Yeah," she confirms. "Except everything I own is invested in the coffee shop."

"Did he explain what he's running from?"

She shrugs, and her gaze drifts to the TV, which is on but muted. "I know it probably has something to do with his gang."

The Lotus Squad. *Jesus*. I'm pretty sure we'll need to draw on the FBI for at least some intel on a violent gang like that. Maybe they have picked up rumbles of something going on in their routine surveillance that might explain why the newly released Lotus Squad member is in such a hurry to leave the country.

It could be anything; a rival gang Ken Choi wronged at some point in time, or perhaps he knows something damaging to his own gang members, or he owes money to them. I don't particularly like any of those options, because they could all put Bess in the crosshairs as well.

Hell, it could be the guy is just milking his sister for what he might see as easy money, using some hyped-up story about being in danger to apply to her good heart. It might have even been him who set the fire, hoping to get the insurance money from his sister. He could've taken the notebook, laptop, and phone records to eliminate any possible connection to him, or maybe just to reinforce his fabricated story someone is after him.

"Do you still have his number?"

"I blocked it after that last call," Bess admits. "He hasn't tried to call me from another number."

"There would still be a record of the number in your phone," I suggest.

She gets up and grabs her cell phone off the little table by the door, and unlocks it before handing it to me. Then she walks over to the window and crosses her arms over her chest as she stares outside.

I easily retrieve the number from her call log on the date we had dinner at Fusion and copy it into a message for Rick Althof with a brief message. Next, I get up and close in behind Bess, putting my hands on her shoulders.

"I'm sorry," I mumble in her hair, recognizing none of this was probably easy for her.

"Why would you be sorry?"

"For making you feel as I imagine you might after sharing all that information."

She turns and lifts her face to me, placing her hands on my chest.

"You didn't. But, Hugo, I hope you can see now why it's for the best not to get involved with me," she pleads. "What you see is a quiet, simple coffee shop owner, but I come with a dark and complicated history I can't seem to outrun. You don't want that in your life."

I shake my head. "Your history may be complicated but it isn't dark. Your brother's choices and mistakes aren't yours to bear, even if they affect you. So no, I don't see how getting involved with you would not be for the best, and aside from that, it's too late. I'm already in up to my neck."

"You're making this so hard," she groans, abruptly pulling from my arms.

She creates some distance as she returns to her spot on the small love seat, curling her legs underneath her, and cradling that pillow in her arms again like a damn shield.

"This doesn't have to be hard at all," I argue. "In fact, it was probably the easiest of decisions; getting involved with you. Nothing you've told me changes that. And—unless my powers of detection are suddenly failing me—you're pretty much up to your neck into us too."

She starts shaking her head in denial, but then suddenly buries her face in the pillow. Not sure whether she's crying, I squeeze in beside her and lightly rub her back.

Startling me, she abruptly tosses the pillow aside and twists around, swinging a leg over to straddle my lap. Before I can utter a word, her hands are in my hair and her mouth covers mine.

From zero to combustible in a heartbeat.

Her mouth plunders as she presses her body against mine. I can feel every inch of her, from the tip of her fiery little tongue to the rigid nipples against my chest and the damp heat between her legs.

Holy shit.

I can't decide where to put my restless hands, finding a treasure trove of curves and valleys as they roam her body. One finally settles under her sweater and on a breast. I fill my hand, catching the turgid little nipple between my fingers and tugging lightly. The other slides down the back of her pants and grabs on to the soft globe of her ass cheek firmly.

"Off...off..." she mumbles against my lips as she tugs on the hem of my shirt.

My mind has trouble catching up with this turn of events, but I'm a guy—I'm conditioned to go with this particular flow—no actual thought required.

With joint—albeit clumsy—effort, my Henley is up and off, and we've moved on to removing her top. Me one-handedly, because I don't want to let go of that round ass that has featured in my fantasies for some time now.

But the moment she whips her sweater over her head, the sight of her fantastic tits six inches from my face demands all my attention, and both my hands.

Her body is a playground, and I'm over the fucking moon to explore every feature. As she rolls her hips, teasing herself and my raging hard-on, my arms wrap around her torso to hold her still so I can shove my face in her generous cleavage.

Ahh fuck, cinnamon and sugar.

I'm just about to test if she tastes like that too, when the phone in my pocket starts buzzing. It's as effective as a bucket of water.

"Ohh," Bess groans when I gently shift her away from my cock and dig in my pocket for my phone.

"Alexander," I answer, quickly clearing my throat of the frog that made me sound funny.

"Catch you at a bad time?" Brenda asks.

I love that woman like a sister, but she's nosy as hell and there isn't much that passes her by.

"Nope," I cut off her inquiries and get to the point. "What's up?"

"Althof left for Spokane where he's meeting with the feds, and I don't want to disturb Savvy, who finally went home half an hour ago. Got a call from the hospital that Chance Tanek is awake."

"I'm about ten minutes out and on my way."

Bess is already climbing off my lap when I end the call.

"Sorry—"

She waves her hand to cut me off.

"No, it's fine. You have to go."

She's far from fine, which is obvious from the way she struggles with her sweater in the rush to cover herself up. I'm worried if I leave now, she's going to build up those shields she dropped for a bit, but I'll just have to break them back down again next time.

I have to go talk to Chance.

I'm still not convinced two fires so close to each other in time and proximity can be a coincidence. So, I want to see if he can shed some light on the auto shop fire at least.

By the time I pull my shirt back on and grab my coat from the chair, she is back at the window, her arms folded around herself.

"Bess…"

She swings around, a tight smile on her lips and a blush on her cheeks.

"I'm sorry I got carried away," she says in a soft voice.

Two steps bridge the gap and I cup her face with my hand.

"Don't you dare apologize for the best fucking make-out session I can remember. But I have to warn you, there's no turning back now I've had a taste, Twinkie."

As much as she's trying to keep a straight face, I can see the light twitch at the corner of her mouth. A mouth I quickly press a hard kiss to before I reluctantly let her go.

But before I walk out, I feel the need to share one more thought.

"For the record, I've never just seen a quiet, simple coffee shop owner. That's what you do, not who you are."

CHAPTER 13

H*ugo*

"It wasn't me."

"You said that before," I remind him, trying to keep the interview moving forward.

Chance Tanek insisted his brother be present while I question him. I don't have an issue with Clem, who thus far has been listening and not contributing, but his brother keeps turning to him with the repeated claims of his innocence when I need to keep him focused on my questions.

"You were mentioning you stopped by Strange Brew first on that day," I prompt him, turning him back to the day of the fire.

"Every day, 'cept Sundays 'cause she's closed. I go there in the morning, before the place gets busy, and she usually has a paper baggie for me with some food."

Of course she does.

It doesn't surprise me in the least, Bess is known for her kindness and generosity.

"So she gave you food that morning?"

He nods. "Yeah, because I remember heading over to the garage. When it's cold I take the food to eat it in the small storage room at the back. Nobody goes in there."

For the first time Clem pipes up.

"I just use it for old junk and file storage, but it's usually locked." Then he turns to his brother. "How'd you get in?"

Chance lowers his eyes and focuses on his trembling hands restlessly fidgeting with the edge of the sheet.

"I kept the key, but I don't know where it is now. It must've fallen when I was running. Dropped my food too."

"Running?" I attempt to pick up the thread again. "Why were you running?"

"From the guy with the gun."

I know Chance probably can't help the way his mind skips all over the timeline I'm trying to pry from his alcohol-poisoned brain, but I just want to shake him. To think I left a hot-blooded woman wrapped around me for this.

"Whoa, back up a little. Where was the guy with the gun?"

"At the back of the garage," he explains. "I was just about to unlock the storage room when he came jogging out the back door. A second later, I had a gun pointed at me. I dropped everything and took off."

"Did he shoot at you?"

He shakes his head. "I don't think so. It all happened so fast."

"Was it anyone you know? Have seen before?"

"Nah. Had his hoodie covering his head and a scarf or something covering his mouth and stuff."

"But you saw he was wearing a hoodie?"

"Black one," he says, nodding.

It's possible he's making this masked, gun-toting guy up to divert the focus away from him, but I don't get the sense he's lying. The guy really isn't in any mental shape to be fabricating stories.

"Anything printed on the hoodie? A logo or an image. Did you see anything else? Pants? Shoes?"

"No, but before he spotted me, he was heading for the SUV parked in the alley."

I almost roll my eyes; this is like pulling teeth.

"What SUV?"

"Looked brand new. BMW XM." Then he turns to his brother. "Remember Dad's Porsche 911 Targa? It was that same color; that petrol blue metallic."

Even as he describes the vehicle, I put the information in my phone, intending to send it straight to Rick Althof.

"Are you sure it wasn't a customer's vehicle?" I ask, playing devil's advocate before I get too excited.

I know Althof has looked at the traffic cameras at both the traffic lights at Main and Elm and the one just south of the garage for that morning, but hadn't found any activity out of the ordinary at either location. That time of the day there wouldn't have been much traffic yet anyway, and so far, Rick was able to eliminate the few vehicles that did show up on the feed.

Having a description for the vehicle is huge, provided the BMW was involved.

"Fuck no," Clem answers. "The only person I know in town with a Beemer is Gail Merrick, our mayor's wife, she drives that white mother-of-pearl sedan and the only time I've had that piece of crap in my shop was when she lost part of her muffler in the church parking lot. She takes it into the dealership in Spokane to get it serviced."

By the time I leave the hospital twenty minutes later, I'm pretty sure I have squeezed all the information I can from Chance Tanek.

I believe his claim of innocence. Even sober, the man can barely keep a straight thought, so I don't buy that he'd be able to plan and execute a perfect arson drunk out of his brain. The other thing is, he couldn't give a detailed description of the guy with the gun but was able to tell us the make and model of the vehicle because the color reminded him of his father's car. That's the kind of thing that seems genuine to me. Of course, finally, there's the not so small issue I don't believe in coincidence; my gut tells me these fires are connected, but I'll be damned if I know how.

The clock on my dashboard shows it's already six. It'll be after seven by the time we eat if I have to cook, so tonight is take-out night.

I quickly check in with Carson to see what he feels like for dinner.

"Pizza."

The instant response is not a surprise.

"Call them, I'll swing by there to pick it up. And Son, order me a medium of that spinach, roasted pepper, and chicken one they have."

"You don't want the loaded pie?"

That's our standing order; they load that pizza with every meat, four or five different cheeses, and a pile of jalapeño peppers. We usually share an extra-large between us.

It's not that I don't *want* the pie, but this afternoon, while sitting on the small sofa with Bess straddling my lap, her hands roaming all over my bare torso, I noticed I have officially entered the dad-bod stage. Clothes hide a lot of sins but my shirt was on the floor. The basic structure is still there—somewhere underneath—but the years of neglect and convenience have definitely left some padding.

"Trying to change it up," I tell my kid. "But you order whatever you like."

As soon as I hang up with him, I dial Althof.

"Did you get my texts?"

"Sure did. Brenda found a picture of the SUV in that color and put out a post on social media to see if anyone recognizes it, and patrol has been notified to keep an eye out. I just got back from Spokane, and KC and I are trying to pull together video feed from traffic or security cameras, expanding the search radius."

"Call Battaglia Security," I suggest. "Most of the private or business security cameras were installed by him. He may be able to tell you which doors to knock on."

"Good idea."

"Make any progress with the FBI in Spokane?"

"Yep. Talked to SAC Jason Mancuso who said he was familiar with Ken Choi, and was aware of his recent parole release. He seemed very interested to hear what happened to Bess, offered to look into Ken's whereabouts, and dig around a little to see if there are rumblings on the street about any possible beef."

"That's helpful."

It's tough getting any kind of timely response from the Seattle PD. They tend to be busy with crime on their own turf, and checking into something for the sheriff's department of a small county clear across the state just isn't high on the list of priorities. With the FBI's involvement, information we need, aside from what the feds have themselves, I'm sure will be more forthcoming.

We're a small, understaffed department and are not really equipped to deal with a lot of major crimes. We rarely ever had to, but in recent years, those numbers have gone up, and our capacity to deal with them is stretched.

"I should run," I state. "Gotta get some dinner home to my boy. But call me if you need me."

"All right, later. Oh wait... Guess who I bumped into at the FBI office?" He barely even pauses before adding the answer, "Tessa Androtti. Remember? The State Patrol's CID agent in charge of that case here last year?"

Blond, ballsy, and built like a brick shithouse, yeah, I remember her. Smart, albeit a bit abrasive, but she was hard to miss.

"What about her?"

"She was there interviewing for a job. Sounds like she left the CID."

My ears perk up.

We've added a few new deputies in the past year, but someone with her background and experience would be a real asset to the department. Much like Althof himself was.

I just don't know if we'd have enough in the budget.

"Is that so?"

"Sure is. She'd make a hell of an asset," Rick echoes my thoughts.

She sure as hell would.

∽

Bess

I WAS JUST FINISHING up the dinner Doug and Arno insisted I share with them in the dining room, when Savvy showed up.

Being the incredible hosts they are, Doug immediately

pulled up a fourth chair, and Arno came back from the kitchen with dessert for four instead of three.

Conversation at the table is casual, but I can tell from the looks Savvy aims my way, she isn't very happy with me. I'm pretty sure the guys notice as well, so as soon as we finish the beautiful Charlotte Russe cake Arno made, I thank them and excuse myself. Heading upstairs to my room, as expected, Savvy is close on my heels.

She doesn't waste any time and launches her opening salvo the moment she shuts the door behind her.

"You told Hugo, but you failed to tell me, your best friend"—she pokes at her own chest before continuing—"your brother was released."

It sounds more an accusation than a question, but I answer anyway, taking a seat on the edge of the bed.

"I did, only because he overheard part of a telephone call."

She dismissively waves her hand, pacing around the room.

"Yeah, I know. He mentioned that. But what I don't understand is why on earth you would keep that from me?"

"It's complicated," I start, but already that doesn't satisfy Savvy, who can get like a dog with a bone.

"Then uncomplicate it for me," she snaps.

I remind myself her reaction is one out of love and concern, and try not to react to her tone.

Assuming Hugo hasn't had a chance to talk to her after my heart-to-heart with him earlier, I fill her in on the information I shared regarding my brother.

"So, either he got sprung and immediately managed to really piss someone off, or this is something that precedes his conviction, and being in jail may have actually kept him safe," Savvy summarizes.

"I'm not sure what is going on, other than he mentioned he's in big trouble."

"And apparently doesn't think twice about dragging his little sister right smack-dab in the middle of it," she fumes.

"You think he could be connected to the fire too?"

She scoffs. "Not a doubt in my mind. There are no coincidences," she states confidently.

Hugo said something similar.

Dammit, I guess I was hoping maybe she'd offer up alternative suggestions, so I could at least pretend my brother hadn't sold me out.

I lie back on the bed and cover my eyes with my forearm against the glare of the ceiling light. The mattress moves when Savvy flops down beside me. Her hand finds mine and she squeezes my fingers lightly. I turn my head to find her looking back at me.

"I'm sorry I was pissed, but I worry about you. How am I supposed to have your back, when I don't even know there's a threat?"

"I know, I just…"

I let the sentence drift off; I don't really have an answer, only excuses.

"By the way, how are you feeling?" I ask her, eager to change the subject to something other than my pathetic excuse for a life.

"Hell, girl, was that supposed to be a segue?" she comments, chuckling as she pushes herself up to sitting. "I've heard smoother attempts from my father, and that's saying something. The man is as slick as a ball of barbed wire."

"I am fine. However, talking about slick men," she adds with an inquisitive raised eyebrow. "You and Hugo?"

Now it's my turn to snort out a laugh.

"And that was supposed to be smooth?" I accuse her, sitting up as well as I dangle my legs off the side of the mattress. "He is...persistent."

Never mind that I'm an absolute limp noodle when it comes to willpower around that man, but I'll keep that to myself. There was nothing limp about the loss of control that somehow propelled me onto his lap.

Nothing limp at all.

"I'd ask you what that shameful blush is about, but I don't think I wanna know. I have to work with the man, you know?" she jokes, lightly bumping her shoulder against mine.

I'm saved from attempting to make excuses for my cheek's reactive capillaries when Savvy's phone rings.

"Let me quickly take this."

I use the interruption to dart into the bathroom to splash some cold water on my face and use the facilities. When I return, Savvy is off the phone.

"That was Hugo, he wants me to call Tessa Androtti. She was the CID agent on the murder case last year."

I vaguely remember her. The shock of finding out someone I'd known for many years was in fact a serial killer blurred everything else to do with that scary time. I still get the chills, thinking how close Carson had come to losing his life to that man. Hugo had been beside himself.

But I do recall something about that woman had been a bit intimidating.

"Why?" a hint of green curiosity prompts me to ask.

"Apparently, she's in the market for a new job. So, I should probably get on the horn before someone else snatches her up."

"Are you going to offer her a job?"

I don't know why I want Savvy to deny it, it's blatantly obvious that's exactly what she's planning to do.

"As soon as I can get a hold of her," she confirms, holding up her phone. "I will be in touch later, and don't go anywhere without notifying Hugo or me."

"Yes, Mother," I mock.

"And if you get bored," she adds, as she hugs me at the door. "Start putting together some mood boards for me."

"Mood boards? For the nursery?"

She's already a couple of steps down the stairs when she stops to look back at me.

"Not the nursery, Tate says she's got that covered."

She grins, wiggling the fingers of her left hand where an unfamiliar sparkle hits my eye.

Then she adds, "My June wedding."

"Wait, what?" I yell after her as she jogs down the stairs.

She doesn't stop, but I can hear her joyful laugh all the way out the door.

Wow.

A wedding, and only two months away. I didn't even get a chance to congratulate her.

I head back inside the room and grab my phone from the coffee table, intending to send her a quick text when I find a message waiting from Hugo.

> Carson wants to know why I'm in such a good mood.
>
> I think I'll keep it to myself. ;) Sleep tight.

GOOD GRIEF, the man doesn't even have to be in the same room to fire me up.

Sleep tight, my foot.

CHAPTER 14

B*ess*

A NEW DAY, a new attitude.

That's my resolve this morning.

Yes, I have a gigantic bump in my road, but I've battled and beat worse problems. Why am I letting this current situation get the best of me? I'm resilient, I think I've proven that, and I have too much going for me to roll over and play dead. That's simply not my style.

I need to keep busy, tackling issues as they come up one by one, instead of trying to solve everything all at once.

Besides, I have my best friend's wedding to help plan, and her baby to welcome a few months after that. I want to look forward to that. Plus, there is this thing with Hugo to explore, and from what I could tell yesterday afternoon, there's quite a bit of enticing real estate to cover.

It's amazing how different the world can look after a decent night of sleep.

I caved last night, and took one of the pills Dana prescribed. It knocked me right out and I woke up refreshed and with a more positive perspective.

After a quick shower, I checked my phone to find a message from my insurance company, confirming they're sending out an adjuster this morning. My plan is to meet him at Strange Brew after I grab a quick bite downstairs.

"Going out?" Doug asks when I walk into the dining room with my coat over my arm.

"Yep, I'm running some errands today. Plan to meet the insurance guy at the coffee shop shortly, and hope…" I cross my fingers, "…I'll be able to get into my apartment to start cleaning up."

"Will you be staying there?"

"Oh, that would be amazing, but I'm not sure I can get things in order that soon. Don't get me wrong," I quickly add, realizing that might not have sounded very grateful. "I love staying here—the room is beautiful, the bed is comfy, you guys are amazing—but I miss my things and my dog."

"No need to explain." He smiles as he pours me a coffee. "I completely understand. But know you are more than welcome to stay as long as you'd like."

"Thanks, I appreciate that. Hey—" I suddenly shift gears when a thought occurs to me. "You do weddings here from time to time, right?"

"Occasionally. We can't really facilitate bigger events, so we don't get a ton of interest from outside of Silence. It's mostly locals who know the place."

I don't really know what Savvy and Nate envision for their wedding, or whether they already have a place in mind, but I can't imagine they'd be looking at doing something big and elaborate on such short notice, and it can't hurt to ask.

"Just as a general inquiry; what is your availability this coming June?"

"As in, this year?"

I scrunch my nose. "Yeah."

"Yours?" he asks, a twinkle in his eyes. "I happened to see that handsome lawman come out of your room yesterday."

Damn blush, I can feel it crawling up my cheeks.

"I'm asking for a friend. Honestly," I add for emphasis, when he slowly pulls up an eyebrow. "I'm just doing some groundwork here. I haven't had a chance to sit down with her and go over what she might want."

"Well, from memory, I don't think we have anything substantial scheduled for June, but let me look into that and I can let you know."

While I eat my breakfast, I glance out of the dining room's French doors.

This place *would* be perfect for a wedding.

The Carriage House has a large stone patio surrounded by a neatly trimmed boxwood hedge, a few Japanese maples —those will look fabulous in June since they leaf out early in the season—and a beautiful garden with roses and rhododendrons beyond. All of it should be in bloom.

A simple wedding; I envision the ceremony here in the dining room, the ornate fireplace would serve as a perfect backdrop for the couple. Those French doors would be wide open to the patio where high tea could be served in lieu of a full sit-down dinner. While the guests were outside eating, we could clear the dining room down to the beautiful wooden floors for a little dancing after.

I can see it all.

I'm not a fan of the insurance adjuster.

The grumpy man was barely able to acknowledge me when I met him outside the coffee shop, yet as soon as Emmet shows up, he's suddenly Mr. Cheerful.

I'd almost forgotten to let Savvy or Hugo know I was coming here. I called from the car but was unable to connect with either of them, so I left each a message. Knowing they'd have a shit fit if I came on my own, I got a hold of Emmet, who was thankfully available to meet me here.

"Luckily it didn't spread up here, but this apartment definitely needs remedial cleaning. Here's the name of a company I've dealt with before that specializes in this kind of work."

The adjuster hands Emmet a business card. The guy has been addressing Emmet the entire time on our walk-through, and it is starting to get on my nerves in a big way. I've held on to this morning's good vibe as long as I could, but at this point it's rapidly eroding.

"I'll take that, thank you," I intervene sharply, snatching the card from the older man's fingers. "Since this is *my* apartment, *my* business, and *my* name on your policy that *my* money pays for," I remind him.

I've clearly shocked him; he looks like he just bit into a lemon and doesn't particularly enjoy the flavor.

"Of course," he concedes primly before finishing up his inspection in silence.

Maybe it would've been better to bite my tongue and let his dismissive treatment of me slide. The reality is, I need this man to sign off on my insurance claim, so I can start repairs.

When we get back downstairs to the coffee shop, he pointedly turns to me.

"This area too is a matter of remedial cleaning, but obviously the kitchen is of most concern. I will email you my detailed findings once I have them written up."

"Can I at least get this company to start upstairs?" I ask, waving the card he provided.

"Since all of this belongs to you, you can do whatever you like," he says in a disingenuous tone. "But you would have to finance it out of pocket, since the decision on your insurance claim can't be finalized until law enforcement has finished their investigation."

I want to slap the superior smirk off his face and have to shove my balled fists in the pockets of my coat. He's enjoying this.

Since I don't want to give him anything else to gloat about, I muster up a smile of my own.

"Excellent. I look forward to hearing from you," I manage.

But the moment he walks out the front door, I deflate like a balloon, plopping down on the closest chair.

Out of pocket? I have enough in my business account to pay the mortgage, keep the lights and heat on, and make sure my employees get paid for the coming month, but without revenue, there isn't much more. I also have a little tucked away in a 401K, but that only goes so far.

"Damn, that doesn't sound too promising," Emmet observes.

"It's not."

Hopes I might open back up for business any time soon seem dashed.

So much for my new bright and shiny attitude.

Hugo

"Any progress on those fires?"

Don Merrick, mayor of Silence, is standing in the doorway of my office.

Immediately I feel my blood pressure rise.

I already don't like the man, but he really pisses me off when he walks in here without so much as a hello and demands an update on one thing or another. He seems to forget the sheriff is an elected official and the sheriff's department is funded by the county. It isn't the town of Silence or its mayor who pays our salaries or controls our budget.

But Merrick still walks around like he owns the place. Doesn't even bother checking in at the front desk and barges right through. He's an arrogant, narcissistic dick, who won the mayoral election on a platform of pretty lies and bombastic promises. There's only one person Don Merrick cares about and that's Don Merrick.

Savvy is much better handling the asshole. She's far more diplomatic than I have the patience to be. Besides, I'm getting a headache from agonizing over the proposal I finally was able to send Savvy moments ago. It's for the county commission to justify the additional budget Savvy plans to ask for to cover the second investigator position she'd like to offer Tessa Androtti.

"You should check in with Sheriff Colter about any ongoing investigations," I suggest, struggling for a civil tone.

"She's not here," he points out.

Something I was well aware of. She left forty-five minutes ago for an ultrasound appointment.

"Then I'm sure Brenda would be happy to take your message for when Sheriff Colter returns."

"Yeah, that doesn't work for me. I need you guys to put some muscle into that investigation. Get it solved so something can be done about those buildings. They're an eyesore right on Main Street. It's the first thing tourists see when they roll into town."

I almost snort out loud. Sure, we get some tourists when the leaves are out and the salmon are running, but people who come here are generally interested in the outdoors and only come to town for a bite to eat or to get groceries. Silence is hardly a must-stop on Tripadvisor's list of places to see.

I manage not to laugh in his face, but I can't hold back a comment.

"Our main priority is keeping the people of Silence as well as their property safe, and to that end everyone is working as hard as they can."

"Apparently, not everyone, since Sheriff Colter is nowhere to be found," the prick has the audacity to say.

The temptation to knock the arrogant, pretentious bastard on his ass is great, but that won't improve the cooperation between city hall and the sheriff's department. Although, it would make me feel a heck of a lot better.

"Sheriff Colter is probably putting in more hours than anyone else. Definitely more than she should."

"Ah yes, I heard she got herself pregnant." He says it like it's a point of shame, something dirty. "Hardly appropriate for someone upholding the office of Sheriff of Edwards County, but that's what the people voted for."

"Absolutely, they have. It's most of those same people

who voted you in too," I point out. "And it's all of those people our department is trying to keep safe, which is what I should be focusing on right now."

That's probably as far as I can go without turning this into an all-out war with the man, which definitely won't serve the people. Luckily, he's at least smart enough to recognize the veiled threat not to push the issue.

"Very well, I will let you get back to it, but make sure your boss is made aware of my concerns."

"I'll pass on the message."

He's about to leave my office when he stops.

"Oh, and before I forget; what's with this neighborhood watch? I had Keith Jespers stop my truck when I was on my way home last night. In the middle of the street," he adds.

Keith Jespers is our pharmacist who—along with a lot of the other business owners—volunteered to keep an eye on any strange behavior around the downtown area. Stopping vehicles is going a step too far. All they're supposed to do when they have a concern is report it to us.

I should probably give Brant—Savvy's father—a quick call to make sure he's aware one of his volunteers is overstepping.

"That shouldn't have happened. I'll take care of it," I assure him.

He nods but feels the need to add, "See that you do."

The moment he's out of sight, I press the heels of my hands into my eye sockets, pushing back on the headache forming there.

What I dislike more than paperwork is dealing with our mayor, and this afternoon I've had to do both. I'd much rather be out there in my cruiser, doing the actual work instead of sitting on my ass all day, but I guess that's part of the job too.

"Is he gone?"

I lift my head from my hands to find Savvy poking her head in.

"I thought you were at your appointment?"

She slips inside and takes a seat on the other side of my desk.

"I just got back five minutes ago. Brenda warned me so I hid out in the kitchen."

"Coward."

She grins back at me.

"Hey, any other day I'd have had your back, but I wasn't gonna let the mayor put a damper on today."

I notice she's still grinning ear to ear, obviously very pleased about something.

"How was your ultrasound?" I venture a guess it probably has to do with that.

"Good. Everything looks perfect."

"And..." I prompt her.

She beams. "And we're having a boy."

"Congratulations!"

I get up and round my desk to give her a quick hug.

"I suppose that's what you were hoping for?"

She shrugs.

"I would've been happy either way, but I know Nate was secretly hoping for a boy."

"Well, I'm excited for you both. I hear Hugo is a good strong name for a boy," I joke.

"So is Thor, but I'm sorry to say neither are on our short list of names."

As a kid I hated my name and was teased mercilessly growing up. But when your middle name is Ferdinant, Hugo is the lesser of the evils. Family tradition demanded I be named after my grandfathers, a tradition I gladly broke when we had Carson. I wasn't about to burden the kid with a name like Theobold Walter Alexander.

"Oh, and when the time comes, feel free to hit me up for any tips on how to deal with adolescent boys," I add. "I feel I've got enough material for a book by now."

These days things have settled down tremendously with my son, but there have been some rough spots over the years.

"I bet you do, and I'm sure we'll be taking you up on that when the time comes, but let me carry the kid to term first."

"That's fair."

"So...what did he want?" She steers the conversation back to the mayor's visit.

"He's worried Main Street is not tourist-friendly with two boarded-up buildings and wants us to hurry the investigation. Oh, and he's not happy about the neighborhood watch."

I don't mention what he said about Savvy herself, because that'll just raise her blood pressure and she doesn't need that right now.

"I bet he's not happy. Dad told me this morning Keith Jespers tried to stop him from getting behind the wheel at two o'clock this morning. It was in the alley that runs between Main and Victoria Street, and Don Merrick appeared to be unsteady on his feet, possibly drunk."

"That's not the story he gave me," I share, chuckling.

"I'm sure it wasn't. Also, according to Keith, it was not his Lexus parked in the alley, but Merrick junior's truck. And guess where he'd come from?"

"The Kerrigan?"

I mention the pub on the other side of the street from Strange Brew, because that's where I've seen the mayor stop in for a drink before.

"Oh no. He was coming out the back gate of a house on Victoria Street. Missy Gentry's house, to be more specific."

Missy Gentry is the forty-something widow of Arthur Gentry, who owned the Lizard Peak cattle ranch about ten miles north of town. Arthur had been almost eighty when he fell off his horse herding cattle and broke his neck three years ago. Missy sold the ranch before his body was good and cold, pocketed a nice chunk of change, and bought one of the old, stately townhomes on Victoria Street.

I never understood why that woman would want to stick around Silence, since she's not from here originally, and spends a lot of time putting down what this town has to offer. But perhaps now it makes a little more sense.

I wonder what Missy's best friend, Aurelia Merrick, thinks of the mayor's late-night visit.

"Can't say it surprises me," I admit.

"Me neither," Savvy concurs. "Those two are a perfect match, although I feel for his wife."

I can't argue with that. Betrayal sucks.

"Talking about wives..." Savvy gets to her feet. "I just stopped by the coffee shop to check on Bess."

It takes me a second to clue in, then I stand as well, leaning forward with my hands on my desk.

"Bess? What's she doing at the coffee shop? She was supposed to call when she went anywhere."

"She's fine, she met the insurance adjuster and Emmet is with her. She did call and left me a message when I was getting my ultrasound. She said she left you one too."

I immediately grab for my phone, which I usually keep in my pocket, but come up empty.

"Shit, must've left it in the cruiser."

"Wait," Savvy calls after me when I start for the exit. "What about the commission proposal!"

"Check your inbox," I yell back before darting past the front desk and out the doors.

Bess looks up when I walk into her small office off the kitchen, where she appears to be boxing up paperwork from her filing cabinet.

I don't hesitate to pull her in my arms and plant a kiss on her.

"Hey," she mumbles against my lips, before pulling her head back slightly. "I did leave you a message."

I smile at her. "I know. Savvy told me, and I saw once I got to my vehicle where I'd left my phone. My bad."

Aware of Emmet right outside, I reluctantly let her go.

"How did it go with the adjuster?"

"Well…" She sighs, making it clear the answer isn't exactly favorable. "Did Savvy mention the insurance won't pay out on my claim until the investigation is finalized?"

"She didn't, and that really sucks. I'm sorry."

I'm not really surprised; most insurance companies aren't in a hurry to pay out if they can help it.

"Yeah. But the good news is, I can pull together just enough money to pay the remedial cleaning company the adjustor recommended so I can get the apartment and the coffee shop in shape. Once the insurance pays out, I'll be able to tackle the kitchen and hopefully replenish my retirement savings."

She delivers it with a big smile, appearing pretty pleased with herself.

"And," she adds, "I've figured out a way to open at least the coffee shop. I'm going to seal off the kitchen with heavy duty plastic and tarps, and I can do some baking upstairs in my apartment once that's done. We'll just have limited pastries and won't be able to serve actual lunches, but the shop could reopen and bring in some revenue to keep itself afloat."

I have a lot of thoughts on the subject, but I wisely keep them to myself until I can properly process them. One of them is that she shouldn't be wasting money paying for a room in a B&B when she could be staying with me. But I sense now may not be a good time to address that.

"Sounds like you've got things covered," I observe instead.

"I think I might."

"How long are you gonna stick around here?"

"A couple more hours to get ready for the cleaners; they'll be here tomorrow."

"And Emmet is gonna stay here with you?"

"Yes!" Emmet himself calls out from the other room, confirming the lack of privacy.

"Okay, in that case, I've got a few things I need to get done, but I'll swing by here when I'm finished."

CHAPTER 15

B*ess*

WE GOT a surprising amount of work done for one afternoon.

Courtney, the woman I had on the phone at Cleaning Restorations earlier, had been super helpful when I explained my situation. She mentioned she'd just processed a cancellation for next Monday and would be able to have a crew here then. She also went into some detail about things I could do myself to make the process a little easier and faster. Saving them time would save me money, so I happily took her advice.

Basically, Emmet, Lola—she showed up later—and I removed everything of importance that could not be run through a washing machine or hosed down. That was important paperwork, pictures, a few paintings my mom left me, books I treasure, and some odds and ends.

At Courtney's suggestion, we packed everything into a few sturdy storage bins I asked Lola to pick up from Ginny at the Nuts & Bolts hardware store. I also tasked her with checking the self-storage place on the south side of town to see if they had a small rental unit available, where I could temporarily store the stuff we're packing up.

Next, we moved on to shoving pillows, throws, towels, linens, all my clothes from my closet and dresser, and even my curtains into large plastic bags. Most of those—except some clothes I may need in the short term—will also go to the storage unit until I have a chance to take the bags to the laundromat.

Lola just left with four bins and five garbage bags thrown in the back of her rusty old pickup. I would've dropped them off at the storage unit myself, but it would've taken a few trips. Also, as Lola pointed out, it would've left my car reeking of smoke for heaven knows how long.

As it is, the pungent odor is sticking to my clothes and in my hair, despite the fact we've had windows and doors open to air things out most of the day. I'm about ready for a nice long shower, but after I ask Doug or Arno if I could perhaps use their washer and dryer.

"Are you sure you're going to be okay?" Emmet asks, pulling down his mask.

Ginny had suggested those when Lola stopped by her store, and we've all been wearing one. Not perfect, but judging from the dirt and soot stuck to us and covering the masks, it was better than nothing.

"Positive. Hugo said he'd be here shortly," I share.

The man messaged me five minutes ago to let me know he was on his way. I'm not entirely sure why he insisted on coming back here—I have my own wheels—but I'll find out soon enough.

"If you're sure, I guess I'll see you tomorrow. I'm assuming you need me back here?"

I have to say, I'm so freaking lucky with my employees. Both of them. Talk about stepping up; both Lola and Emmet have done that in a big way these past days. Their support has gone above and beyond what the modest salaries I pay them deserve.

Once all this is done and dusted, and we're back to functioning the way we should, I'm going to need to flex my budget somehow to give each of them a raise. It's the least I can do.

"If you don't mind," I tell Emmet. "I'd like to at least go into the kitchen to toss out all perishables and anything else we can fit in the bin in the alley before they pick up the garbage. Otherwise, it's just going to sit out there until next week, smelling."

"What time do you want me?"

"Around nine would be great."

He throws me a mock salute and a lopsided grin, and reaches for the garbage bag I'm filling with paper cups, plastic lids, and other stuff I've been pulling from the cupboards behind the counter in the coffee shop. It really hurts, having to dispense of all my inventory, but as Courtney informed me, none of it is considered safe for use anymore.

"Leave it. I'm just going to finish this cupboard and then I'll toss it out," I assure him.

There is still some room left in the bag after I empty the rest of the cupboard, and I eye the plastic bin which stores our coffee beans. That's my gold, a carefully balanced blend I've spent years developing and mix myself. Those are pricey beans, but sadly, they too will have to be tossed. Too much has happened, too many people have been through here, and too many hands have touched things. I can't risk using them.

It's a bit of a struggle tipping the bin into the garbage bag without spilling beans all over the floor, but I manage to get it done. Of course, now the bag is heavy as hell and I struggle to drag it to the side door. I guess I could leave it for Hugo, but stubborn determination has me haul it outside myself.

Lifting it up high enough to tip over the side of the dumpster in the alley requires a Herculean effort. There, it teeters precariously, but when it threatens to topple back on top of me, an arm reaches over my shoulder, shoving it resolutely into the dumpster.

I swing around, fully expecting Hugo, but instead I find my brother. My instincts kick in and I shove at him with every ounce of strength left in my body and try to dart past him inside. He's still faster, and manages to grab hold of my arm, swinging me around to face him.

"Please, Bess. They know everything."

If there is anything that can stop me from fighting him, it's those words. I freeze instantly.

I get my first good look at Ken and realize how amazing it is I recognized him in the first place. He's aged, and not just the twenty years since I last saw him. He's gaunt and his eyes look old, desperate, and I can't stop my heart from bleeding just a little for him.

"What do you mean *everything*?" I hiss at him.

"E-very-thing," he enunciates slowly.

It's like a cold fist reaching into my chest and squeezing my heart.

This is a nightmare.

"How?"

The moment he lowers his eyes, I know it was him.

"Why?" I ask my brother, who may have well just signed my death sentence along with his own.

He shakes his head, looking as terrified as I feel.

"Almost twenty years is a long time without being able to talk to someone you trust, Bess. He was my cellmate for nearly ten of those years. How was I supposed to know he'd try and sell that information to Shane?"

Shane is Shane Lee, leader of the Lotus Squad. He and his brothers, Mike and Joon Lee, were the brains and the engine of the gang. At least they were back then when they recruited my brother.

It was a lifetime ago, yet hearing his name, feeling this fear, it might as well have been yesterday.

"We need money and we need to get out of here," he insists.

"We? Why? You led them here, didn't you?" Suddenly vibrating with anger at the injustice of it all, I shove him as hard as I can, causing him to stumble back a few steps. "You led them right to my front door."

"No." He shakes his head vigorously. "They already knew."

I can almost hear the tumblers fall into place in my head.

I'm about to tell him what an idiot he is for coming here, when I hear my name called from inside the coffee shop. Just as I turn around, I catch sight of Hugo turning down the hallway and coming toward me.

I whip my head back to find my brother gone. Vanished into thin air in a fraction of a second.

"Hey...is everything all right?" Hugo asks behind me, and I swing my entire body around to him, wearing a big smile.

"It's all fine."

Hugo

The relief is immediate when I see her standing right outside the door.

She seems a little strange though, almost like she's looking for something or someone. But the next moment she walks in the door, shutting it behind her as she goes up on her toes to kiss me.

The perfect distraction, instantly erasing any perceived weirdness.

"Are you ready to go?"

"Uh...yeah, I guess. Go where?" she wants to know.

"Dinner at my place."

I don't tell her she won't be going home after; I'll tackle that when we get there.

Luckily, Doug and Arno were understanding and accommodating, allowing me to pack up her things and pay her bill. She'll be ticked off about that too, but whether she likes it or not, she's going to have to learn to accept some help. That is, if she wants to stay afloat until her insurance comes through to cover her costs.

"I have my car here, so I'll have to follow you."

"Leave it here, we can grab it later," I suggest, putting a hand on the small of her back as I guide her firmly to the front door.

I'm eager to keep moving, worried the moment we stop she'll dig her heels in again. If I've discovered one thing about Bess, it's that she can change her mind on a dime and likes to throw up real or perceived road blocks. I'm hoping not to give her a chance by staying in motion. At least until we get to my place. Once there—and without a vehicle to facilitate an escape—I'll have time to convince her to stay.

To my surprise, she doesn't say much as we grab her things, lock up Strange Brew, and get in my truck. She stares out the window on the way home, a pensive, almost faraway look on her face. When I lightly touch her arm, she almost jumps out of her seat.

"Are you sure you're okay?"

She forces a tight smile on her face. "It's been a long day, I guess I'm more tired than I thought. Maybe it's best if I—"

I quickly interrupt before she can finish that thought.

"Why don't you have a nap while I cook? Unless, you'd rather have a shower first, of course."

She grabs a hank of hair, wincing as she sniffs it.

"Shower it is," she decides.

Ragnar goes ballistic when we get home, almost knocking Bess on her ass as we walk in the door. She doesn't seem to mind, and gives the dog plenty of loving before I remind him he needs to go out for a pee. Bess grabs the opportunity to head up for a shower.

Of course, my well-laid plans fall apart the moment Bess goes upstairs and finds her own things I already moved into the primary bedroom.

"Why is my stuff here?" she calls from the top of the stairs.

"I was going to talk to you about that over dinner," I offer, looking up from the bottom.

"Seems to me the time to talk would be before you decided to break into my room and kidnap my things," she snaps, building up steam.

Admittedly, I'd rather have her fuming mad than subdued, like she was on the way over here. Call me weird, but I enjoy her fire.

"For the record, I didn't break in, I was given access. And, I didn't technically kidnap your stuff, I simply moved it to a more convenient place." I hold up my hand to stop her when she gears up to react. "Please, let me finish. Obviously, in an ideal world I would've talked to you first, but you had your hands full at the shop, and I thought I could be helpful dealing with your room at The Carriage House. You need every penny you have, and staying there is a waste of money when you have a free place to stay here."

I take a few tentative steps up the stairs.

"You can have my room; you'll have your own bathroom. And before you worry about expectations, there are none. Carson is gone for the weekend and I'm gonna crash in his room."

My son reminded me this morning about the open house this weekend at the University of Washington, the school he has his hopes set on. With everything going on, I'd clearly forgotten about it.

"Where is he?"

One of the things I really like about Beth is her connection with my son. She really cares about him and it has nothing to do with me. I'm convinced they would have this connection, even if I wasn't in the picture.

"He was invited a couple of weeks ago by Larry Pierce, his buddy Cody's dad, who was able to get his hands on some Mariners' tickets for Saturday night. It just so happens to coincide with an open house at UW this weekend the boys wanted to go to, so they are making a weekend in Seattle out of it."

By now I've made it to the one-but-last step before the landing, and am at eye level with Bess, who no longer looks angry.

"I forgot. He mentioned it last week. I can't believe he'll be off to college in September," she mutters.

"Neither can I. It'll be quiet around here."

"I'm still mad at you."

"That's okay, I can handle it," I assure her, putting my hands on her hips and tugging her a little closer so she's within kissing distance. "Go have a shower while I get dinner going, and you can yell at me some more after."

"Fine," she mumbles, but her arms slide around my neck when I lean in for a kiss.

I haven't mentioned the main reason I wanted her closer to me, but that'll have to wait until after her shower.

I'm not looking forward to it.

CHAPTER 16

SHE IS BARELY EATING the pasta I threw together.

"That bad?" I tease, trying to lighten things up a little.

Despite the lively dust-up on the stairs, over dinner Bess is back to being quiet and seems miles away, distractedly playing with the food on her plate.

"No, it's good. I'm sorry, I guess I don't have much of an appetite," she apologizes, putting down her cutlery.

I get up from the table, gather up my own empty plate and her almost untouched one, and leave them by the sink. Then I walk back to her and hold out my hand. She looks at it and then at me.

"What are we doing?"

"The dog needs a walk and we could use some fresh air," I suggest.

There is only a brief hesitation before she places her

hand in mine and lets me pull her to her feet. I help her in her coat, shrug into mine, and clip the leash on Ragnar, who is already panting by the front door.

I scan up and down the road as we walk down the path to the sidewalk. This street is quiet, only a handful of houses on either side, so we don't get a lot of traffic through here. It wouldn't be hard to spot a person or a vehicle out of place.

I'm not sure whether it's the fresh air making a difference, but I notice Bess is suddenly a lot more alert out here too. Good, she should be aware of her surroundings at all times, and I need to stop dragging my ass telling her why that's more important now than ever.

"We made some progress today on the arson investigation," I start, snagging her attention. "Not the one at the coffee shop, but at Main Street Mechanics," I clarify. "We found a vehicle that was seen outside the garage before the fire started. It belonged to someone by the name of Victor Zhang."

I keep a close eye on her to see if she reacts to that name at all, but she doesn't flinch. She seems very interested in the subject though.

"He's local to Spokane and known to law enforcement as a gang member."

She reacts to that information, a slight gasp as her hand twitches in mine.

"It's a small-time gang, local to Spokane but, according to the FBI, they're affiliated with the Lotus Squad, part of their narcotics distribution network."

We stop at the small park at the end of the street to let Ragnar do his business.

"I don't understand," she volunteers. "What issue would they have with Clem?"

"They don't," I respond. "But Clem has something in common with you, an address."

"What are you talking about? His place is down the street from me. I'm at 140 and he's at—"

"104," I finish for her.

Realization flits over her face before it's replaced with something more like fear. I hate making her afraid, but she needs to know what she's dealing with. Whatever it is her brother did to piss his old gang off, it's worth killing over.

Victor Zhang was found dead in the trunk of his petrol blue BMW XM, shot execution style. Rumor on the street is he fucked up on a job he was doing for the Squad, and they weren't too pleased.

I'm keeping those details to myself, but there's a reason I want to keep Bess as close as possible.

"That was meant for me."

I drop her hand and fold her in my arms instead.

"Looks that way."

Suddenly I feel her back go rigid under my hands.

"They're trying to bait Ken. Draw him out in the open," she deduces accurately.

That was the conclusion we came to as well.

And if Ken Choi is any kind of brother—estranged or not—he won't likely sit by idle while his sister is under threat. Only the coldest of monsters would willingly throw their own family under the bus. From what I've been able to learn, Ken Choi was far from a choirboy, but he was not the devil incarnate.

"Probably. You should also know we've not yet been able to locate your brother, but we're keeping a close eye out in case he decides to show up in Silence."

She mumbles something under her breath I can't quite make out.

"What was that?"

She lifts her face, looking up at me with resignation in her eyes as she takes a step back.

"I said, too late. He's already here."

My blood chills, even as my mind already starts filtering through what I might have missed. I don't have to go far back to pick up on signals I may have dismissed at the time.

"He was at the coffee shop, in the alley."

She confirms with a nod.

I try to keep a lid on the flash of anger at her failure to mention anything before.

"Was that the first time?"

The question comes out a bit harsher than I intended.

"Yes. I swear I hadn't heard from him since I blocked his number."

I doubt her blocking his number would've actually stopped him from calling if he'd wanted to. It would've been as simple as using another phone. But I think he decided it would be easier to come see her in person.

The sound of a vehicle coming up the street draws my attention, and I squint to identify the truck, while closing the distance to Bess. Ragnar stops sniffing at our feet and lifts his head as well, emitting a low growl.

My hand instinctively goes to the weapon I have clipped to my belt. I'm about to push Bess behind me when the truck pulls into the driveway of a house, just across the street from me, and the neighbor's adult son and his girlfriend get out.

Exhaling audibly, I relax my hand and lift my arm around Bess's shoulders, tugging her close while I tighten my hold on the dog's leash.

"Let's take this conversation back home."

Bess

"Here."

Hugo hands me the tea I asked for when he offered me a drink.

Ragnar is already asleep, sprawled out on his back with his legs up in the air at my feet. How he can sleep like that, I don't understand, but it seems to be his favorite position. He clearly has no shame.

"Thank you," I mumble, still a little subdued after I shocked even myself by my admission to seeing Ken.

It just didn't feel right, keeping that information from Hugo when he's being so caring and transparent with me. The last thing I want is for him to take risks he's not prepared for. Information is half the battle, and he needed to know.

"So, just to recap," he says, taking a seat next to me on his roomy couch as he pulls back the tab on his beer. "He still wants to disappear and needs your money, but now he wants you to go with him."

"Yes."

"And the reason for that is because your brother, in his infinite wisdom, spilled some incriminating information he should've kept to himself about the Lotus Squad to a cellmate, who then turned around and sold him out. I mean, for them to go so far as to involve you in such a public way, by trying to burn down your place of business, it must've been some pretty damning information."

I nod, because...what else can I do?

I've given him as much of the story as he needs to understand the dynamics of what is going on. There are just a few details I'm hanging on to. Information that might do more harm than good, since it would surely bury my brother, and it would've all been my fault. After all, if not for me, my brother wouldn't even be in this situation.

"And you don't know what it is he has on them?" Hugo asks me again.

"My brother never shared gang business with me," I answer evasively.

That's not a lie, but what he shared had nothing to do with gang business. Although, I have a feeling that's a technicality Hugo won't be able to appreciate once he finds out. Because I can't bring myself to believe he won't. Eventually.

I sip my tea quietly, giving Hugo a chance to process the information while he has his beer. The silence doesn't last too long before he tosses back what's left in his can and gets to his feet.

"I'm gonna have to make a few phone calls. Feel free to turn on the TV if you like."

Without another word, he gets to his feet and, tossing his empty can in the trash in the kitchen, heads for the basement stairs.

He's angry. I know it. But at the moment I sense that's more about the situation than it is about me. However, that can easily change when he finds out the whole truth.

I grab the remote and mindlessly flip through the channels, but nothing catches my attention. Shutting the TV off again, I toss the remote on the coffee table and carry my tea mug to the kitchen sink and rinse it out. Then I slap my hand against my leg and call for the dog.

"Let's go, Ragnar. Let's go to bed."

I'm going to need my buddy if I have any hope of getting even a wink of sleep tonight.

I WAKE up to a hushed whisper.

"Let's go, buddy. My turn now."

Next, the mattress shifts as my furry source of heat disappears, only to be replaced by a set of strong arms and a broad chest. I keep my eyes firmly closed.

"I know you're awake, Twinkie. Your breathing changed and your body coiled up like a loaded spring the moment I touched you."

"What do you want?" I grumble ungraciously, still with my eyes shut tight.

He rolls on his back, taking me with him so I'm now draped on top of him, the shirt I borrowed from his drawer bunched up around my waist and my ass hanging out of my thong. *Lovely*. He doesn't seem to notice my state of undress as he keeps one arm banded around me and, with his free hand, brushes the hair back from my face.

"Sometimes I go into bulldozer-mode. At least, that's what Carson calls it when I become task oriented and forget who's in front of me. That's what happened earlier when it may have felt like I was badgering you, only to walk out on you moments later. I needed to confirm the information, digest and decide next steps, and finally delegate tasks to get us to the objective."

"Which is?" I ask, finding myself snuggling in against him.

"At the very top of the list: ensuring your safety. That's nonnegotiable."

I want to ask about my brother's safety, but I sense that wouldn't be a nonnegotiable issue for Hugo. Not when it could conflict with mine. There's no doubt in my mind he wouldn't think twice about sacrificing Ken if it meant he'd be keeping me safe. If that's not trust, I don't know what would be.

Trust is all he's ever asked of me, and it's the least I can give him.

But before I have a chance to end my guilty silence, his hands grab on to my exposed butt cheeks at the same time his mouth captures mine. His deep growl reverberates through my body as his fingers dig into my dimpled flesh. He doesn't seem to care, and in all honesty, I'm not particularly concerned myself. Not when I feel his body's response to me pressing against my hip.

I love that Hugo is not all hard planes and sharp angles, but his strong body is covered by a comfortable layer I can melt into. In contrast, his dick is pure steel, rigid and unforgiving, and a shiver runs down my entire body with the need to feel him inside me.

"Fuck, you feel so damn good," he rumbles in my ear as he rolls us over once again.

He wedges his hips between my legs, and I arch my back when he grinds his cock against me, the friction making me moan out loud.

Then he stops moving abruptly.

"Are you ready for this, Bess?"

My eyes snap open and lock on his clear blue ones, staring back. Little else exists in this moment and I nod my response. He drops a light kiss on my lips.

"I need the words, Twinkie. I need you to be sure."

My body is raring to go, but I force myself to look beyond my libido and gauge where I am emotionally.

The times have been few and far between since I've taken the opportunity, or had the inclination, to engage in a sexual encounter with anyone, and even on those occasions it was more a matter of going through the motions without much emotional investment.

With Hugo things are different. There is a lot on the line and the investment is huge, for both of us, and so are the risks.

But I want this. I want it so badly. I grab on to his firm ass to keep him from going anywhere.

"I'm so ready."

The words have barely left my mouth when I find myself being divested of my shirt, and next my panties, leaving me buck naked with Hugo on his knees looking down on me. But he doesn't give me a chance to feel self-conscious.

"Jesus, Bess, you're my every *fucking* wet dream."

Then he shoves his sleep pants down his hips, but only gives me a brief glimpse of his fine physique before he drops down, wedging his shoulders between my legs, and blowing every rational thought from my mind with his mouth.

My orgasm takes me by surprise and feels almost like an out-of-body experience. I'm still coming down to earth when, moments later, Hugo nudges my entrance with the tip of his sheathed cock. He locks in on my eyes, and watches my reaction as he slowly and deliberately enters me.

I feel overwhelmed, both covered and filled by him, unsure anymore where one ends and the other begins. I feel safe, alive, complete, and at peace, even as I stretch to accommodate him and every nerve ending in my body is firing signals. My body is a raging storm, as my heart and my mind find balance. And as Hugo starts to move, using his body expertly to drive mine to the summit, I'm hit with a sense of belonging I don't think I've ever experienced.

Later, with my arms surrounding his body—still shaking from the force of our combined orgasms as he tries to catch his breath—and his face pressed into my neck, I try again to give him all of me.

"There's something you should know. I—"

His fingers find my lips, covering them.

"Tomorrow," he mumbles, barely awake.

As his breathing deepens, I let myself give into the draw of sleep.

Tomorrow it is.

CHAPTER 17

H*ugo*

I WOULD'VE LOVED to stay in bed with Bess, who is still out like a light, but I reluctantly relinquished my spot to Ragnar, who'd been whining at the door ever since I kicked him out last night.

After a quick shower in Carson's bathroom—one I should remind him to clean when he gets back from Seattle, it's disgusting—I sneak out the front door, where Roy Battaglia is already waiting for me. He's got a cardboard tray with carryout coffees and a brown paper bag from the diner.

I'd messaged him before my shower to see if he could swing by the Bread & Butter Diner to pick up some breakfast for us on his way here. I'd planned to pick up some groceries today since my fridge is pretty empty, but I'm obviously not going anywhere in the foreseeable future.

"All quiet," he informs me. "I just checked in with my guys. No suspicious activity."

"Good."

Roy was one of the people I called last night, after what Bess told me emphasized the potential danger she could be in.

I still felt her hold back though, and that itself increased my concerns. Whatever it is her brother blabbed his mouth about, it's bad enough for her to keep close to her chest. In addition, I suspect whatever it is, Ken Choi had at least some involvement because I can't see Bess covering for the Lotus Squad, but I believe she'd try to protect her brother. Even against better judgment.

The only reason I didn't spend the night blocking the front door, armed to the teeth, is because Roy and his crew were there keeping a watchful eye out.

The other call I made was to Rick Althof, filling him in on the additional information. I purposely left Savvy out of the loop. At least for now, until we have a better grip on the situation and can present her with plans already in place. Despite not having known Althof long, I am putting a lot of faith in him to handle the investigative side, because there is no way in hell I'm letting Bess out of my sight.

His first course of order is to locate Ken Choi. There is no guarantee he didn't beeline it out of Silence after I interrupted their little chat in the alley yesterday afternoon, but my gut tells me he didn't go far. It's not likely he's staying somewhere in Silence—he'd be too visible—but there are plenty of places to hide out in the woods and mountains surrounding us.

"I've got two guys in the neighborhood during daylight hours, and the rest of the guys will be back tonight," Roy continues, breaking into my thoughts. "Unless something changes."

"I'll let you know if that is the case," I comment.

"Fair enough. I'll just grab my things and get started out here. It might get noisy; I'll have to do a bit of drilling."

Roy is here to install my new security system.

I may be law enforcement, but since one of our own—a Silence native I knew and worked with—attacked my son and turned out to be a killer we were looking for, my sense of security took a good hit. Last night, after discovering we might have elements of a violent gang right here in Silence posing a serious threat to Bess, the decision to get a decent system installed was easy.

I head back inside with our breakfast, leaving Roy to his work. Ragnar, who must've come down to see where I went, immediately picks up on the paper bag in my hand and circles my legs as I try to head up the stairs.

"Back off, buddy. I've got a piece of bacon with your name on it in here, but you've gotta be patient."

As if a five-month-old, food-motivated puppy the size of a bear cub understands the concept of patience.

"Who was at the door?" Bess asks when I walk in.

She's boosted herself up on an elbow and is squinting one eye at me from under her sleep-tousled hair. A red sleep crease runs down the cheek she had pressed into her pillow earlier. She looks fucking amazing in my bed.

I'd love to keep her here, just like this, but I know before long both our phones will start ringing once Savvy gets to the office and finds out about last night. I really want to make sure I get a proper meal into Bess before the chaos erupts.

"Roy Battaglia. His guys kept an eye out last night, and he's installing a security system here today."

Her second eye snaps open and her lips form a thin line, showing me she's not thrilled about that.

"Before you say anything," I quickly add. "I've been thinking about having one installed since Carson was attacked last year, I just never got around to it. This is a perfect opportunity."

It's easy to see she's not convinced, but at least she's letting it go. Not that it was negotiable anyway.

"What's in the bag?"

She pulls herself up and tucks a pillow between her back and the headboard.

"Bread and Butter breakfast bowls with a side of bacon to share with the pooch."

I set the bag and the tray with coffees down on the nightstand and sit on the edge of the bed beside her, leaning in to kiss those perfectly plump lips.

"Morning. Did you sleep okay?"

Her mouth pulls into a little smile, and I like the faint blush suddenly putting color in her cheeks. I'll bet she's remembering what came before we both crashed hard.

"Yeah, I did."

"Good."

I hold her eyes a bit longer, enjoying the view and the connection, when Ragnar announces the end of his patience with a woeful howl.

"All right, boy. I promised."

I hand Bess her coffee before unpacking the food.

"Sit," I order the dog, who, to my surprise, immediately drops down on his haunches.

"Good boy."

I toss him a piece of bacon he snatches right out of the air.

"You're going to spoil my dog."

"Nah." I hand her one of the bowls and the bamboo cutlery it came with. "It's called training. He gets nothing for free."

To demonstrate, I repeat my earlier command and wait for the dog's compliance before tossing him another piece.

"You lucked out," I tell her as I dig into my own breakfast. "He likes his food enough to do just about anything to get it. He's a pretty smart dog, which means he's going to enjoy you training him, but the downside is he'll probably bore easily as well. You've already experienced the outcome of that."

"Yes. One I don't care to repeat," she points out.

If I'm honest, I enjoy having the dog around. But not as much as I enjoy having his owner around. Both of them can stay as long as they'd like.

The whining of a drill firing up outside is a sobering reminder of why Bess is here in the first place.

Then my phone rings.

∾

Bess

I'm surprised to see Nate's truck parked in front of Strange Brew, and the front door of my coffee shop wide open.

I spoke to Savvy earlier and she never mentioned anything about Nate coming. Mind you, she had other things on her mind, like yelling at me for not calling her immediately after Ken showed his face. She'd already given Hugo the same treatment.

Savvy isn't a yeller; she doesn't usually get fired up to the point she's almost in tears, but she did this morning. My guess is it's probably pregnancy hormones, although that wouldn't explain my own wobbly emotions.

I glance over to catch Hugo's profile. He's noticing the truck and the door as well.

"Did you know he was going to be here?"

"No idea," he rumbles, as he pulls into a spot two away from where Nate's truck is parked.

Hugo is already not too happy being here. I insisted on coming, pushing forward with my plans to get the place as ready as I can for when the cleaners show up on Monday. He would've rather I'd stayed holed up at his place, hiding out until all of this blows over, but I have a business to run. At least, I hope I still have one when all is said and done.

I didn't tell him yet.

I intended to, but between Savvy calling, Roy needing access to the electrical panel, and me needing to get ready so I wouldn't keep Emmet and Lola waiting at the coffee shop, there wasn't enough time.

"Stay put," he orders moodily as he starts getting out of the truck. "I'll get you out."

I'd love to remind him how I feel about being ordered around, but the man is trying to protect me, so rather than poking the already grumpy bear, I sit and wait for him to do his thing. Which basically is scanning up and down the street before opening my door. Then he tucks me under his arm and rushes me inside Strange Brew.

Nate and Emmet, decked out in protective gear, come walking out of the kitchen, carrying a blackened piece of drywall between them when we enter.

"What is happening?"

It's Nate who answers me, pulling down his mask to flash an understated grin.

"Heard the insurance adjuster already went through and

you've got cleaners coming in Monday. Might as well get all the dirty work done all at once, so we're getting a head start on your kitchen," he explains as they walk out of the front door and toss the drywall in the back of his truck.

I'm not sure what to say, so when Nate walks back in, I stick to a simple, "Thank you."

"Pure self-interest," he replies in passing. "Savvy's been a bear without your pastries to soothe her sweet tooth."

"People wanna help, Twinkie," Hugo states beside me. "Let it happen."

Touched by the support of my friends and happy Hugo appears to have gotten over his snit, I briefly lean my weight into him.

Then I shrug off my coat and drop my purse on the nearest chair, grab a face mask from the box, and go to work. Hugo is right behind me.

PHIL, Savvy's stepmom, shows up around midday, lugging in two large boxes from Pie Central and a twelve-pack of water.

She also produces a stack of folded papers from her large leather tote she hands to me.

"I wasn't sure which one you'd want."

Confused, I unfold the papers to find a Viking brochure she must've printed off the website. My old range was a Viking, and it's one of the top commercial brands out there. The only reason I'd been able to afford mine was because I bought it secondhand. No way I'll be able to afford a new one.

"I'll probably be looking for pre-used," I explain. "It all depends on what the insurance company values my old one at."

"Fuck insurance," Phil states bluntly. "They're gonna drag their asses and try to cut corners and find ways to shortchange you. Believe me, I've had to deal with them before." She shakes her gray curls. "No, this isn't about insurance money. I have a proposal for you. More of a favor than a proposal, actually. It involves your walls."

"My walls?"

She nods eagerly, her smile wide.

"I want to rent them."

I'm even more baffled now than I was before.

"For chrissake, Phil," Nate mutters around the half slice of pizza he shoved in his mouth. "Quit talking in riddles. The woman is not a mind reader."

"Right. Well, I don't know if I mentioned it, but I've been trying my hand at painting. Just dabbling, really."

"Nonsense," Nate interrupts again. "Her paintings are fantastic and would probably sell for a pretty penny."

"Yes, well..." Phil stammers, clearly a bit embarrassed by the praise. "I wasn't going to do anything with them, but lately I've been toying with the idea of starting a community food bank, or a community emergency fund, or even both. Something by the people of Silence, for the people of Silence. Any money I make from the sale of my paintings would go toward setting up a program like that, and others could join me if they wanted to. Selling their crafts or art, or maybe donating goods or services. But I thought, since Strange Brew is pretty much the hub of the town, perhaps I could rent some wall space in your coffee shop to peddle my wares, so to speak. The new range could be first and last month's rent?"

My excitement started growing the moment she made mention of a food bank, because I know there is an increasing number of people here in Silence whose food security is not what it should be. For all the common reasons: automation culling the workforce, a rising cost of living against lagging wages, a growing graying population on fixed incomes. The effects are hitting Silence just like anywhere else.

I'd love to be part of an initiative like that. It's right up my alley. Plus, free artwork on my walls, turning Strange Brew into a gallery on top of a coffee shop, is a fantastic bonus.

"Yes."

"But I completely understand if you'd rather not get involved," Phil rambles on as if I hadn't spoken. "I know you already have your hands full. Although, I would happily volunteer my time to offset the additional work…"

I let her run on while turning my attention to the sheets of paper she handed me. I flip through the pages until I find what I'm looking for.

Then I turn the brochure toward her and tap my index finger on the picture.

"I want that one," I interrupt her.

"Yes?"

Her face is one of eager anticipation, and it's difficult not to laugh at her excitement.

"She already said yes once," Nate provides dryly. "How many different ways do you want to hear it?"

His comments earn him a general chuckle and a very sharp elbow from Phil.

"Can it, smart-ass." Then she turns a smile on me and holds out her hand. "So, we're in business?"

I clap my hand in hers and confirm, "We are in business."

Then I mentally cross my fingers.

CHAPTER 18

H*ugo*

"Nothing?"

I'm standing out on the deck, watching Ragnar practice lifting his leg on every blade of grass in the backyard.

"No. The feed is too grainy to make out the license plate. All we know is it's a black or navy, older model Toyota RAV with the spare tire on the back."

Bess went straight upstairs to have a shower after we got home, while I let out the dog who'd been cooped up all day. I took the opportunity to call Althof for an update.

Apparently, he found what he thinks might be the vehicle Ken Choi is driving. It was caught speeding through the intersection on Cooper Drive at Victoria shortly after I found Bess hauling out the garbage. Cooper Drive is where the back alley running behind the businesses on the coffee shop side of Main Street comes out.

"It's probably stolen," I point out, frustrated at the lack of progress. "If he's got any sense, he'll be switching out vehicles every chance he gets."

"I put a BOLO out on the RAV, and I'll keep an eye on incoming stolen vehicle reports."

"And what's the word on the Lotus Squad?"

"Mancuso is checking in with the Seattle PD Gang Task Force. Those guys will likely have confidential informants on the inside, who may be able to shed some light on what the hell is going on. Or at the very least, give us an idea of the whereabouts of the gang's main players."

Jason Mancuso is the Spokane FBI agent Rick met with earlier in the week. I haven't met the guy—he must be new to the Spokane office—but it's always useful to have connections in other branches of law enforcement.

"Good. Keep me up-to-date."

"Will do. I assume you're not planning to come in tomorrow?"

Tomorrow is Sunday. Carson is scheduled to be back from Seattle somewhere around dinnertime.

Shit. I really would've liked to have seen this resolved before he gets home, but that may have been wishful thinking. Unfortunately, sitting on my ass doesn't help matters either, so I should probably go in for a bit and put some added muscle into this investigation.

"I'll probably be in at some point."

"Are you sure? What about Bess?"

"She'll come with me. No safer place than the station."

I'm not sure how Bess will feel about that. I believe she had plans to sit down with Phil to hash out ideas for Phil's charitable venture. But those will either have to wait, or move to the station, where I'm sure we can find an empty space for them to use.

"Fair enough," Althof concedes before he abruptly signs off. "Talk later."

I slide my phone in my pocket and brace myself against the railing, waiting for Ragnar to tire of sprinkling the lawn, two drops at a time.

In the meantime, I wonder if perhaps I should give Larry a call, see if he can keep my son for a couple of days. Carson could crash with Cody, like the kids used to do when they were younger, but something tells me a sleepover at a buddy's when you're seventeen doesn't quite hold the same appeal.

My son is becoming a man, he's proven as much over the past year or so, and it's a little bittersweet to see him forge a life of his own. It's a bit sad Emily didn't get a chance to witness this last surge into adulthood, she's the one who deserves the kudos for raising such a great kid.

For too much of Carson's life I let work absorb me, letting Emily take on the brunt of parenting and running the household. I'm not proud of the fact I took her for granted for more years than I should've gotten away with, but I'm grateful I had a chance to try and be a better husband.

Unfortunately, that was only after Emily was diagnosed with Triple-Negative Breast Cancer. A particularly aggressive form of breast cancer against which she barely had a chance. The fast-growing lump in her breast was discovered by her lover, the physical therapist in Spokane she went to see every week for the better part of a year to help her with a rotator cuff issue. He's the one who whisked her over to the MultiCare Deaconess Hospital to get it checked out.

It was a blow, in more ways than one, and I was so fucking angry about all of it—the betrayal, the lies, the cancer—but part of that anger was also directed at myself. I dropped the ball on our marriage first. Sure, I may not have slept with another woman, but my work was my mistress and she demanded all my time. I was so full of the importance of what I was doing, I casually brushed off any concerns Emily brought up about our marriage, our family. To the point where she no longer bothered telling me how unhappy she was, she just went and did something about it.

Yeah, I was pissed and hurt and, *fuck*, humiliated, but I couldn't lay all the blame at her feet. I had to own some of it myself. So as my wife was battling that godawful disease, I made sure to be the husband she'd always deserved.

Unfortunately, she didn't get to enjoy him for very long.

"I was wondering where you'd gone."

I turn around to watch Bess stepping outside with her almost black hair still damp from her shower.

Ragnar, who hears her voice, finally comes bounding up the steps of the deck to greet her.

"I was waiting for that one to finish marking every square inch of the yard," I grumble.

My complaints make zero impression on the dog, who seems perpetually happy, with tail wagging, tongue lolling, and what looks like a smile on his face.

"Are you okay?" Bess asks, stepping up to me and putting a hand on my arm.

She has a look of concern on her face as she scrutinizes mine.

I guess my trip down memory lane must be showing. Reaching out, I slip my arms around her and tuck her head under my chin. Only a faint hint of sadness over what was lost lingers as Bess molds herself against me. She feels right in my arms, and I realize how fucking lucky I am to be getting a second chance to do this right.

Bess

"Nothing more you can do at this point anyway."

I look across the kitchen island at Savvy, who dropped by as we were putting away the remnants of our dinner.

There weren't a ton of supplies in the house, but I was able to scrounge up enough to throw together a couple of quesadillas. If we are going to be holed up here much longer, we're going to need some groceries. Maybe we can pick a few things up tomorrow.

"I know, but it helps to visualize when we're in the space," I try to explain.

"You're just going to have to visualize it another day," Savvy fires back dismissively.

I think she's still ticked she had to find out from someone, other than me, about Ken showing up last night. She's worried, I get that. So is Hugo, which is why the two of them are ganging up on me about spending tomorrow at the sheriff's station.

The prospect isn't particularly appealing, but I can't really complain too hard since I'm the reason Hugo is going in on his day off.

So, I suck it up and concede.

"Fine. I'll give Phil a call."

Hugo, who is putting away the baking tray I used for dinner, throws me a cocky grin over his shoulder. I roll my eyes in response and grab my phone off the counter.

"Of course."

Phil is one of the most laid-back people I know and

agrees immediately to meeting me at the sheriff's station instead of the coffee shop.

I like that she's casually unconventional, refreshingly outspoken, and doesn't care much what others think. It's the kind of easy confidence you might expect from a veteran of the music industry, but despite her colorful background, she's really embraced her new chosen life in Silence. Her desire to invest in the community is evidence of that, and I really look forward to collaborating with her.

While I'm on the phone with Phil, I notice Hugo and Savvy having a quiet conversation in the background.

Just as I end my call, I catch the last few words of something Savvy is saying.

"...bring him in on murder charges."

"Murder?" I gasp, grabbing on to the front of my sweater as my chest feels tight.

Savvy winces as she and Hugo exchange a look. Then they turn to me, but my focus is on Hugo, who is wearing a look of guilt.

"What murder?"

"Remember I asked you about the owner of the vehicle they found that was seen behind Clem's shop around the time of the fire? Victor Zhang?"

I nod.

"I didn't want to mention to you we found him in the trunk of his car. Dead."

"Killed," I clarify, my blood running cold through my veins.

"Execution style," Hugo confirms.

"Because he torched the wrong place," I guess, feeling the oppressive weight of fear press down on me.

Oh, I was scared before—I'm all too familiar with the kind of violence the Squad can wield—but the execution of this Victor Zhang, and stuffing him in the trunk of his vehicle to be found, is a clear message. Shane Lee is dead serious about his revenge and not in the mood to entertain explanations, and that doesn't bode well for my brother or me.

"First we find your brother, then we'll find them," Savvy says encouragingly. "We've got the cooperation of the FBI, and we're throwing every resource we have at it."

My smile of gratitude in her direction is a little weak. As much as I value their investigative talents and appreciate the effort they're putting in, I'm not so sure they'll be able to get to Shane Lee, who is the head of the snake in the Lotus Squad. It's been tried before, but he's a slippery eel and a charismatic leader; he'll have plenty of minions like my brother willing to take the fall for him.

I remember sitting in the courtroom when my brother was led in. My abject disbelief when he chose to plead guilty, not even putting up a fight to charges I knew for a fact could not be attributed to him. I'd come prepared to fight for him, but he didn't even bother putting up any kind of defense for himself.

After he was convicted and sentenced, I'd gone to visit him in prison, wanting an explanation. That's when he told me what he'd done, and why I could not breathe a word of it.

I didn't, unlike my brother, who unburdened to someone he thought he could trust. Hugo and Savvy have given me absolutely no reason not to trust them, but still I have not breathed a word. Doing so would sign my brother's fate, as well as my own.

But I'm not sure how long I can hold on.

"Well, I should be heading out," Savvy announces as she gets to her feet. "Nate was planning to get the firepit going outside, and Tatum offered to make some hot chocolate. But I'll see you two in the morning."

She walks over to me and grabs me in a firm hug.

"Hang in there," she whispers by my ear. "Hugo will look after you if you let him."

I don't know if he heard what she said, but as he walks back in after showing Savvy out, he's got a smirk on his lips.

"What?"

He shrugs his shoulders but continues coming my way until we're toe to toe.

"Will you? Let me look after you? Although, the way I've been wanting to look after you all night is probably not what Savvy meant."

The sexy rumble of his voice and the heat in his eyes directly translate to a warm dampening of my panties.

The rush of fear I felt earlier is already fading. We're locked up tight behind a security system Battaglia Security is monitoring, a team of Roy's men are patrolling the neighborhood, and the dog has been fed and walked.

So when this man I've been lusting after for longer than I care to admit offers to look after me in that tone of voice, I'm eager to find out how.

Leaving him standing in the kitchen, I turn on my heel and head for the stairs. I'm halfway up when I hear his heavier footsteps rush up behind me, and suddenly I'm swept off my feet.

He carries me into the bedroom where he lets himself fall back on the bed, taking me with him. His hands immediately slip under my sweater, sweeping it up and over my head. Next, he unhooks my bra before rolling us over so he's on top. His kiss is thorough as his hands snatch away the lacy fabric and then reach down for the buttons on my jeans.

I love the way he growls in my mouth when his touch encounters a part of me he likes, as he does when he slips a hand down the front of my panties and his fingertips encounter my slick folds.

Abruptly, he rips his mouth from mine and sits up, tugging my jeans and underwear down my hips. I squirm in anticipation, waiting for him to get naked as well. Instead, he lowers himself—fully dressed—between my naked thighs, pushes my knees out so I'm spread wider, and latches his mouth to my aching core.

I'm quickly overwhelmed by the lashing of his tongue, the tug of his lips, and the deep penetration of his fingers. Lost in an avalanche of sensations, I grind myself into him, pleading and reaching for completion. When it comes, my body jerks with the violence of it, leaving me shaking and gasping for air.

When I finally catch my breath and open my eyes to look down, I find Hugo's blue eyes looking back.

"Beautiful," he mumbles.

It's obvious he observed me through the throes of my orgasm, and self-awareness immediately creeps in. But before I can reclaim some modesty, he lowers his head and gently licks along my crease, flicking my sensitive clit with the tip of his tongue.

Then with a smile on his lips, he presses a kiss to the inside of my thigh.

"I could live on the taste of you."

CHAPTER 19

H^{ugo}

I PEEK into the large meeting room where Bess and Phil are focused on a laptop on the boardroom table in front of them. They don't even notice me.

I'm on my way to Savvy's office. Apparently, Special Agent Mancuso showed up a few minutes ago, and Althof is on his way back. I'm crossing my fingers the fed is bringing us some good news, because we've been spinning our wheels most of the morning.

Mancuso gets to his feet as soon as I walk into the office.

"Hi," he says, holding out his hand. "I don't think we've met yet. Jason Mancuso."

"No, we haven't. Hugo Alexander."

His handshake is firm, but he doesn't try to break my fingers, which counts in his favor. I hate guys who are trying to prove themselves that way. They may as well whip out their dick and a measuring tape. *Dumb*

"What did I miss?"

"Not much yet," Savvy notes. "We'll wait for Althof to get here instead of repeating things."

No sooner has she spoken, when Rick walks in, breathing heavy like he's been running.

"Tell me," he prompts, not bothering with introductions or greetings.

I don't blame him. I know he's been going nonstop since this case landed on his desk, and probably feels like he's chasing his tail. Other than a dead firebug, the witness accounts of a drunk, and a lot of theories, hearsay, and assumptions, there isn't a hell of a lot of concrete evidence to hang this case on. Hell, we can't even put our hands on people we'd like to question.

"One of the Seattle Gang Task Force's CIs came through with an interesting bit of information," Mancuso starts. "As I assume you know, the Lotus Squad was founded by the Lee brothers, Mike, Shane, and Joon. Shane, the middle brother, has always taken the lead, with Mike, the oldest, managing the business side. From what we can tell, the younger one, Joon, didn't really have a set role within the organization. If anything, he was an enforcer. The muscle, if you will."

"Was?" Savvy picks up on.

The agent turns to her and confirms, "Was. He fell off the face of the earth twenty-one years ago. Just disappeared. Plenty of rumors went around at the time—he'd stolen money and taken off, the brothers had a falling out, a rival gang took him down—but nothing was ever confirmed and no sign of him was ever found."

I immediately think of Ken Choi, and the secret he supposedly spilled to a cellmate that prompted his own gang to come after him. I also wonder what, if anything, Bess might know about the missing Lee brother.

"You think Choi knows something about the disappearance," I suggest to Mancuso.

"I *know* he does," is the answer. "And what's more, Shane Lee thinks he does. The CI overheard him order Ken Choi be found and brought to him alive, and to use whatever means to flush him out of hiding."

"And they're trying to use his sister to do that," I observe.

A sober nod is his response.

"When was this?" Rick asks. "How old is that information?"

"Apparently, this was about a month ago. Which would fit the timeline of events here in Silence."

"Do we know who he sent out?" Savvy wants to know. "Names, pictures, anything to help us look?"

"Yes," Mancuso confirms as he bends down to pull some papers from a briefcase by his feet.

He hands out copies of what looks to be a gang hierarchy, listing known gang members and, if known, their role in the organization. I'm shocked at the size. There are easily thirty or so names listed in the upper echelon of the Squad alone. That's not counting the second page with another list of names marked as foot soldiers. It looks like the Lee brothers did okay for themselves with the large network they built.

"I'll forward a link to a secure cloud folder that holds all the individual profiles, but the file was too big to print out."

"I'd appreciate that," Savvy thanks him.

"One other thing," Mancuso mentions. "My boss was pushing for us to take over this investigation…"

I can almost hear Rick Althof's teeth grinding. Although our office has always welcomed outside help, nobody is a fan of getting booted off their own investigation.

"But I've been able to convince him to hold off and let me stick around here to keep a finger on the pulse and help out where I can."

The help is very welcome.

Especially since Savvy informed me earlier it looks like we're going to have to wait to approach Tessa Androtti with an offer to join our department. One of the county commissioners has to undergo some kind of medical treatment, so this week's scheduled meeting was postponed.

In all honesty, I wouldn't object if the FBI decided to take over the entire investigation, because that would allow me to focus on keeping Bess safe. Heck, I could take her away somewhere; we could lay low until any threat is eliminated.

That wouldn't be bad; maybe somewhere warm, with a beach, and with only the bare minimum of clothing needed, if any.

I'm rudely yanked from my daytime fantasies when Savvy calls me to attention.

"Hey, Hugo. I said, are you on board?"

My blank look betrays my ignorance on the subject.

"Not sure where you were for a moment, but it looked like someplace good. Care to share?" Savvy teases.

"Not on your life," I grumble, causing her to laugh at my expense.

"I was suggesting Rick take a couple of hours to go home, shower, have a nap and a meal, while you get Agent Mancuso a copy of our case file and maybe walk him through the crime scenes to get him up to speed with where we are."

Crap.

I'd told Bess we'd hit up the grocery store for some supplies, and I still have to figure out what to do about Carson, who is coming home tonight. It doesn't look like Bess is going anywhere but back home with me. We are nowhere near in the clear yet by any stretch of the imagination.

"Sure," I answer grudgingly.

Moments later, with Althof gone home for a break and Mancuso off to the restrooms, Savvy turns to me.

"What was that all about?" she asks a tad sharply.

"What was what all about?"

"You hesitated."

"Bess," I reply honestly. "I don't like the idea of leaving her alone."

"I'll be here."

"I know, and it's fine. It was just logistics. I'll probably be a while and she'll be here waiting. We were supposed to grab some groceries because the fridge is empty, and also, Carson is back tonight and I'm not sure what to do about that. But I'll figure it out."

"Carson is seventeen. Why don't you call and let him help you work that part out. Or, if Nate's okay with it, he can crash at ours. Tatum could ride to school with him and save us a drive. As for the groceries, I was going to stop and grab a few things on my way home. I can take Bess."

Again, I hesitate.

"You can trust me, you know," Savvy adds with a smirk. "I wear a badge and a gun and everything."

I would trust Savvy with my life any day of the week, but this isn't about me.

It's about Bess.

∼

Bess

"I really appreciate this."

My friend tosses me a grin. "Not a big deal."

I asked her to make an extra stop at The General Store on Elm Street to see if maybe they have a hand mixer. It's one thing Hugo's kitchen is missing, and I'd really like to do a little baking, starting with the quiche I'm hoping to make us for dinner tonight. I already have all the necessary ingredients in the cooler bag in the back of Savvy's SUV.

"Hang on. Let me get out first," she says as she pulls into the parking bay in front of the store.

Similar to what Hugo does, she rounds the front of the vehicle and looks up and down the street before opening the door for me.

"I'm starting to feel a little awkward with this whole routine," I confess as I get out.

"I know, but we're merely being cautious. It's unlikely anyone is going to try anything in broad daylight in the middle of town anyway, but better safe than sorry."

I can't really argue with that, at the risk of sounding ungrateful, everyone is looking out for me.

As I am every time I walk into this store, I am completely overwhelmed with the sheer volume of products it carries. There isn't a square inch of shelf or wall space left that isn't packed with a random mix of items ranging from toothpicks to engine parts. The General Store is a world of its own, and walking in here is like stepping into an alternate universe. One of knickknacks and nostalgia, quality and kitsch, history and innovation jumbled together on every shelf.

Nobody comes out to offer help. If you want help, you find your way to the counter at the back of the store, where most of the time you'll find Mabel Jenkins knitting another afghan or baby sweater to be donated to a family in need somewhere.

That reminds me, Mabel would be a good person to approach about Phil's initiative. If there's anyone in the know about the needs of the people of Silence, it would be Mabel.

Not today though. Today I look forward to the challenge of rummaging through the century-old, jam-packed store by myself, on my quest for a handheld mixer. A little highlight in what are pretty bleak days.

"Do you even know if they have one?" Savvy asks behind me, sneezing when I lift a folded fur partially covering a box I can't identify.

"Nope, but don't yuck my yum," I warn her, sad to find the box contains a wrench set and not the object of my desire.

Savvy does not share my love for this place, which is why I'm so appreciative she's indulging me. She's commented many times over the years how the place is a fire risk, no longer structurally sound, and a hazard to the public's safety. She's probably right on all those accounts, but even as our sheriff, she'd have a hell of a time trying to close down this treasured store. She'd have a riot on her hands, and I might be leading the mob.

"Fine," she grumbles. "But I'm about to pee my pants here. This baby has decided on top of my bladder is its new favorite hangout."

"So go to the bathroom," I prompt her. "I'm sure Mabel will let you use it."

"You'll have to come with me, I can't leave you alone."

I snort in amusement.

"Alone?" I direct a pointed look at one of the many

mirrors on the ceiling. Mabel's own security system allows her to keep an eye on every nook and cranny of this store.

"Trust me when I say, Big Sister is watching us."

In the mirror's reflection I catch Mabel putting down her crochet hook to wiggle her fingers at us.

"Oh, all right. But don't you go anywhere," Savvy concedes.

"Where am I gonna go?"

But she's already moving to the back, shuffling sideways through the narrow aisles, and I resume my search.

"Goes faster if you ask," Mabel's disembodied voice calls out.

"I know, but what's the fun in that?" I yell back.

My eye catches something on the shelving unit in front of the store window. It's a set of individual pudding forms that look like pretty little Bundt cakes. It would look really neat to bake cupcakes in those. They'd come out with a little divot in the middle I could fill with a compote or fresh fruit.

I reach to pick one up when a sharp rap on the window outside draws my attention. Bending down, I peek between the two shelves.

I'm shocked when I see my brother standing outside the window. He's waving for me to come outside and is nervously looking over his shoulder.

"Please," I can barely hear his voice, but his plea is unmistakable.

Regardless of the bad things he's done, he's still my brother, and I'd be lying if I said I don't still love him. Despite the pull on my heartstrings, I stop myself from running outside. I'm not an idiot.

But when he suddenly spins around as a white van pulls up, coming to a sudden stop, the bottom falls out of my stomach. I already know nothing good can come of this when the side door of the van slides open, and two guys dressed all in black jump out.

"Savvy!" I yell, even as I catch sight of some kind of automatic weapon in the hands of one. "Savvy! We've got trouble!"

I can hear commotion in the back of the store as I watch my brother raising his hands. The two guys rush him, grab his arms, and half drag him to the waiting van.

Instinct has me running for the door, when I'm yanked back by the hem of my coat and hear Savvy hiss behind me.

"Get down and out of the way."

Just as I duck to the side, I catch a glimpse of the van doors closing. When Savvy pulls open the door, I hear the engine rev as it takes off.

Taking my brother with it.

CHAPTER 20

B*ess*

"What are you doing?"

I ignore Savvy's snarl and buckle up.

She was going to take off without me. So, when I poked my head out and saw her running for her cruiser, I didn't think twice and took off after her, pulling open the passenger door just as she was jumping behind the wheel.

"It's my brother in that van," I point out as she peels away from the curb to give chase with sirens and lights going.

"Hugo's gonna fucking kill me," she mutters as she grabs for her radio. "Unit seven in pursuit of vehicle involved in a kidnapping. Heading southbound on Elm east of Victoria following a white Ecoline cargo van, license CJ95093. At least three suspects, armed and dangerous, and one victim."

As my ears roar with a cacophony of noise—including

the adrenaline-fueled pumping of my own blood—I'm beginning to question the wisdom of this endeavor. My friend—albeit Edwards County's sheriff and therefore skilled as well as armed—is very pregnant, and I have no weapon nor skill to be of any consequential use.

But from the way Savvy is bent over the steering wheel, whipping around corners in dogged pursuit of the speeding van and barking directions into her radio, I don't think anyone could get her to stop now.

Something hits the side mirror on my side with a crack, splintering the top of the molded frame.

"*Shit.* Get down," Savvy yells, shoving at my shoulder. "All the way down, they're shooting."

I immediately undo my seat belt and make myself as small as possible under the dashboard, clutching my purse, which suddenly starts ringing. Reaching in, I find my phone and answer.

I don't get a chance to say anything more than hi, because it's Hugo and he immediately starts yelling.

"What the fuck do you guys think you're doing? Are you trying to get yourselves killed? In case you didn't notice, you're under fire. Tell Savvy to fucking fall back, we're coming up right behind you."

"O-okay," I stammer.

I've never been really intimidated by Hugo, but then again, I never heard him this furious before. Just as I prepare to relay the message to Savvy, the cruiser makes a sharp turn and I lose my balance, slamming headfirst into the center console.

Then there is a squeal of tires, followed by another abrupt turn, tumbling me to the other side.

"Bess? What the fuck, Bess? Answer me!"

A little disoriented, I scramble to find the phone that

slipped from my hand in the chaos. As soon as my fingers encounter the familiar silicone casing, I grab on and bring it to my ear.

"I'm here, I lost my balance."

"Who are you talking to?" Savvy fires in my direction.

"It's Hugo, he says he's right behind us and for you to drop back."

She darts a quick glance in my direction and I catch her wince, right before she returns her attention to the road.

"Tell him to pull up beside us. The idiots are turning up the dirt road to the old quarry. They're heading into a dead end."

"Put me on speaker," Hugo barks in my ear.

I do as he asks and slide my phone on top of the laptop mounted to the center console, so he and Savvy can yell at each other instead of me. Reaching up, I gingerly explore the side of my head I banged with my fingertips, it feels wet, and I discover split skin over a nice goose egg. *Wonderful*.

But my attention snaps back to Savvy when I hear her curse.

"Fuck, he's jumping."

Jumping? Who's jumping?

I couldn't stop myself from poking my head up to look for myself if I tried, just in time to see Ken hanging off the open door of the van bumping through the gates of the old quarry in front of us.

Then my blood freezes as I watch him let go in the middle of the open quarry, his body almost bouncing off the hard ground.

A scream is torn from my chest as Savvy hits the brakes to avoid hitting him, almost knocking me over again in the process.

Her sharply issued, "Stay," slides right off my back as I reach for the door handle and stumble out of the vehicle.

Savvy gets to Ken first, her weapon drawn. Dismissing any potential danger, I drop down on my knees next to my brother's still body.

"Jesus, Bess," my friend grumbles behind me.

I do a quick scan of Ken's body for blood or, God forbid, holes. Then I gently swipe at the shock of graying hair so I can see his face and am surprised to find his eyes open.

"Are you okay? Ken?"

"My leg."

The words are ground out through clenched teeth.

I turn around to take a closer look and this time I notice the dark stain spreading on the inside of his pant leg about thigh height.

"Savvy, he's bleeding."

"Already calling it in," she assures me. "Put pressure on it, while I get my kit."

At this point I don't even know what happened to the van and the armed kidnappers and I don't care, I'm more concerned with the blood I feel slipping from between my fingers.

While Savvy goes to grab her first aid kit from the cruiser, I lean my full weight on my hands, trying to keep as much of my brother's blood inside his body.

He moans in pain, and grabs one of my wrists with his hand, squeezing with surprising strength.

"Not a word, Bess," he hisses.

"Ken..."

"I mean it, you can't tell them."

His face is scrunched up in pain but his eyes are pleading.

"This is crazy, Ken," I argue. "We can't outrun this and

now it's putting other people in danger. They were shooting at me; at people I care about."

"I just got out, Sis, I can't go back."

Dammit, he's killing me.

Blinking my tears back, I shore up my resolve.

"I'm sorry, I have to, Kenny."

Time to end my guilty silence.

HUGO

Fuck, fuck, fuck.

I just saw Bess jumping out of Savvy's cruiser and darting for her brother, and I could do nothing. I don't even have phone contact anymore.

Instead, I'm stuck in the passenger seat of a Bureau-issued Escalade with Mancuso behind the wheel, who is dead-set on going after the white van which just blew past us in the opposite direction.

What a shitshow this is.

I turn my body and strain against the seat belt to try and catch another glimpse of Bess as the fed seems to hit every fucking bump on this dirt road, but Savvy's sheriff's cruiser is blocking the view. I have no choice but to trust my boss to keep the woman I'm fast losing my heart to safe.

Who the fuck am I kidding? My heart was lost before I even knew how well she fits me in every way. The thought of anything happening to her makes me sick to my stomach.

At least I don't have to worry about Carson. I called him earlier and he said they were about two, two-and-a-half hours out. I explained the situation, told him I felt it was safer for him not to come home, and floated the idea Savvy suggested of him crashing at Tate's house. I would've thought he'd jump all over that, being a teenage boy and all that, but he surprised me by asking Cody's dad if it was okay for him to crash there. I got the impression the boys had a good time this weekend.

I'm actually glad that's the route my son decided to go. Since he and Tatum started dating, he's been spending almost all his free time with her, neglecting his friends. As much as I like Tate, I don't want Carson to lose his buddies.

"Heads-up," Mancuso warns, giving me just enough time to grab onto the handle above the door before he whips around the wheel to turn a sharp left.

The van up ahead is swaying from side to side, making me wonder if the rough ride back there blew out one of their tires.

"Cavalry is here," the agent mumbles, as a couple of our cruisers are speeding toward the van from the other side, lights flashing.

I guess the driver of the Ecoline panicked when suddenly the vehicle veers sharply, first to the left but then he overcorrects, and the van hooks to the right, careening off the shoulder and into the ditch below. It rolls a few times before coming to a stop on its roof.

I'm out of the SUV with my weapon in my hand before the wheels stop rolling and start sliding down the steep embankment on my ass. Mancuso joins me, and so does Rick Althof—he must've been monitoring a scanner at home and caught up with us—as we run toward the crashed vehicle.

The driver is crawling out of the window of the flattened cab, and the moment his feet hit the ground, and Mancuso yells, "FBI. Don't move another fucking inch!" the punk is off and running, the fed on his heels.

"At least two left," I call over to Rick, who is mimicking my cautious approach from the other side of the rear of the vehicle.

One of its back doors hangs open and a pair of legs is visible, but nothing seems to be moving inside. Still, armed and dangerous is not something to take lightly and if, as I suspect, these guys are Lotus Squad, they don't shy away from violence, even against law enforcement.

"Sheriff's office!" Rick yells, crouching down to give them a smaller target to aim at, should they start firing. I do the same. "You, in the van, come out, slowly with your hands high."

The legs don't move, and nothing else seems to either. If these guys were in the back of the van the entire time, it's quite possible they were seriously injured or killed in that rollover. But I'm not taking any chances.

I'm on the side of the door that is closed, providing me with a bit of cover from whoever is inside. As Althof continues to yell instructions to the suspects inside, I start approaching the back of the vehicle, hoping that since I can't see anyone, they can't see me at this angle either.

Once I reach the rear, I press my back against the door and inch my way to the open side, keeping an eye on Rick, who stands up and trains his weapon inside the vehicle. I crouch low, giving myself an angle whoever is inside may not expect. Then, with a sharp nod to warn Althof, I turn and move into the opening.

The guy whose legs were visible from the outside has his upper body wedged under one of those big metal tool boxes. No part of him is moving.

It takes me a second to locate guy number two. He

must've been tossed into the cab and appears to have impaled himself on a metal or steel pole. This one is awake—wide awake—his eyes like dark saucers in a stark white face as he looks back at me.

"Do we have medical coming?" I yell over my shoulder.

"On the way," Rick responds from right behind me.

Then he pokes his head over my shoulder.

"They look a mess."

Twenty minutes later, the guy with the pole is in an ambulance, on its way to meet up with a Life Flight Network helicopter to take him to the level one trauma center in Seattle.

Mancuso came back just as the ambulance got here, half dragging the handcuffed driver, who only had minor injuries compared to his buddies. He went in the back of Lloyd's cruiser to get checked out at the hospital in town on his way to the station lock up.

The third guy didn't make it, his neck broken in the rollover. The coroner is on his way to pick up the body.

"You're staying?" I ask Althof.

He nods. "I'm waiting for the coroner. Once he's done, I want to poke around the van a little. See what I can collect. Feel free to get a head start on interviewing the driver. I'll be in as soon as I can."

Mancuso and I hop into his SUV and start making our way back to the station.

I already spoke with Savvy earlier, who assured me Bess was okay, and they were at the hospital with her brother, who'd been shot in the leg. I was glad to hear she was all right, but I'd feel a fuck of a lot better seeing it for myself.

"Actually, would you mind dropping me off at the hospital instead?"

Mancuso glances over.

"I just wanna check on things there."

"Isn't Sheriff Colter already at the hospital with Choi?" he asks, a hint of amusement in his tone.

"She is," I confirm.

"And so is his sister," he adds.

"Yes."

"I'm guessing it's her you want to check on," he concludes, proving himself to be perceptive.

I guess it's a good quality for an FBI agent to have.

"You would be correct."

Ten minutes later, he pulls up in front of Silence Memorial Hospital to let me off. When I walk into the lobby, I spot Savvy right away. She sees me too. She's standing by the front desk, on her phone, and points me in the direction of the waiting space on the other end.

It's been less than an hour since I last saw her bolt out of Savvy's cruiser, but that hour felt like an eternity. Long strides carry me across the lobby.

She notices me and is already getting to her feet when I reach her. She's in my arms a second later, her head tucked under my chin, and her hands sliding under my jacket and around my waist.

We stand like that for a few moments, my heart quietly settling as I breathe in her scent. Then I lift my head and look down at her, noticing a cut and some bruising on the side of her forehead, just inside the hairline. I lightly touch the area with the tip of my finger.

"What happened?"

"I hit my head on the center console when I was ducking

bullets," she says dryly, like dodging gunfire is a regular occurrence.

Immediately I feel my earlier anger building again. Angry at Bess for putting herself in danger, and furious with Savvy for allowing it.

I turn my head to shoot an angry glare across the lobby.

Bess's hand pats the middle of my chest.

"Get over it," she urges. "I didn't really give Savvy a choice, and given the chance, I'd do it again. What I couldn't have lived with is letting my brother be carted off to be executed like a dog."

"You put yourself in danger," I grind out.

"I'm aware, and I'm sorry if you were scared for me, but I had no choice."

I scoff at that.

"Of course, you had a choice."

She shakes her head and looks at me with a sad expression on her face.

"Not really. You'll understand when I tell you all of it."

CHAPTER 21

B*ess*

WITH KEN in surgery to repair the damage the bullet did to his leg, there is no time like the present, but I didn't realize how hard it would be to get the words out.

After burying my secrets for two decades, it's as if my mouth won't wrap around the truth.

I'm a liar. Even if it was lying by omission for the most part, I was purposely deceitful to people I deeply care about.

The two I love deepest are watching me, waiting for me to expose the darkest and some of the most painful experiences of my life. Their eyes are kind and patient, but I'm not sure how long they will be.

Unsure where to start, I force my memory back to the beginning.

"I was eighteen. Still living at home with Mom, who was

very strict when I was eager to explore the world. She wanted to protect me from the kind of world my brother had joined. At the time, being so sheltered, it seemed like he led an exciting, maybe even adventurous life."

Our argument that day was the same one we'd had several times before. I'd wanted to go see Ken, but Mom forbade me. Every other time it would end with me conceding to my mother's will, and I'd stay home, restricted to the occasional phone call with him. But this time, I left anyway, my mother in the doorway behind me, pleading for me to stay, as I grabbed the keys to the old klunker I'd worked so hard to buy.

Independence lured and became harder to resist by the day. I had my first taste when I brought home the first paycheck from my after-school job at a well-known Seattle coffee shop. Then came the rusty Dodge Neon I was able to buy off Mr. Wainfleet down the street for fifteen hundred, hard-earned dollars.

But now I was ready to push my boundaries further, expand my horizons, and I was going to start by visiting my brother in the apartment he'd been boasting about in our calls.

I was willfully ignorant, intent on seeing my brother as some kind of modern day Robin Hood, instead of the hardened criminal he had become. I missed him. Missed bickering over the last piece of bacon at breakfast, missed his cheeky wink as he managed to con Mom into letting us do something she'd initially refused us. I even missed his loud music blasting through the house, making it impossible for me to listen to mine.

But my brother wasn't home. His friend was. I'd only met him once before; Ken had taken me for pizza one night when Mom was working late, and his friend had shown up halfway through our dinner.

Joon Lee was very good-looking, and was clearly used to getting what he wanted. But I didn't enjoy when his attention landed on me. I remember thinking at the time he had a predatory look in his eyes.

I saw that look again the moment he opened my brother's door.

Despite my innocence at the time, I knew I was in trouble, even before his hand shot out and I was yanked into the apartment.

No amount of yelling, screaming, clawing, or fighting seemed to deter him from doing what he had set his mind to do. There were no neighbors who came to my aid. No one heard me, or if they did, they willingly ignored my screams.

I went somewhere else, disconnected from my body, and locked myself inside my head where I was in control.

The first thing I remember after was my brother leaning over me.

"Come on, Bess, I need you to get dressed and get out of here. Please, hurry."

My body was shaking so hard I had trouble covering myself up so Ken was forced to help me. I remember him walking me out to my car, telling me to drive straight home, and not talk to anyone.

"Tell me he killed that fucker," Hugo snarls, snapping me back to the present as he jumps to his feet.

I catch sight of the anguish on Savvy's face and the rage on Hugo's. They had not interrupted me once, until now.

"I didn't know at the time," I convey. "I never saw him again. Not at the apartment that night, or any time after."

Savvy grabs on to Hugo's sleeve and urges him to sit back down.

"How did you get home?" she gently asks me.

"Ken ended up having to drive me in my car. I remember Mom wasn't home and I went straight upstairs. He ran a bath for me, took care of my clothes, and then left before she came home."

"And no one ever approached you about him?"

"No. I mostly stayed close to home after that, and rarely went out by myself."

"You never even told your mom what happened?" she probes.

I shake my head. "No. She never knew."

I didn't see the point. What was done, was done, and all it would've accomplished was to upset her. She'd tried so hard to keep me safe, I'd rather she think she succeeded. There'd been one point I was tempted. Mom had been in the ICU battling sepsis after what should've been a routine gall bladder surgery, and things were not looking good. She told me if there was anything I wanted to tell her, to do it then. She died eight hours later, knowing nothing more than she'd kept her little girl safe, and I'm glad for it.

"Did you at least see a doctor?" Hugo suddenly asks.

"No. Not until a few years later when I was in college and was having some symptoms I thought might be related, but that turned out to be cancer."

"Cancer?"

The outburst comes from both of them.

Oh, God. I'm making a mess of this.

"Endometrial cancer, but that was eighteen years ago. I'm fine now. I'm so sorry," I add, apologizing for yet another little part of myself I haven't let them in on.

I'm oh for two at the moment, and I haven't even gotten to the most egregious of my lies, or omissions. It'll only increase the divide I can already feel growing. Something Savvy's next comment only confirms.

"Jesus, Bess. Is there anything else we need to brace for?"

"Yes," I answer her honestly. "One more thing, probably the most important thing you need to know."

Hugo surges to his feet and turns to the window, his arms crossed in front of him and his back to me. The body language couldn't be clearer if he'd hung a sign around his neck. But I started this, and I need to see it through. It's the right thing to do, even if it comes two decades too late.

"When Ken was arrested, one of his charges was for a violent home invasion. I didn't find out until he already had a trial date that home invasion took place on the same day he found me in his apartment."

I lean forward with my elbows on my knees.

"My brother was with me, looking after me at the time those people were assaulted and robbed in their own home. He'd refused to speak to me, but I'd been ready to speak up on his behalf, and was shocked when he pled guilty to all charges."

"Are you saying he pled guilty for something he didn't do?" Savvy wants clarified.

"Yes. And when I asked him why, he told me he was better off in jail, and that if I were ever to speak a word to anyone about where he really was that night, I would get him killed."

"Because he found Joon raping you and killed him," Hugo states, his voice oddly level.

"Yes, but I swear I didn't know until then. I never asked what happened to him and we never talked about that night. Maybe some part of me suspected, I'm not really sure what I thought at the time, but that was the first time he told me straight up he'd killed him."

With the worst of it out in the open, I'm surprised to find Savvy still sitting in front of me, instead of turning her back like Hugo did.

"I've kept silent for twenty years, but I can't do it anymore. Not when people I care about could get hurt in the process."

"It's a little late for that."

My eyes dart to Hugo, who is staring at me over his shoulder with regret all over his face. I feel my heart sink to the pit of my stomach, and am at a loss for words.

Hugo makes it clear none are wanted when he rips his eyes from mine and turns on his heel, heading for the exit.

"I'm so sorry," I finally manage to whisper to his retreating back.

I get to my feet and prepare to go after him, when Dana walks into the waiting area.

"Your brother is awake."

∼

Hugo

"Give me a fucking name, you piece of shit!"

Frustrated, I slam my fist down on the rickety table in front of him. Rather that than plant it in his face, which is what I really wanted to do.

The driver is nothing but a spindly kid, no older than late teens, early twenties, but with seasoned, flinty eyes that constantly dart around the small room, constantly gauging and assessing his options.

The trouble with these gang kids is their fear for retaliation from their gang is greater than their concern about anything law enforcement can do to them. We've been working on him for a few hours now, and the kid won't confirm who gave them the order. He's not talking at all, just staring back with those almost mocking eyes.

It just got to me.

"Easy," Althof warns in a low voice behind me. "Let's take a break."

He shoves me out of the door, and I immediately head to the restroom to splash some water on my face.

When I got here, Mancuso was taking a break from interviewing the punk and Rick was about to head in. I volunteered to join him, eager to get to the bottom of this mess.

I would've rather talked to Ken Choi, who seems to be at the center of all of this, but it would probably be a while before we'd be able to interview him. Besides, I needed to get out of there, get some air.

I ended up walking here from the hospital. I needed the half hour it took me to tamp down the rage burning through me.

Anger at a man who unfortunately has already been dead over twenty years, otherwise it would've been my pleasure to rip his fucking limbs from his body and beat him to death with them.

Anger at a brother who, in his attempt to protect his sister, burdened her to a life shackled to a lie she had no choice but to perpetuate.

And yes, anger at Bess for not letting me share that burden with her.

But what really burns me hard is first discovering she'd been raped. There are things I would've done differently had I known that. I might've been more cautious, gentler in the way I touched her. Then to find out she had cancer and never shared that either. Not when Emily was fighting and losing her battle, and at no time after. Those kinds of experiences seem pretty essential to what makes a person who they are, and now I'm left to figure out what to do with that information.

I can't deny a brief gut reaction of *not again* flitted through my mind when the subject of cancer came up. Part of me wonders if Bess was afraid that information might have impacted how I see her.

Does it make a difference? Does any of it change the way I feel about her?

I lift my head and look in the mirror over the sink, my face wet with the cold tap water I splashed on it.

Nah. I love her, have for a while, and it's only grown deeper the closer we've gotten. Despite my slightly bruised ego, that hasn't changed.

Rick is waiting for me when I step out.

"What was that all about?"

"Sorry. I'm frustrated."

"That much was obvious," he returns dryly. "You were a bit more intense than I'm used to. What gives?"

I hesitate, knowing what I'm about to share could potentially get Bess in some trouble, and at the very least will expose things about her that really shouldn't be for public consumption. But it was Bess's call to make that sacrifice to help resolve this case, and it's important information that paints a clearer context.

I look down the hall toward the front desk area and notice a few curious glances. The hallway is a little too public for this kind of sensitive subject.

"Grab Mancuso and join me in the meeting room. I have some new information."

On my way there, I duck into the kitchen for a quick cup of office dredge and find Brenda there.

"I heard about Bess's brother, how is he?"

I get the sense that's not what she wants to know, but I answer her anyway.

"As far as I know, he should be okay."

I grab a mug and pour myself coffee, watering it down as best I can with the creamer I find in the small fridge. I'll probably be up half the night drinking coffee at this time of day, but it's not like I was going to go home with this case heating up the way it is. In any event, I need my head clear for what is to come.

"And Bess? I'm surprised she's not with you."

I knew Brenda was fishing for more. She has a great sixth sense for picking up on dynamics playing out under the surface, and is relentless in sniffing them out.

I don't want to feed into that, so I stick to the basics.

"She's okay, still at the hospital with Savvy," I share, quickly adding, "I've gotta run. They're waiting for me."

Then I dart out the door.

With any luck, she'll be off for the day by the time I come out of the meeting.

The last thing I need is to bump into fucking Don Merrick right outside the meeting room.

"There's no one at the front desk," he starts in an accusatory tone.

"That's probably because it's after five on a Sunday afternoon," I point out. "But Brenda is still around, if you were looking for her."

"Actually, I was looking for the sheriff, but you'll do."

I almost laugh at the blatant diss, but don't want to give him the satisfaction of acknowledging it. Besides, I'm already strung tight, I don't want to give him a chance to get under my skin.

"It's come to my attention there's been a major development in this case, and I'd like to know how soon you can wrap this up. I have an important investor visiting in a few days and the last thing I need is another fire or kidnapping or high-speed chase right through town to scare him off."

How fucking ignorant can you be? This douche is more concerned about investments than he is the citizens of this town. Already fired up, this is enough of a trigger for me.

I lean in and very nearly poke my finger in his chest.

"You have gotta be fucking kidding me."

CHAPTER 22

B*ess*

GREAT, now my brother won't speak to me either.

He knows I talked the moment he spots Savvy following me into the room.

All I get is a glare before he turns his head away.

"I find it rich you are pissed at me for sharing, when you're the one whose loose lips got us into this mess in the first place," I tell the back of his head.

When he doesn't react, it only fuels my anger.

"What would you have me do, Ken? Go on the run with you? How would that have solved anything? What kind of life would that be? I already have a life, right here. I have friends, people I care about, a business I built by myself. I don't want to run. I want to stay and fight to keep it."

Savvy nudges me when nothing from my brother is forthcoming. "Come on."

Grudgingly, I allow her to lead me out into the hallway where I let my emotions get the better of me.

Mom always taught me not to rely on any man but to carve my own path in life. Well...looks like she was right. In the span of an hour, the two men who hold my heart—for whom I would easily have done anything—chose to turn their backs on me. It's not even that I'm all that disappointed: how could I be if I was already half expecting this for an outcome?

But I am hurt, although that might be a bit of an understatement. Heartbroken is probably closer to the truth.

"I don't know why I'm bawling," I mumble, keeping my head low so my hair covers at least part of my face from nosy passersby.

"Well...let me see," Savvy offers. "Your business was torched, your home is unlivable, a violent gang is on your heels, your brother was kidnapped before your eyes, your boyfriend walked out on you—probably just needed some time to process, but still—and now your brother is laying yet another guilt trip on you. I say you've earned a good cry."

I wipe my nose with the sleeve of my sweater. Not exactly ladylike, but neither is walking around with tears and snot running down my face.

"I know what you need, a good hug," my friend declares, abruptly turning to wrap me in a tight hold.

I indulge for a moment before disentangling myself. "What I could use is some puppy snuggles."

Oh no...*Ragnar*.

We left home this morning thinking we'd be back by lunch. That poor dog has been alone all day. With everything going on, I totally forgot about him. I wince at the thought of all the damage he could've done to Hugo's house in that time.

"I've gotta go," I blurt out, beelining it for the exit. "Ragnar's been alone all day," I add over my shoulder.

"Hold up," Savvy calls behind me. "I can't leave your brother and you can't go alone; you don't have wheels. Let me call someone."

Ten agonizingly long minutes later, when I see KC pull up outside the hospital in his patrol car, I dart outside and jump into the passenger seat. KC was about to get out, but I tap my hand on the dashboard.

"We've gotta go."

"Just a minute."

Savvy followed me outside at a slower pace and walks over to the driver's side where KC rolls down his window.

"Give her a ride to Hugo's place and walk her to the door. Then I want you to wait outside until Battaglia's guys show up, and after that I need you back here."

"Sure thing, boss."

"You..." Savvy points at me. "Stay inside and lock up until Hugo gets there. Understood?" she orders sternly.

"Yeah, yeah, fine. Can we go?"

THE SMELL HITS me the moment I walk in the door, and I brace myself for what I'll find as I punch the code to set the alarm.

Walking through to the living room, I groan when at first glance I notice white fluff on the couch and the floor around it, and trailing down the stairs is a strip of toilet paper. When I move farther into the room, something crunches under my foot, and I bend down to pick up about two-thirds of a well-chewed remote control.

There is evidence of Ragnar everywhere, including the

big dump he took in front of the back door, but no sign of him. I quickly clean up the poop and turn on the exhaust fan over the stove, hoping it'll help get rid of the smell.

Considering he's been alone for about eight hours now; the damage is relatively minimal. At least down here. A throw pillow, obviously the remote, somebody's gym sock, a Tupperware container holding butter Hugo kept on the counter—the butter eaten, I presume— and, so far, one toilet roll, but I haven't been upstairs yet.

I gather the toilet paper as I head up the steps, discovering a half-chewed bar of soap on the landing. The bedroom door I distinctly remember closing is open. Scratches in the paint mar the bottom of the door and the post. I hold my breath as I stick my head inside, and am surprised to find the room virtually untouched, other than the dog, splayed out in the middle of the bed, comatose on top of my sleep shirt.

At my, "Hey, boy," he flips over and lifts his head, one ear inside out. Then with a happy bark, he leaps off and almost knocks me on my ass.

"Do you need to go outside?" I ask him as I give him a good rub.

Feeling lucky I can easily fix or replace what he damaged, I follow him downstairs, where I find him already waiting by the kitchen door. I punch the code into the keypad by the door before I open it, letting Ragnar bound outside to do his business, while I start picking up the decimated throw pillow and various bits of plastic off the floor.

The garbage can under the sink is close to overflowing by the time I stuff everything in, so I pull out the bag, tie it up, and carry it out the back.

Hugo parks his rolling bins on the side of the deck, so I head down the two steps and drop the bag in the bin. I'm just closing the lid when Ragnar comes out of nowhere and darts past me. He jumps up against the wooden fence separating Hugo's property and his neighbors, and starts barking his head off.

It's dark, the only light out here comes from inside the house, and I can't see what he's barking at—for all I know the neighbor is out there or some kind of animal—but it's suddenly making me feel very uneasy. Invisible fingers creep up my back and I'm already retreating up the steps to the back door when I try to call the dog back.

"Come on, boy. Let's go. Inside! Ragnar, come!"

When he finally turns and comes bounding back, I peer beyond him into the shadows and just catch sight of someone climbing over the fence. Panicked, I rush the dog inside and slam the door, my fingers shaking as I try to throw the lock and arm the alarm.

I jump when Ragnar starts barking again, running for the front door, where someone starts banging on the other side. Fueled by fear and adrenaline, I run after the dog, scoop him up in my arms, and dart up the stairs where I lock us into the bathroom.

Ragnar is still growling from deep in his chest, and I'm shaking so hard, my teeth start to chatter. My hand digs for my phone in my pocket, only to discover I never took it out of my purse, which is still on the hall table by the front door.

At the sound of a loud crash and glass breaking from downstairs, Ragnar immediately wrestles loose and starts barking at the door, but I wedge myself between the toilet and the tub, my heart lodged in my throat.

~

Hugo

. . .

"She was in an impossible situation, you realize that, right?"

I'm surprised that comes from Althof. He never struck me as a particularly sensitive guy but, apparently, he's picking up on some remaining negative vibes I must be sending out. I really need to check that.

Still, it irks me he feels he needs to defend Bess to me.

"Of course I get that."

Not what you'd call a gracious response, but I'm trying to fucking roll with the punches here. Give me a break.

"You know what this means," Mancuso interjects. "She's in as much danger as her brother is. If Shane Lee knows Ken killed Joon, and why, and he's aware Bess knew about it the entire time, he's gonna hold her equally responsible. These guys don't mess around with people they feel wronged them."

"But in that case, why this cloak-and-dagger game? Why not put a straight hit out on her instead of lighting a fire when she's not even there?" Rick puts forward. "Or for that matter, why not shoot Ken right where he stood on the sidewalk instead of going to the effort of having him snatched off the street."

All good questions, and now I really feel fucking stupid for having walked out on Bess at the hospital. I was so hot under the collar, I never even thought through the implications of the bombshell she dropped. Some fucking protector I am.

Mancuso speaks up, "Because I suspect Shane Lee wants to do the honors himself, and he wanted a chance to have both Ken and Bess in front of him for maximum effect. We were right in thinking they were using Bess to flush out her brother, since he was the more elusive one, and probably counted on being able to pick her up easily once they had him. My guess? He'd have made Ken watch them violate and then kill his sister, before killing him. The ultimate revenge."

The picture he paints is too vivid in my mind and I slam my fist into the wall in a rage.

"Real sensitive, Mancuso," Althof observes in a deadpan voice. "You must be a barrel of laughs at parties."

"Shit. Sorry, man," the agent apologizes, and then adds, "I've gotta take this," when his phone starts ringing.

"I'm off," I announce, heading for the door.

The need to get to Bess is burning a hole in my gut.

"Where to?" Rick calls after me.

"To grab Bess at the hospital."

No way I'm going to leave her in close proximity to her brother and make it too easy for those Lotus Squad fuckers to snatch them both. She'll be safer the farther I can keep her from Ken.

"The hospital?" Brenda, who was lurking in the hallway, pipes up. "She's not there anymore. KC just called in; he gave her a ride to your house."

"Thanks," I mumble, brushing past her in my hurry to get home.

Just as I push through the door to the parking lot, I hear my name called and running footsteps behind me.

"Hold up," Mancuso pants as he catches up with me by my cruiser. "That call was from my contact in Seattle; they've lost Shane Lee. Nothing since last night."

I don't like that. I don't like that at all.

"I need to get home to Bess."

I'm about to climb behind the wheel when my phone starts ringing. It's Battaglia.

"Yeah."

"We've got trouble at your place. I'm on my way there now," he rattles off.

"Bess is there by herself."

His curt, "I know. We're on it," is followed by a sharp click.

"What's going on?" Mancuso asks as I jump in the cruiser.

"Something's going down at my place," I snap as I jam my keys in the ignition.

"I'm coming with you," he announces, jogging around to jump in on the passenger side.

No sooner does his ass hit the seat when I tear out of the parking lot, hitting the sirens when I turn onto the street.

I'm about to grab my radio, when a call comes in dispatching all available units to my address for a suspected home invasion.

Jesus. They're inside my fucking house.

"We're no use to her dead," Mancuso comments when I turn a corner too fast and the back end of my SUV slides sideways, wheel squealing.

I see Roy's vehicle and one patrol car parked in front of the house when I turn onto my street. Swinging around them, I pull into the driveway. I slam the SUV in park with the wheels still turning, bringing it to an abrupt stop. Mancuso swears under his breath, but I ignore him as I jump out.

The front door is open and I run inside.

"Bess!"

Nobody is in the living room or the kitchen, but there's glass everywhere from the broken sliding door. Someone crashed through there. Out in the backyard I see the bobbing beam of a flashlight.

"Bess!" I call out again.

"Alexander," Mancuso's voice sounds behind me.

When I turn, he points up the stairs and I rush toward him.

She looks so small, standing at the top of the stairs with that crazy fucking dog in her arms. I take the steps two at a time and sweep her and the dog up in my hold.

"Are you okay? Tell me you're all right," I mumble as I carry her into my bedroom and set her down next to the bed.

Ragnar immediately tries to scamper off, so I quickly close the door to make sure he can't get out. Then I return to Bess and gently run my hands over her body to look for any injuries,

"I'm okay," she whispers, her voice as shaky as mine. Her teeth are chattering. "I hid in the bathroom. I was stupid, I let the dog out because he'd been cooped up so long. He'd had an accident in the kitchen already and he needed to go. I wasn't thinking. I'm sorry," she rambles as I stroke the hair back out of her face. "Then Ragnar went crazy, and I saw someone coming over the fence. I got us inside, locked the door, and hid in the bathroom."

"Good," I try to soothe her with a calm voice, even though my heart feels far from calm, it's beating out of my fucking chest. "You did good."

She drops her forehead to my chest and I cup a hand on the back of her head, keeping her right there, against my heart.

Fuck, that was close. Too close. We can't stay here.

A soft knock sounds before Roy pokes his head around the door.

"Everything okay in here?"

"Yeah. What's happening out there?"

"My boys just got here and were suspicious of a vehicle sitting in front of that little park down the road. It's dark out, they figured; why would anyone be hanging around a park at this time of night? Anyway, one of them went to check on it, the other kept an eye out, and then suddenly your dog started going crazy in the backyard. It alerted my crew, they came running, heard a crash at the back of the house and one stayed at the front, banging on the door and calling me. The other went around back, just in time to see two guys in your backyard, scrambling to get over the fence."

"Descriptions?"

"Dressed in black, average build, one around five nine, five ten, the other maybe six feet."

"And?" I prompt him for more, all the while keeping Bess sheltered in my arms.

"He was on their tail to the edge of that small ravine and then they split up. He says he followed the shorter of the two, but lost him in the dense brush."

"Shit."

"Yeah. Your deputy is checking out that vehicle by the park. It's still there, so either it wasn't theirs or they abandoned it."

"How the hell did they find her here?" I voice my thoughts out loud.

Roy shrugs. "I bet you they had eyes on the hospital, saw Bess leaving and followed. Waited here at the park until they saw KC's patrol car leave, not knowing we had a security team monitoring from across the street."

That makes sense, but it brings me back to my earlier thought that we cannot stay here. That means I need to draw back from the investigation completely and pack our bags. Next, I need to get us out of here unseen.

"Have you met Special Agent Mancuso?" I ask Roy.

"He came out and introduced himself."

"Can you ask him to come up here?"

Roy nods and backs out, closing the door.

Then I put my hands on Bess's shoulders and set her back a step.

"We can't stay here."

Her eyes are wide, but she nods her understanding. I'm sure she'd come to that conclusion on her own.

"I know a place, but we can't take any chances we're being followed. I'm pretty sure whoever was trying to get at you had or has eyes on the house, which means we have to create a diversion and move quickly."

She nods again, a little firmer this time. "I'll start packing."

There she is, a spine of steel.

CHAPTER 23

B*ess*

"Morning."

Squinting against the bright sunlight streaming in, I peek at Hugo sitting down on the edge of the bed, already dressed. In his hand he has a mug that says, *Rock On*, and is emanating the most beautiful aroma of any morning.

I push myself up and hold out my hand.

"Coffee..."

I close my eyes and take a sip, letting the memories of last night's frantic scramble flood back. The rushed packing, sneaking into the garage and hiding in the old pickup with Ragnar's panting steaming up the windows until one of the security guys and a female deputy pretending to be us drove off in Hugo's cruiser. They were supposed to head for a roadside motel outside Winston, about halfway between Silence and Spokane. The hope was for them to lure the bad guys right into the arms of Special Agent Mancuso's colleagues, who would already be waiting at the Riverview Motel.

By the time we got the signal the coast was clear, the street was quiet, and there were no vehicles parked outside the house, other than a single patrol car.

Instead of heading south, toward Spokane, we headed north. I imagined a hunting shack somewhere in the mountains when Hugo mentioned he knew a place, I wasn't expecting an entire house. A familiar one at that.

We only drove ten minutes out of town when he turned the pickup onto a dead-end mountain road with two houses I'm very familiar with: the Colter place, and the house Savvy built but sold to Phil when she first moved to town. She only lived in the house for a short while before moving in with Brant Colter on the farm a mile or so up the road, but she uses the place as a guest house for visitors and built her music studio over the garage.

Phil and Savvy's father were waiting for us when we turned into the driveway.

I swear the main reason I slept like a log, after being scared out of my gourd last night, was because I couldn't have felt any safer with Hugo and the dog, a state-of-the-art security system, Sheriff Colter senior and his collection of guns just up the road, and nobody knowing where we are. Not even Savvy.

"Apparently, Phil keeps the place stocked with the basics," Hugo informs me. "And Ragnar already loves it here. Lots of new smells and plenty of greenery for him to mark."

"What time is it?"

I look around for my phone but can't find it.

"It's nine thirty, and your phone is on the kitchen counter, charging."

Nine thirty? I can't remember the last time I slept in that late. I'm usually up before the crack of dawn to start...

"The coffee shop," I cry out, scrambling out of bed. "The cleaning crew was coming at nine this morning."

Hugo plucks the sloshing mug of coffee from my hand.

"Taken care of," he calmly states. "Lola and Emmet are looking after things."

"How..."

"Lola called early this morning, you were still deep asleep, so I answered your phone."

The urge to object dissipates as quickly as it rises, and I plop down on the edge of the bed beside Hugo, reclaiming my coffee mug.

"So what's the plan? What are we gonna do all day?"

I realize what a suggestive question that is when I catch the positively lecherous look on Hugo's face.

"I could think of a thing or two."

Not that his expression left much to the imagination, but his comment cements where his head is at. I would've thought I'd be annoyed by that kind of innuendo, but I'm not. In fact, I'm finding it a turn-on he seems to find it difficult to keep his hands or his eyes off me. I can honestly say I've never—to my knowledge—been the subject of someone's blatant desire like that. I'll admit, it's a bit heady.

I'm seriously contemplating spending the entire day in bed with my handsome Viking, when the dog starts barking and a voice carries through the house.

"Yoohoo! Anybody here?" I can hear Phil call out from the other side of the house. "I hope y'all are dressed and decent and home, because I've got my hands full here and your dog is fighting me for the damn bacon."

"I'll go," Hugo says, pressing a firm kiss to my lips. "You get dressed. It'll be fun undressing you again later."

I watch him leave the room, appreciating his casual attire of faded jeans and loose-hanging flannel shirt over a white tee. As much as I appreciate the dark jeans and navy shirt of his uniform, I like this laid-back look even better on him. It exposes a side of him I'm eager to explore. I have visions of long hikes, barbecues, campfires, and quality time spent with friends.

It takes me five minutes to splash some water on my face, give my teeth a quick brush, finger comb my messy do, and get dressed. I find Phil sitting at the kitchen island, a mug of coffee in front of her, chatting away with Hugo. He immediately turns his head with a faint smile on his lips, reaching out for me and pulling me to his side.

I find I no longer blush or get embarrassed at the public displays of affection. Quite the opposite, actually, I enjoy the way he publicly claims me, almost challenging those present to make anything of it. And I claim him right back, leaning into his side with my hand on his stomach as I smile at Phil.

"So what did you bring?"

"Just a couple of things I thought you might need."

Hugo snorts. "A couple of things? It took me two more trips to haul all the groceries inside. You'd think we were preparing for Armageddon or something."

"Don't exaggerate," Phil scolds him with a wave of her hand. "I just thought Bess might want to make use of this well-outfitted kitchen and try a few new recipes."

Hugo pulls open the door leading to the laundry room and pantry, and points to the floor. The small space is packed full with a giant sack of flour, a big bag of regular and one of icing sugar, several large containers with spices, baking powder, powdered milk, chocolate chips, various kinds of nuts. Stacked on the washer and dryer are containers with fresh fruits, a couple of brand-new baking trays, a box of piping bags and tips, and a roll of parchment paper.

"There's eight pounds of butter in the fridge," Hugo informs me.

I shoot Phil an incredulous look, even as my hands start to get restless.

"Well...I have a vested interest in getting you up and running as soon as possible," she announces, getting up off the stool and making her way to the front door where she stops and looks back.

"And just so you know, I'll be happy to taste test anything made by your very talented hands."

Then she slips out the door before I can even form the words to thank her.

Hugo chuckles. "That's not all, she brought over enough food we could hole up here for a month and wouldn't have to come up for air."

I'm still eyeing all the goodies she left me in the pantry when Hugo comes up behind me and slips his arms around my waist. Then he drops his chin on my shoulder and his gaze follows mine at my baking bounty.

"What are the chances I can drag you away from here and back into bed?"

I bark out a laugh.

"Yeah," he mumbles, dropping a light kiss on the shell of my ear before letting me go. "I was afraid of that. Cock-blocked by a bag of flour."

~

Hugo

"I'm listening," I assure Savvy.

But only barely, because the sight of Bess in the kitchen in her element, her face flushed as she hums some vaguely familiar tune as her hands create magic, is a tad distracting. As are the unbelievable aromas filling the house. There is not a chance in hell I'll ever get back the six-pack of my youth if this is my future.

My boss texted me a few times this morning, demanding to know if Bess was all right after last night's scare, which I assured her she was. But this time she called with some updates on the case, which I was eager to hear.

I already spoke first thing this morning with Carson, making sure I caught him before he'd hear about what happened at the house through gossip. He was obviously upset, but I was able to assure him we were both fine and any damage to the house would be fixed. Last night, Roy Battaglia had already offered to talk to Nate about replacing the back door. I also talked with Cody's dad, Larry, who very kindly offered Carson could stay as long as needed, which was a weight off my back.

But I hadn't spoken to anyone other than Phil and Bess since then and started feeling quite disconnected from what was going on in the world out there.

"What's happening?" I prompt her.

"Well, other than the fact I haven't had a fucking wink of sleep, there's been no luck so far on the subjects. That vehicle left down the street from your place turned out to be stolen earlier last night from the employee parking lot at a fast-food restaurant in Winston. The theft wasn't discovered until the end of the owner's shift. My guess is the goons had a secondary vehicle somewhere else in your neighborhood. One they could get to in an emergency if, for whatever reason, they needed to split up or the first vehicle was made. I've got a few deputies canvassing the neighborhood for anyone who may have seen something or security cameras that may have picked up their movements."

"It's pretty much a moot point though," I suggest. "Whatever vehicle they may have used will have been discarded by now. In fact, I wouldn't be surprised if they were a couple of getaway vehicles ahead of us."

"I know," Savvy agrees, "it's likely, but they've made mistakes before, and I don't want to risk skimming over steps and potentially missing something important."

I can't argue with her on that, but sometimes I hate how slow the wheels of justice can turn. Although, you won't hear me complain about having Bess to myself while we wait.

"But they haven't shown up at the motel yet. Your decoys are going to hang out there for a bit longer and Mancuso's team is monitoring. If anyone shows, they'll be all over them."

I hope they do, but at this point I don't think they'll simply walk up and knock on the door. I'm pretty sure they'll be a lot more careful in their approach than they were at my place.

"One interesting development though," she adds. "Apparently, Mancuso had a talk with his supervisor and got approval to offer Ken Choi a deal."

At that, my ears perk up. Bess's brother could do a lot of damage to the Lotus Squad if the feds could convince him to roll over on his former gang members.

"Think he'll take it?"

"Don't know," Savvy returns. "I haven't been able to get a

word out of him. Heck, he even refused to speak to Bess last night."

"Priceless. The asshole blabs to a fellow inmate, putting himself and Bess on a hit list, and now he wants to blame her for trying to save them both?"

"I know," Savvy soothes. "He's a dick, but I'm hopeful Mancuso can get somewhere with him. Give the guy a chance to get himself and his sister out of this situation."

"I sure hope so."

"I'll let you know," she promises, ending the call.

My anger at her brother evaporates when I glance over at Bess, who is piping icing on the carrot pecan cake she said she was making next. She's so engrossed in doing what she loves, a little smile plays on her lips. Man, I could watch her dance around the kitchen forever. What's in her heart is reflected on her face.

When her eyes catch on me a moment later, she lays it all on the table for me with just a look.

My mouth spills over.

"God, I love you."

CHAPTER 24

B*ess*

THESE PAST FEW days have been absolute magic.

That is, if I tune out the circumstances that got us here.

We've explored the woods all along the creek hiking. I caught my very first brook trout under Hugo's tutelage, which we cleaned and grilled for dinner. I've been able to fine tune some recipes I'd been working on, the results closely scrutinized by Hugo and Phil. We walked with Ragnar up to the Colter place and introduced him to Brant and Phil's growing farm menagerie. We've played card games, watched a few movies, built a bonfire under the stars, and talked, a lot.

We covered a lot of ground, most of it related to what I kept to myself for far too long. Cancer, growing up with an overprotective mother who didn't want me to make the mistakes she had, having a brother affiliated with organized crime, and yes, we also talked about the rape. It turned out to be a tougher subject for Hugo than it was for me but, of course, I've had years to process what happened, yet it's still fresh for him. But it was good, cleansing in a way, and it feels good to have someone I've shared every dark corner with, who has stuck by my side.

Hugo opened up as well, and managed to shock me when he shared about struggles in his marriage I hadn't been aware of. Turns out things weren't always as perfect as they looked from the outside.

Of course, the other thing we did plenty of was have sex.

Copious amounts of sex. I'm pretty sure I've had more orgasms in the past couple of days than I'd accumulated over the rest of my life.

What can I say? Not only is Hugo exceptionally talented and nicely equipped, but he's also the man I love. What's more, he loves me, and I've never in my life felt as free and unburdened to enjoy the attention focused on me. Being the center of attention under any other circumstances would make me cringe, but not with Hugo.

He loves me.

I almost hit the floor, along with my carrot cake, when he made that declaration. I was not expecting that.

I'd hoped one day he might, but not this quickly. It's amazing to me that not that long ago, I was resigned to loving this man from afar for the rest of my life.

Now look at us, snuggled up in bed in a state of post-coital bliss, watching the sun rise outside the window.

"What do you want to do today?" Hugo asks, his breath brushing my forehead.

"I'm not sure. I think there may be enough eggs left for me to make a quiche today."

He squeezes me in his arms. "You know you don't always

have to be responsible for all our food, right? Your skills may be way superior to mine, but I've been known to throw together a decent meal from time to time," he points out.

I turn in his arms and rest my chin on his chest so I can look at him. "I'm aware, but food is my love language. Always has been. And there's nothing better than feeding people I love."

That earns me another squeeze and a smile I feel down to my toes.

"I just wish Carson was here, so I could feed him too."

I've been thinking about Hugo's son a lot, feeling guilty for keeping his father from him. I even tried to suggest Hugo should go home to be with his son, but that idea was abruptly dismissed.

"As much as I love you wanting to feed my son, I'm sure he's not starving," he suggests. "Besides, he seems to be having a good time at Cody's, so I'm not so worried about him."

I grumble a little, putting my cheek back down to his chest.

"Still...as much as I enjoy being here with you, how long can we keep this up? You should be working—Savvy's carrying too much on her shoulders already—and I need to get back to running my business, I've been generating zero income since the fire."

"Tiring of me already?" he teases.

I pull on a couple of stray chest hairs in retaliation.

"Don't mock me; it's a valid question."

"Yes, it is," he concedes. "But as we heard yesterday, the FBI tracked down and captured the two gang members they believe tried to break into my house, and are actively questioning those suspects in hopes they'll give up the individual who put out the order. Also, Mancuso seems to be making some headway with your brother. Things are progressing, albeit slowly."

I press a kiss to his chest before disentangling myself and swinging my legs out of bed.

"I hope so, because pretty soon I'll be out of funds to pay my staff, and without Lola and Emmet, I don't know if I'll ever be able to get Strange Brew back up and running."

Hugo rolls on his side and props himself up on his elbow.

"All the credit to Lola and Emmet for the way they've stepped up but, Twinkie, you're the heart and soul of Strange Brew. It is now, and will be long after Lola and Emmet have moved on."

Then he suddenly surges up and jumps out of bed as well, scooping me up in his arms.

"Now, can I interest you in a shower?"

IT'S ALREADY ALMOST noon by the time I turn off the blow-dryer, shake out my hair, and allow myself one last glimpse in the mirror before leaving the bathroom.

I hardly recognize myself, this glowing, confident woman staring back at me. I may be imagining things, but even my hair seems to have a deeper shine to it. For no reason other than my own satisfaction, I dress with a little more attention than I have in the past few days. My newest pair of barrel jeans I've had to wash three times already to get the smell of smoke out, a clean white T-shirt, and the intricately crocheted sweater vest Dana bought me for my thirty-ninth birthday, but haven't had a chance to wear yet.

Feeling good about myself, I walk down the hallway separating the main bedroom suite from the kitchen and living room, when I hear the sound of voices on the other side of the wall. I'm pretty sure one of them belongs to Savvy.

"How did you know where to find us?" I'm already asking as I freeze right inside the kitchen when I see not only Savvy, but the FBI agent standing by the island.

Hugo immediately comes for me and slips an arm around my shoulders.

Savvy shrugs at my question. "I knew you guys wouldn't go far, so when my dad canceled standing dinner plans with some cockamamie excuse, and Phil avoided my phone calls altogether, the wheels started turning."

Of course they did, it wouldn't be Savvy if she wasn't driven to get to the bottom of every mystery. I guess that's why my friend is the sheriff of Edwards County.

"Okay, fair enough, but what are you doing here?" I indicate the space around me. "And with a guest," I add, before turning to SAC Mancuso. "No offense."

He shrugs easily. "None taken."

"Doesn't that defeat the purpose?" I push on.

"Exactly what I was hoping they could fucking explain," Hugo grumbles, shooting stern glances at Savvy and the agent.

"Your brother is ready to make a deal," Mancuso responds, taking the lead.

"He is? What does that mean? What kind of deal?"

I'm surprised he's even considering talking.

"It means he's willing to share any and all information related to Shane Lee and the Lotus Squad, details that should help us take down the organization piece by piece, in return for protection under the WITSEC program."

"Great," Hugo reacts. "But that doesn't explain why you're here."

"Because he demands to talk to Bess first."

Hugo

"It's dangerous."

She smiles at me and puts a calming hand on my chest.

We're in the bedroom, where she dragged me after I went off on Mancuso for even entertaining that idea.

"So is trying to hide when it's just a matter of time before Shane Lee finds us as well. This is not a tenable situation for the long term. This is an opportunity for me to take an active role instead of passively waiting for others to fix my problems. It's a chance to take back some control."

I hear her.

Fuck, I even agree with what she's saying, but that doesn't mean I have to like having her out in the open again, vulnerable to threats. Shane *fucking* Lee is still out there and hasn't been accounted for, neither have God knows how many members in the Lotus Squad ranks. The danger is no less than it was before Ken Choi decided to finally do the right thing, and I really resent the fact he's determined to put his sister in that vulnerable position once again.

"I want a chance to talk to him,' Bess pleads. "Listen, this will likely be the last opportunity I have. You heard Mancuso, he'll be in protective custody until he disappears into the witness protection program. I'll never see him or talk to him again. He's my blood. My *only* blood."

I can't stand to see the tears glistening in her eyes, even as she fights hard to hold them off. Dropping my forehead to hers, I blow out a breath, releasing some of the tension in my body.

"You're right," I give in. "But we're not running out there without a solid security plan in place for you. I don't care if we have to hire added security to do it, but I'm not willing to take any chances. You'll have to give me that."

The grateful smile she beams up at me means a lot. But even more so do the words that follow.

"Then make your arrangements for my safety. I trust you implicitly."

I sweep her up, branding myself on her in a fiery kiss. Then I grab her hand and lead the way back to the kitchen, where Savvy and Mancuso are patiently waiting.

Then I lay out my own demands.

"Ready?"

I glance over at Bess, who is almost unrecognizable wearing the slouchy beanie with unfamiliar blond waves draped over her shoulders, as well as a pair of bold-framed sunglasses hiding her expressive eyes. Bess already had the glasses, but the wig and beanie are courtesy of Phil, who apparently kept some accessories from her previous life as a rock star.

As for myself, I've tucked my flannel shirt in the waistband of my jeans, and am wearing Brant Colter's beloved Stetson. He entrusts me with both the hat and his old Ford Bronco.

While Bess and I hiked along the creek up to the Colter place, Savvy and Mancuso stayed at the house to throw off anyone who may have followed them. Half an hour later, they returned to town to make sure security measures are in place at the hospital where Ken is still under guard.

Savvy had called ahead to let Brant and Phil know we were on our way. Initially, her father wanted to drive the Bronco with Bess and me hiding in the back seat, but Savvy nixed that, explaining for Bess and I to walk into the hospital unchecked, our best chance to do so would be in some kind of disguise, looking like we belonged.

Given that we'll be driving the Bronco, it made sense to look like Brant and Phil. Not that we'd pass close scrutiny, but hopefully just enough for people to skim over us and not look too closely.

"Ready," she confirms, sounding confident.

But when I grab her hand to give it a little squeeze, I find it clammy.

"It'll be okay," I try to assure her as I pull the vehicle out of Brant's garage.

She flashes a smile.

"I know. It's not that. I'm just worried about what to say to Ken. It'll be the last thing he hears from my mouth, and I want it to mean something."

My opinion—as strongly as I feel it—has no place here, so I keep my thoughts to myself. As far as I'm concerned, Ken Choi does not deserve any consideration. The guy is once again putting his sister in the crosshairs. But he's not the only family I have.

No sooner do I turn onto the main drag into town, when a green pickup turns out of a driveway on the other side of the road. I watch in my rearview mirror as it tags on behind me. I can only make out a driver, a guy wearing a ball cap and a pair of reflective shades that make it hard to distinguish any features.

That didn't take fucking long.

Letting go of Bess's hand, I reach for the gun I have tucked under my thigh. Steering one-handed, I keep the weapon I have in my other hand on my lap.

"What's happening?" Bess wants to know.

"Just being cautious, that's all."

Still, she jumps at the sound of my phone ringing from the cup holder where I tossed it.

"Could you get that for me?" I ask her. I don't have any hands to spare. "Put it on speaker."

"Relax," Roy Battaglia's voice comes through. I can hear he's smiling. "You're looking a little tense behind the wheel."

I narrow my eyes on the driver of the truck in my rearview mirror and watch as he slowly raises his hand and wiggles his fingers.

"You son of a bitch. You could've given me a heads-up," I grumble.

Roy laughs. "I did, but apparently you don't check your messages. If you had, you'd also know one of my guys in a silver RAV will tag up at the base of Elm Street and follow you the rest of the way to the hospital. I'm going to stay a couple of vehicles behind once he tags in. The point is, you can relax, we've got your back."

The line goes dead and Bess breathes out a sigh of relief.

Good, I don't want her to worry.

But there's no way I'm letting go of my gun.

CHAPTER 25

H*ugo*

WITH MY LEFT arm tightly around Bess's shoulders and my heart in my throat, I walk across the parking lot and into the hospital.

I'm not used to having to trust others, but the objective is to get inside the hospital as inconspicuously as we can, and I can't do that with a gun in my hand.

We get a few curious glances as I walk us briskly through the lobby, to the elevators off the hallway at the other end. Savvy made sure Ken was moved from the recovery room after his surgery, to a room at the far end of the second floor, making it easier to keep him secure. Savvy said she'd keep the hallway clear so we could slip inside Ken's room unnoticed.

What we hadn't accounted for was the goddamn mayor picking that moment to tour the hospital with his investor buddy. Trust Don Merrick to fuck up our attempt to stay under the radar.

"Ah, Chief Deputy Alexander!" his voice booms through the lobby, turning heads. "What a coincidence. I had planned to stop by the station later for an introduction, but you've saved us a trip."

On the other side I catch a glimpse of Savvy poking her head out of the hallway before she ducks back out of sight. She's probably avoiding Merrick.

Squeezing my eyes shut, I pull Bess in tighter and turn us around. I'd only draw more attention to us if I tried to avoid the mayor.

"Mayor Merrick," I bite off between clenched teeth.

It's the first glimpse I get of his guest; a large, rotund man, I'd guess about sixty, decked out in dressy western gear, complete with snakeskin boots and bolo tie, wearing the largest fucking Stetson I've seen in my life. I'd say more flash than substance, except the guy has got to tip the scales over three hundred pounds.

"Arlo, I'd like you to meet Silence's finest, Chief Deputy Hugo Alexander."

Merrick smiles wide, completely fucking ignoring Bess, who I'm keeping plastered to my side.

The guy holds out a meaty hand I can't ignore.

"Arlo, is none other than Arlo Hudson, of Hudson Developments. He's thinking about building a deluxe senior living community here in Silence, putting our little town on the map. I'm showing him all our town's amenities."

"Pleased to meet you," I mutter under my breath, taking back my hand.

I'd like to know where he's planning on putting that development, but that's for later concern. Right now, I'd like to get Bess out of the open.

"It's the old country charm that drew me here," the man drawls in a thick Texan accent. "Hard to find that genuine character these days."

Then his eyes drop to Bess. "And who's this lovely—"

"We actually have an appointment we're late for," I quickly intercede, already turning us in the opposite direction. "Sorry to run. Nice meeting you," I add over my shoulder as I rush Bess across the lobby.

Savvy is waiting and pulls us into a supply closet.

"What the hell was that all about?" she hisses, shutting the door and closing us into a space barely big enough to hold the three of us.

"Merrick's big investor is a Texas developer wanting to put Silence on the map," I share with a hefty dose of sarcasm. "The idiot might as well have put a spotlight on us, for fuck's sake."

I'm riled up, my hand rubbing Bess's shoulder restlessly.

"Calm down," Savvy orders. "You guys wait here for a minute. I'm going to make sure we're still clear and will come get you."

The moment she leaves, Bess turns to me and lifts a hand to my face.

"You good?"

I blow out a breath. "Yeah. But that could've gone sideways. Just so you know, I can't stand that pompous ass of a mayor of ours. Not only is he a self-important baboon, but he's the worst kind of misogynist as well. He didn't even fucking acknowledge you."

Bess snickers at my disgruntlement.

"He never has before, and I didn't expect him to start now," she calmly informs me. "Besides, this was one situation where I was grateful to be invisible, so don't burst a vein on my account."

She's a constant surprise to me. Every time I make the mistake of thinking of Bess as small and vulnerable, she proves herself to be strong and resilient, and definitely a bigger person than I am.

I'm about to tell her so when a soft knock sounds on the door, and I hear Savvy's voice say, "It's me."

When she fits herself into the modest space, she fills us in.

"It's all clear, but we'll forfeit the elevator and take the stairway," she announces. "I'll lead, Bess behind me. Hugo, you take the rear. Let's go."

I untucked my shirt so I have easy access to my weapon, which I shoved in my waistband when we got out of the Bronco. Moving as the last in line, I have one hand on Bess's back, and my other resting on the butt of my gun, my eyes constantly scanning for any person or movement that seems out of place.

We get to the stairwell without incident, to find Deputy Lloyd McCormick standing guard. My guess is, someone will be keeping an eye on the elevator too, monitoring anyone going upstairs.

This has got to be hitting the department's overtime budget in a big way. It's been all-hands-on-deck for a while now. Getting that extended budget approval by the county commission can't come soon enough, because we desperately need to add some bodies to the schedule. Unfortunately, that too will have to wait.

Ken's room is the first on the right, closest to the stairwell. Probably picked for the easy access and the option to keep him somewhat isolated from any other patients. An agent I don't recognize is posted outside the door, and one more is inside the room, along with Mancuso, who is in front of the window. The vertical blinds are partially closed, keeping the light in the room fairly dim.

I only have a vague recollection of Ken Choi from the few times I encountered him when he was a teenager, and of course I've seen his mug shots, but I have a hard time recognizing the gaunt man semi-reclined in the hospital bed.

He's not looking back though, his eyes are fixed on his sister, who hesitates a few steps into the room.

"I'd like to talk to my sister alone."

Choi's voice is raspy, like that of an old man.

"Can't do that," Mancuso states.

"Come on, man. Where are we gonna fucking go? Hover outside the door for all I care, just give me a few minutes."

"Hugo stays," Bess speaks up, reaching a hand behind her.

I grab on and take a step closer.

Choi's eyes slide over his sister's shoulder and land on me.

"You her man?"

"He is," Bess answers firmly before I can.

Clearly she's done with men talking over her head like she's not there. Good for her.

"Fine. He can stay, I've got a thing or two to say to him, but the rest of you out."

Savvy turns to smile at Bess.

"We'll be right outside."

Then she moves past us into the hallway. Mancuso no more than grunts before he follows, motioning the other agent out of the room as well.

It's just the three of us now, and suddenly the silence feels heavy.

"The cop says I won't be able to contact you after," Ken addresses his sister. "Ever."

"I was afraid of that," she softly acknowledges.

He nods his head, looking at Bess with something that looks a lot like pain in his eyes.

"They want me to tell them everything I know, to be their rat and help them bring down the Squad. Mancuso says it may be the only way you'll have a chance at a normal life."

His eyes come back to me for a moment.

"You gonna be there for her?"

"For as long as she'll have me," I assure him.

BESS

"Is that what you want, Bess?"

His features become distorted from the tears filling my eyes.

"You want this life?"

I know he wants to hear me say it. To help him come to terms with what ultimately has to be his decision.

"I love my life," I share honestly, moving around the bed to take one of his hands in mine.

The palm of his hand is callused, but I welcome the warm friction against my own. I file the sensation away to draw on as a tangible memory of the brother I'm about to lose again.

He glances down at our joined hands before his eyes come back up to meet mine.

"I'm sorry…I haven't been much of a brother."

He shrugs, his eyes sliding past me to the window, when they suddenly widen.

I'm just starting to turn around when Hugo yells, "Get down!"

At the same time I hear the sound of glass shattering, his heavy body hits my back, taking me down to the ground.

My ears are ringing and my cheek is ground into the linoleum, Hugo's weight is robbing me of air, as I watch Ken drop to the floor on the other side of the bed. Our eyes lock as chaos ensues in the room around us. People rush inside. There's yelling, the sharp crack of gunshots, and the sound of screams in the background.

I'm starting to get disoriented, no longer able to see clearly as I struggle to breathe. Suddenly the weight is lifted and Hugo rolls off me.

Or rather, is rolled off me, by Mancuso, who is wearing a grim expression.

"We need medical assistance!" he yells as he starts dragging Hugo out of the room.

I suffer a similar fate, when I'm grabbed under my arms and pulled into the hallway.

Savvy crouches down beside me, brushing the hair out of my face.

"Bess? Where are you hurt?"

Hurt? Am I hurt?

"I don't...I don't think so."

I'm not even sure what happened back there, but other than maybe a few bruises, I don't think I was injured.

I push myself up to sitting, and catch sight of Ken on the other side of the hallway, his back against the wall and his face even paler than before. Mancuso is by his side. Then my eyes are drawn to a huddle of medical staff crouched over someone on the floor ten feet away, and those long legs sticking out look all too familiar.

"Hugo..." I mutter, trying to scramble toward him on hands and knees, when Savvy pulls me back.

"Let them work on him."

"What happened? What's wrong with him?"

"He was injured."

"What do you mean?"

Then my brother speaks up across from me.

"Your man took a bullet meant for you."

CHAPTER 26

B*ess*

"No."

I turn my back on Savvy.

"Look," she persists, "until we've made sure there are no other threats, you'll be safer somewhere else."

I can be equally stubborn.

"I'm not leaving voluntarily."

Not a chance in hell. The man took a bullet that was intended for me, I'm not about to leave him by himself.

"Bess, come on. Nate is on his way to the school to pick Carson up and bring him here."

"And the last thing that boy needs is to see me turn tail. I love you, Savvy, but you're wasting your energy."

We're in an empty room on the first floor where Hugo was taken to have a tube placed in his chest.

The bullet hit him under the right shoulder blade, fractured a rib, and nicked the right lung before lodging just under his clavicle. His right lung collapsed, which is why they're putting in a chest tube. It's supposed to drain air and blood from around the lung so it can reinflate.

Thank God for Dr. Sharma, who handled the injury like it was par for the course, and not highly unusual for this small-town hospital. Two gunshot wounds in a week must be a rarity.

I'm on pins and needles, wanting to see for myself Hugo is going to be okay, but having my friend hovering restlessly is only amping up my anxiety.

"Go," I tell her. "Check on progress, do what you need to do. There's no need to babysit me. You said the FBI team had the situation under control."

Apparently, the shooter had been posing as a utility worker, doing inspections on the electrical poles along the street. He'd been up in a cherry picker in front of the hospital. Roy Battaglia's team intercepted a young kid running out of the hospital lobby when the shooting started. They figure he was a lookout and probably alerted the shooter when Mayor Merrick held us up in the middle of the lobby.

I was surprised to hear Mancuso tell Savvy the shooter was none other than Shane Lee himself. The agent suggested he probably got tired of his soldiers not delivering on his orders, and decided to come out and do the job himself.

A decision that cost him dearly when a bullet from one of the agents returning his fire ended his life.

I should feel relief, but I don't, and I likely won't until I can look into Hugo's eyes and have him tell me he is going to be okay. That's the only thing that matters in this moment. Everything else gets shoved to the back of my head until later.

"Where's Dad?"

Carson barges into the room, panic in his eyes when he locks them on me.

"Bess?" His voice is small and wavers.

Nothing but a small boy in a man's body, terrified out of his mind he's going to lose yet another parent before he's even finished high school.

I surge to my feet and wrap him in my arms.

"He's going to be okay," I whisper in his ear as his shoulders shake in my hold. "I promise you; he's going to be fine."

From the corner of my eye, I see Nate pull Savvy out of the room, closing the door on us.

I'm not sure how long we stand here, Carson letting go of his emotions while I struggle to hold on to my own.

"What happened?" he eventually asks, wiping at his face with his sleeve.

"He was protecting me," I share, not hiding from the truth as I slowly release him. The boy deserves to know. "And was shot in the back. Right now, the doctor is placing a tube in his chest so his right lung can inflate again, but we're hoping he won't need any additional surgery and will heal on his own. I expect Dr. Sharma to drop in and give us an update any time now."

"Are you okay?"

"Yes, honey. I'm fine."

Good Lord, what a sweet boy he is. His parents really did a good job with him, and hats off to Hugo for making sure his son was nurtured emotionally after losing his mother.

Carson is a sensitive kid—something I assumed was inherited from Emily—but now that I'm getting to know his father better, I can see that same sensitive side in him. Although, Hugo has more trouble expressing his, and instead walks away from an emotional confrontation, like he did when I opened up about the secrets I'd kept.

"Did you have a chance to talk to Tate?"

I know those two have a lot in common—Nate's daughter, Tatum, lost her mother to an overdose only about a year ago—and it's been good for them to have someone in their own age group who's been through a similar experience to talk to.

"Yeah, Nate picked her up too. She was going to wait in the truck."

"Good."

I'm restless, but I do my best to present a calm front and force myself to sit. No sooner does my ass hit the seat when my phone starts vibrating in my pocket. I don't recognize the number but answer anyway.

"Hello?"

"Bess?"

Hearing my brother's voice is a relief. A team of FBI agents whisked him away after what happened in his room, and I was told he was taken into protective custody. We never had a chance to finish our conversation.

"Ken..."

"Listen, I talked one of the agents into letting me use their phone, but I only have a few minutes. I never had a chance to say goodbye."

"I know, I had come up with all these things I wanted to say to you. I was going to bring up things I remember of when we were kids, before moving to Seattle, but it doesn't really matter, does it? I'm sure you have those same memories, or maybe you have different ones."

"Good times, Sis," he mumbles.

"Yeah, good times."

"I have regrets—" he starts, but I cut him off.

"As do I, but you know, in the end the only thing that matters is I love you. I always have, and no matter where you are, or who you are, that will never change."

It's silent for a beat, and then I hear him clear his throat before he comes back on.

"I feel the same," he returns gruffly. "Have a good life, Bessie."

"You too, Ken," I choke out, hearing the line go dead.

This time it's Carson—a little taken aback by my sudden flood of tears—who comforts me with a warm hug. I barely get a chance to explain what my emotional outburst was about, when Dr. Sharma pokes his head around the door.

"You can see him now."

Hugo

It feels like I got trampled by a herd of buffalo and it hurts like an SOB to breathe, but it was so worth it when I see Bess walking in, holding my son's hand.

The nursing staff put the head of the bed up, so I am more sitting than lying down, which makes it a little easier to get air. It also makes me look a little less helpless, although I still have a tube sticking out from between my ribs and my face is covered with an oxygen mask I was warned not to remove.

My, "I'm okay," is no more than a whisper, almost drowned out by the hiss of the oxygen.

"Hey, Dad."

"Hey, kiddo. Sorry for the scare." My voice sounds a little stronger this time.

Carson shrugs it off, squaring his shoulders, but I notice his red-rimmed eyes, and I hate that I put him through this. He's seen too many hospital rooms in his young life already, and walking into mine must trigger a host of bad memories for him.

I notice how close he stays to Bess, and that does my heart good to see. Even after Emily died, Bess was someone he trusted, would occasionally open up to. Knowing if something had happened to me, he'd have Bess in his life. She would look after him, of that I have no doubt.

"Hey, Twinkie," I greet her, meeting those pretty dark eyes.

She doesn't speak and simply nods, taking my hand and pressing it against her face.

"Does it hurt?" Carson asks, filling the silence.

"Like a motherfucker."

Who'd have thought talking would be a workout? It's taking a lot of effort.

My son points at the tube coming out of my right side.

"How long do you have to have that in for?"

"Hopefully not too long. Doc says I'll be here for a few days."

Days I won't be able to look after Bess, which I need to talk to Roy Battaglia about as soon as I have a chance. I haven't even talked to Savvy or Mancuso, so I have no idea what went down after I got shot.

There's so much I need to think of, but my head is so damn fuzzy.

Despite my efforts to keep them open, I feel my eyes drift shut.

∼

When I next open them, Savvy is sitting in a chair beside my bed.

"Where is Bess?"

"Nate, Tatum, and KC took her and Carson to the diner for a quick bite before it closes for the night. Bess didn't want to go, but we made her. She needed some fresh air."

"What time is it anyway?" I ask, noticing at some point the sun had set.

Savvy glances at her watch.

"Almost nine."

It was a little before eleven this morning when Bess and I walked into the lobby, but it feels like a lifetime ago.

"How are you feeling?" Savvy wants to know.

I do a quick inventory and am surprised to discover the pain isn't quite as sharp as I remember it being earlier.

"Breathing a little easier," I admit.

"Yeah, Dana was in earlier and put some meds through your IV she said would probably bring some relief."

I must've been out of it, because I never woke once. But feeling better and thinking clearer, I want to be brought into the loop.

"Is it safe for Bess with just KC and Nate?"

Savvy grins.

"Yeah. We took care of the snake's head and the FBI, in conjunction with the Seattle Gang Task Force, is quickly rounding up the rest of the Lotus Squad echelon. What do you remember?"

I think back to the moment I knew something was off. I'd caught a glimpse of a guy in a boom lift, facing the hospital instead of the electrical post. It took a fraction of a second for me to realize he had a rifle aimed right at us and I immediately reacted, but obviously not quite fast enough.

"Shooter was a utility guy in the cherry picker."

She nods. "Correct. The utility company had been doing inspections along the road yesterday as well, and Mancuso's team made sure and checked out the work orders. When the truck with the lift was out there again this morning, they assumed the work was still ongoing. We later discovered one of the utility trucks was stolen from the yard sometime during the night. They saw an opportunity to get eyes in the room and took it."

Clever.

"So, I assume they picked up Shane Lee?" I inquire.

"More like picked off Shane Lee," Savvy volunteers. "That's what I meant by the head of the snake; Shane Lee was the shooter. One of Mancuso's guys took him out. He's dead."

The agent was right the other day; the gang boss was gung ho to take care of business himself, but ended up making himself vulnerable in the process.

"Mancuso mentioned he suspected as much when Lee went missing. He figured Lee wanted to make Ken watch his sister get killed before he was executed himself."

"Man, he was a cruel bastard," Savvy comments.

"What about the third brother? Mike Lee."

"He's slick. He managed to slip across the border into Canada, so now he not only has the feds on his tail, but the Royal Canadian Mounted Police as well. He's the money guy and has always stuck to the business side of things. It's suspected he may have had an exit plan all along, and funneled the bulk of the gang's money across the border. Looks like he's more interested in maintaining the lifestyle he'd become accustomed to than seeking revenge, like his brother."

Good. Let Canada worry about the guy.

I briefly close my eyes in relief. It sucks to be stuck in a hospital bed where I'm no good to anyone, but it looks like things are under control, even without my help.

"Are you tired?"

"No, I'm good. I just don't like sitting on the sidelines. Especially when we've already clocked what has to be record hours in overtime this past week alone."

I'm the one who normally allocates hours and makes sure we stay within budget, and I already know there'll be a headache waiting when I finally have time to sit down and crunch the numbers.

"About that," Savvy returns. "I guess today's events were good for something, because I got a call earlier from Judge Stephen Crombie."

Judge Crombie is the chairman of the county commission.

"He'd received a complaint," she continues. "It was from the mayor's office, and outlined the blatant incompetence of the sheriff's department given the rise in criminal and violent activity in Silence, and used today's shooting as an example."

Unbelievable, that miserable asshole did not waste any time, did he?

In a surge of anger, I try to sit up, only to be painfully reminded of my injuries.

"Whoa, easy, my friend. You'll be happy to know Merrick's complaint did not have the desired outcome, for him at least. Judge Crombie asked if I felt our budget was sufficient, which I told him it was not. I mentioned the request for additional budget I'd submitted for the next meeting's agenda, which he apparently had not seen yet."

She chuckles and shakes her head.

"Anyway, as a result of Merrick's interference, Crombie has called an emergency meeting for first thing tomorrow morning, and he is going to put forth a motion to allocate us sufficient budget for an additional investigator, as well as two more full-time deputies, effective immediately. He expects the motion to pass without much push back."

"I'm calling Tessa Androtti the moment I get the green light," she adds with a smug grin.

I wish I could laugh, but all I manage is a snort.

"Damn, what I wouldn't give to be a fly on the wall in Don Merrick's office when he gets wind of this," I comment.

"Me too, my friend. Me too."

CHAPTER 27

B*ess*

"LET'S GO, BUDDY!"

I watch as Carson tosses the ball once more for Ragnar, who is having the time of his life here.

Here being Phil's house on the creek.

She suggested I stay for the time being and I gratefully accepted, since construction started this week at Strange Brew, and Lola has been staying in my apartment to keep an eye on everything. Also, it doesn't feel right for me to stay at Hugo's place while he is in the hospital.

Since Carson has been virtually glued to my side from the day his father was injured, he ended up staying here with me. His idea, not mine, and after clearing it with his father, of course.

Carson loves it, because he has a nice big TV in his bedroom and his own bathroom on the opposite side of the house from the primary suite. He's already been out fishing with Savvy's dad and last night went horseback riding with Tatum on the farm.

It's the weekend, so no school for him, but we are supposed to be at the hospital at ten thirty to pick up Hugo, who is coming home today. I'm not sure what home yet, because I haven't had a chance to discuss Phil's generous offer to use the house for Hugo's recovery with him.

I know he is frustrated with the slow progress, even though Dr. Sharma had warned him this kind of injury is not one you bounce back from in a day or two. He's already been in the hospital for four days, and was told, at best, he could return to part-time modified duties—i.e. a desk job—in two weeks, and depending on how he does, to full duty in four to six weeks.

My man did not like hearing that, so I fully expect to be bringing a bear home, wherever we end up.

It's amusing how everyone assumed, by some unwritten agreement, I would be looking after him. Don't get me wrong, I wouldn't have it any other way, but it strikes me as funny how he and I have so quickly become a foregone conclusion.

"Carson!"

This time when I call, he comes running, Ragnar on his heels.

"Want me to drive?" he asks when I lock the door behind us.

My Prius is still parked behind the coffee shop, but I've been driving the old Bronco, courtesy of Brant Colter, while Carson has been getting back and forth to school in his pickup, which Hugo had borrowed and parked in Phil's garage the night we got here. I'm not even sure where Hugo's truck is at this point.

Maybe tomorrow we can sort out the vehicle situation; at least pick up my car at the coffee shop and return the Bronco to our neighbors up the road with some fresh muffins as a thank you.

"Yeah, that's fine. Let me just make sure Ragnar has fresh water."

Climbing into the passenger seat of his pickup, I'm hit with a smell so pungent, it makes my eyes water.

"I'm guessing you forgot to put your soccer gear in the garage to air out after practice last night?"

"Sorry," he mutters, quickly pulling his duffel bag with sweaty, and very stinky, equipment from the back seat, and running it into the garage.

"Better open all the windows," I suggest when he gets behind the wheel. "We don't wanna gas your dad on the way home from the hospital."

I guess it doesn't matter where Hugo wants to recover, we're going to have to come back here regardless to pack up the kid's and my stuff.

The breeze is chilly as Carson navigates down the mountain, but the crosswind helps to quickly clear the offensive odor in here.

Oddly, the smell reminds me of Ken, who was notorious for leaving his sports gear lying around. That was when we were living in Silence, before moving to Seattle, where everything started going off the rails for him. I never wanted to leave here in the first place, but I was a child, I didn't have much of a choice. But I'm glad I found my way back here. Silence has always been home for me.

The drive into town is without incident, for which I'm grateful. We've had altogether too much excitement this past month, although things seem to be returning to normal. With Ken gone, the entire FBI contingency up and left as well. The first forty-eight hours, I had one of Battaglia's guys following me around, but when things quieted down it didn't seem necessary anymore.

I, for one, will be glad to get back to some kind of routine. A new one, that includes Hugo and his son.

Hugo is already sitting in a wheelchair, his bag on his knees when I get to his room, something he apparently isn't thrilled about.

"Nothing wrong with my damn legs," he grumbles when I bend down to greet him with a kiss.

Touching him already comes so naturally, I'm no longer concerned with PDAs. What is surprising to me is how unsurprised people seem to be he and I are together now. It's like everyone already knew, and we...or maybe I should say, I was the only one in the dark.

"Good," I comment dryly as I start pushing his wheelchair toward the exit. "You can show me how well they work after we get you home."

Carson has pulled up his truck outside the doors and hops down to grab his father's gear. I let Hugo get himself up and into the passenger seat without interfering, sensing he won't want me fussing over him, and return the chair to the lobby.

Once we're all in the truck—I'm in the back with Hugo's bag—I broach the subject of where to take him.

"You have two options," I tell him, leaning in between the two front seats. "We can take you home, but then we'll have to pick up the dog and our stuff from Phil's house, or we can stay at her place for a bit. She offered."

He glances over at me.

"Are you gonna stick around?"

"That was the plan."

He nods. "Then I don't give a flying fuck where."

"Phil's house!" Carson votes with enthusiasm.

That would've been my choice too. Not that I don't like Hugo's place, because I do, but I am more at home in Phil's house. I don't feel like I'm trying to fill the void left by Emily. I take up my own space in the roomy bungalow.

Also, at Phil's I have a state-of-the-art kitchen I can claim as my domain.

"You're the chauffeur," I remind him.

I sit back and buckle up, letting my mind drift as Carson drives us home.

It's a ten-minute drive from town, which means I'd be heading down the mountain in the wee hours of the morning. At least I will be, once we have Strange Brew back open, but that won't be for at least another week, according to Lola. She's been monitoring progress and is working on ordering to replenish equipment and supplies we've had to toss out. She and Emmet have also been giving the coffee shop a fresh paint job, and are waiting for me to pick colors for the apartment upstairs so they can do the same there.

Truthfully, I don't know what I want. As much as I loved my apartment before, I don't see it the same way anymore. It used to be my little oasis, my safe haven, conveniently close to the business that was my life. My life used to be contained within the brick walls of that building, but that's no longer the case. I still love Strange Brew and would never give it up, but my life seems to have grown beyond those boundaries.

At least I got word from the insurance company yesterday they'd be cutting a check the beginning of next week. That will mean I'll be able to pay Lola and Emmet without interruption and can hopefully replenish some of my spent savings.

But those are concerns for another day, for now I'm going to enjoy having Hugo home with us.

∾

Hugo

Jesus, even just walking to the fucking bathroom has me panting like I ran a marathon uphill.

How is it possible that someone in the prime of his life and in fairly decent shape is reduced to the fitness level of an octogenarian? If this is the state of my endurance, there's not a chance in hell I'll be taking Bess to bed any time soon.

I've been dreaming about all the ways I want to fuck her. Stuff we haven't had a chance to explore yet, and frankly, things I haven't even fantasized about in years. Some of it would probably be above my capacity, even if I were completely healthy, but it sure would be fun to try.

And every time Bess walks in the room, bends over to pull another of her creations out of the oven, or smiles that mysterious little smile in my direction, my cock jumps to attention. Apparently, the only part of my body that did not get the memo we are temporarily out of business.

On the other hand, this past weekend here—the quiet of the mountains with just the sound of the water, breathing in the crisp mountain air—has been the most relaxed I've been in I don't know how long. Yesterday we sat outside by a small fire Bess built, watching Carson try his hand at fly fishing in the creek. Simply enjoying each other's company.

I've noticed how comfortably Bess and Carson seem to interact. Nothing forced or artificial, but with an ease that shows how much each cares for the other.

They fit. We all fit in a way I didn't think would be possible.

Carson was off to school this morning with an egg sandwich to eat on the way—because of course he stayed in bed 'til the last minute—and a wrap and freshly baked muffin Bess packed him for lunch.

I was about to tell her he knows how to make his own lunches, has done so for years, but I could see she loved doing it, and my son seemed to appreciate the gesture, so I kept my mouth shut. Why mess with something that seems to make both of them happy?

This is a new experience for me, being more of an observer than a participant in the life around me, but to my surprise I not only enjoy it, but am learning a lot. About Bess, about my son, but most of all about myself.

My whole life has been about finding a purpose, improving as well as proving myself, and in doing so I fell out of touch with what really mattered. But here, with Bess and my son, I'm discovering I don't need to prove anything. As long as I'm here, I'm enough as I am.

Bess is sitting at the kitchen island, working on my old laptop, when I come around the doorway. I know she's trying to pull together a wedding for Savvy and Nate in three weeks. No mean feat. Their nuptial plans had been put on the back burner for a while there, but now that things have quieted down, the wedding is once again front and center, and Bess wouldn't be Bess if she didn't jump in with both feet to help make it happen.

"I love you."

She looks up at the sound of my voice and smiles that smile.

"And I love you."

I walk over and sit down on the second stool, taking her hand and turning her so she faces me.

"Move in with me."

She barks out a laugh before catching herself. Then she squints her eyes at me.

"Move in...are you serious? We've only been...it's been what? A month?"

"Move in with me," I repeat.

"Hugo, this is fast. I mean, what about Carson?"

She seems determined to come up with excuses, but none of it matters.

"Fast? Bess, I've known you since you were wearing knee-high socks and pigtails. As for my son; he loves you, and he obviously doesn't have an issue with us all sharing a house, since we're doing that now."

I lean in so my nose is almost touching hers. "Move in with me."

"But I have my apartment..." she stalls.

"Lola can have it—she's already there—and you'll have a bit of extra rental income you can use to pay down the mortgage on the building faster. Move in with me."

"You want me to move into your house with you?"

That's where I pick up on the hesitation. It's not the moving in with me she's necessarily balking at, it's where she's moving, and I get it. Emily and I bought that house when she was pregnant with Carson, he's always lived there, but he'll also be leaving for college soon.

"Move in with me...anywhere," I amend my request.

"Really?"

I can tell from the way her face lights up I finally found the right question.

"Yeah. Hell, we can even see if there's any way Phil would part with this place."

She's beaming at me now, a smile so happy I file away every little detail to memory.

"I love it here," she whispers, adding, "with you."

Then she slips off her stool, steps between my legs, and slides her arms around my neck, kissing me deeply. I groan in her mouth as her tongue teases mine, inviting a heat I wish I had the ability to unleash.

My cock sure is ready, which is something that doesn't go unnoticed by Bess, who abruptly releases me. She sinks down to her knees, her face tilted up and eyes locked on me as she pulls down the front of my sweats. My mouth falls open as her fingers curl around my rock-hard dick and she, almost casually, licks her lips before sliding them down the tip.

"Sweet fucking hell, Twinkie," I groan.

"Am I hurting you?" she asks, slipping my cock from her mouth.

Yes, my sweet, beautiful girl; you are hurting me, but in the best possible way.

"Don't stop," I plead, curving my hand around the back of her head.

My last coherent thought is, *I hope Phil doesn't decide to drop in*, before I lose myself to Bess's mouth.

CHAPTER 28

H^{ugo}

"We meet again."

I look up from my computer to find Tessa Androtti standing in front of my desk.

Getting to my feet, I reach over to shake her hand.

"So it seems." I grin at her. "Good to have you on board."

"Glad to be here, although if you believed my children, you'd think I dragged them into the bowels of hell."

I remember she'd mentioned having a couple of teenage boys when she helped out on an investigation last year.

"They'll adjust. Lots to do here for them with summer right around the corner," I inform her. "Lots of outdoor stuff."

She snorts. "Right now, their main concern is how slow the internet is out here. I'll be lucky to be able to get them out of the house at all."

"How old are they again?"

"Remi just turned fifteen and Linc is seventeen."

"Yeah, I have a seventeen-year-old kid too. He loves his gaming as well but, luckily, he also has an interest in the outdoors. He's even taken up fishing recently, I bet he could motivate them."

"Well, they're a little old to set up a playdate, but maybe we could get together for a burger or something at some point. I've found food is an excellent motivator for my boys."

Shoot. I hope we're just talking about introducing our kids, but there is something about the way she looks at me that makes me wonder.

"You know what? Let me talk to Bess. We have a wedding to attend this weekend, but maybe we can do a cookout at our place the weekend after. We could invite a few more people and properly welcome you and your boys to Silence. The house is up in the mountains and we have a creek, brimming with fish, right in our backyard. I'm sure the boys will get a kick out of it."

"Oh, I don't think I met your wife last time I was in town," she returns, a little taken aback.

"Are you sure? I think you may have met Bess, she owns the coffee shop, Strange Brew. But she's not my wife. At least not yet."

Technically, the house isn't ours yet either, but just last night Phil agreed to sell it to us, provided she can keep her music equipment stored over the garage. At least until the old barn on the farm she has had her eye on has been transformed into her new art and music studio, with added guest suite. A project that, apparently, she'd been toying with for a while already, wanting her studio closer to home.

It was funny to see how easily Brant acquiesced, since I've always known him to be allergic to change. But marrying Phil has really mellowed him out. Where before Phil he had to be forced into retirement kicking and screaming, now he seems to have settled into a different routine with his new wife.

It's a good example for me to draw from, because my story is not that different from Brant's. We're both workaholics, we both lost our wives to cancer, and we both thought marriage was something of the past and not part of our future.

I haven't asked Bess yet. I decided to wait until after Savvy and Nate tie the knot this coming weekend. I'm sure when I do, Bess will come up with a litany of imagined roadblocks—top of the list will, undoubtedly, be it's too soon for us to take that step—but I'll patiently knock each of her objections out of the way, one by one.

"I do remember her, actually. Nice woman, and the best lemon blueberry scones I've ever tasted," Tessa returns with a smile. "Anyway, I should get back to the files the sheriff gave me to look at, but I'm game for a meet and greet any time."

"We'll set something up."

My desk phone rings just as I sit back down. I just started back last Thursday and am already so bored with desk work, a phone call is a welcome change of pace.

"Alexander."

"Chief Deputy Alexander, it's Connie Dixon. I'm terribly sorry to disturb you, but I find myself in a bit of a pickle. I ordered some flowers for the reopening party at Strange Brew this afternoon, since I won't be able to attend. Unfortunately, I accidentally had them delivered here, instead of the coffee shop. Now, I assume you plan to be in attendance, and was wondering if you would mind swinging by to pick them up."

I glance at my watch and notice it's creeping up on 2 p.m. already.

Aside from doing a lot of the planning for Savvy and Nate's wedding, Bess and Phil have hit the ground running on Phil's community fund idea. Strange Brew has been open since last week, but it had taken those two another few days to pull together what they need to plan the gallery.

Being a Monday, the coffee shop is closed to the public, but Bess had an early start this morning nonetheless. She's there now with Phil and Lola, placing all the artwork for the official grand opening of the Silence Community Gallery. The project has been very hush-hush, which is why everyone was told this was a sort of welcome back celebration.

I'd better hustle if I want to pick up the flowers and be there in time for the doors to open at two thirty.

"Too bad you can't be there, Mrs. Dixon. Are you not feeling well?" I ask as I quickly sign off my computer.

"Oh, I'm fine. It's just that I don't venture out too much anymore. I'm getting older, you know."

She is in her late eighties, but she's always been at the front of the line for any community events. This is unusual for her and part of me wonders if the experience with Chance Tanek in her kitchen left her shaken more than she might be willing to admit.

"I'm on my way over, and we'll talk then, okay?"

"You're a good boy, Hugo."

I grin as I hang up. Mrs. Dixon is the only person who can call me a good boy and get away with it.

Except for Bess, of course, but with her it has an entirely different meaning.

I'm smiling as I walk out of the office, waving goodbye to Brenda in passing.

"You're in a good mood," she calls after me.

I just lift a thumbs-up over my shoulder.

Bess

"You're late."

I regret my comment the moment it leaves my mouth.

I've just been running around like a madwoman this morning, putting up all the artwork, while also creating copious trays of bite-sized appetizers we plan to serve. There won't be any pastries or specialty coffees this afternoon, but I was able to obtain a one-day permit to serve alcohol, and Phil rented glassware and ordered a few crates of champagne. That's all we'll be serving, along with a non-alcoholic punch Lola put together.

I haven't even had a chance to change or do my hair—I'm a mess with a ratty mop constantly falling in my face—when Hugo walks in the side door, with Mrs. Dixon in his wake, which I saw too late.

"My fault entirely, my dear," she replies, shaming me even further. "I'm afraid I held Hugo up, gave him too hard of a time when he was kind enough to offer me a ride. I take full blame."

"No, Mrs. Dixon, I'm the one who should be apologizing. I have no excuse for my ungrateful comment, other than it's been a crazy day already, and I should've had a stiff drink instead of opening my mouth."

I hear Hugo's soft chuckle and throw him my best apologetic smile. He's been nothing but supportive and accommodating.

"Why don't you go ahead inside and have a look around, Mrs. Dixon," he urges her, gently coaxing her toward the coffee shop. "Bess and I will join you in a moment."

I see Phil take charge of the old woman and aiming a wink at me. The next moment, Hugo is stalking toward me, forcing me to retreat into the kitchen where he unceremoniously picks me up and sits me down on the counter, still covered in flour.

"Talk to me," he orders, wedging himself between my legs as he cages me in with his arms braced on either side of me.

"I'm sorry."

"Not what I'm asking for, Bess. Just talk to me."

Like he often does when we're discussing something important, he leans his forehead against mine, creating a little bubble of intimacy where anything is open for discussion and honesty is a requirement.

"I think I've been pushing too hard," I confess, letting my body slump. "I've run out of steam and we haven't even opened the doors yet."

"Hey, it's been a bit of a crazy month, and even before that I don't think you ever took a break. Maybe it's time you did, cut yourself a little slack."

"I can't now, I have the appetizers to get ready, arrange them on trays, set them out on the buffet table we have set up. Then I have to change and try and make myself presentable." I glance up at the kitchen clock. "And I have less than five minutes to do it."

He stops me when I try to launch myself off the counter, and frames my face with his large hands.

"Go change, do whatever you think you need to do to clear your mind and get yourself ready. You can be fashionably late. I'll take care of the appetizers and if I need help,

I'll ask Lola. You have a crew of people here who can cover for you."

He presses a hard kiss to my mouth, as I'm about to launch a protest, before he releases me.

"You need to take care of yourself or you won't even make the wedding this weekend."

Oh God, the wedding.

My knees almost buckle at the thought of the list of things I still have to do to make sure my best friend's day is perfect.

His final point hits home; if I don't take a breath, I'll burn out before the weekend.

Hopping down from the counter, I start pointing out what appetizers go on what tray, but it seems Hugo's losing his patience with me.

"They want your food, they don't care what damn tray it's served on," he grumbles. "You're wasting time."

He's right, I am. With one last glance around the disaster zone that is my kitchen, I grab the bag I brought this morning and dart down the hall and up the stairs to use my old bathroom.

In large part the apartment is unchanged, except for a few things that pop out at me. An unfamiliar book upside down on the coffee table, waiting to be picked up again. A sweater hanging off the dining room chair. A footstool I don't recognize by the couch. But what stands out more than anything else, are the plants. Lush greenery invaded every available sunny spot in the room.

It almost looks like a greenhouse in here. I love it. This is what I always envisioned with these beautiful old windows letting in all that light, but sadly, I do not possess a green thumb. I've effectively killed every plant I ever bought. But Lola obviously has a gift.

Standing in the middle of my old apartment, I try to gauge whether I feel any regret, but I don't. I've loved this place, but I wouldn't want to come back. It's crystal clear to me Lola belongs here now.

As Hugo suggested, I'm fashionably late when I walk into the coffee shop—moderately presentable—fifteen minutes later. I could hear the buzz of voices in the hallway but did not expect the crowd of people I find inside. It looks like every single table is occupied and, in addition, people are walking around, checking out all the artwork on the walls.

It looks like they are as impressed as I was when Phil first showed me her beautiful paintings. They are as colorful and unpredictable as the artist herself, using an eclectic blend of art mediums—watercolor, charcoal, ink, oil, pastels, acrylics—to create amazingly realistic pieces. Buildings, landscapes, people, objects, nature, it seems she finds inspiration everywhere.

"There she is!"

To my shock, Mayor Merrick makes a beeline for me through the crowd. I'm tempted to look over my shoulder to see if someone else entered behind me, because this would be the first time the man's ever acknowledged my existence.

Phil walks up behind him, making a face I have a hard time not laughing at. I don't think the mayor is anyone's favorite person.

"I am delighted to see you've decided to elevate the decor with these stunning pieces by our resident celebrity," he gushes, pumping my hand in his clammy one. I make a mental note to scrub my hands after. "This will surely bring in a higher standard of clientele."

Higher standard? Should I be insulted? After all, we already had everyone in this small town dropping in on the regular, so I'm not exactly sure who he's talking about. But before I can question him on the subject, he's already rambling on.

"Had I known, I would've been happy to contribute to this worthy endeavor. I still could."

Phil claps a casual hand on his shoulder, which seems to startle him.

"You know, Don, as I said to you before, I'm pretty sure Bess and I have things covered, but we sure do appreciate the gesture."

That seems to take the wind out of his sails, and with a mumbled excuse of needing a word with someone, he slinks off, his tail between his legs.

"What was that all about?" I ask Phil.

"Oh, he just doesn't like the attention on anything other than himself, that's all," she explains. "In fact, he suggested changing the name of the coffee shop to give it a bit more cachet." She makes a face and adds, "His words, not mine. I think he secretly wants his name connected to the community fund, so he can go down in history as the town's great benefactor."

That wouldn't surprise me.

"So other than that, how has the response been so far?"

"Already sold a painting."

I turn to her with my mouth wide open. "Are you kidding me?"

She grins wide.

"Nope. The big triptych of Silence."

The triptych she's referring to is technically three paintings that together form a panoramic view of the town and the entire valley. It's a large piece, which is why we put it up on the long wall.

"Who bought it?"

She looks around. "He seems to have disappeared. It was an older gentleman. I can't recall ever seeing him in town before, but he said his name is Peter Abel. Lola took his payment and said he told her he'd be back in the morning to pick it up."

"That's amazing. That deserves a toast," I announce.

"What are we toasting to?" Hugo asks as he approaches.

"Phil sold a painting."

She bumps my shoulder. "We sold a painting," she corrects me. "The first clank of coins hitting the bottom of our Silence Community Fund."

Hugo reaches over, plucks a couple of glasses of champagne off the table, and hands them to us, before grabbing one for himself. Then he lifts his glass to us.

"Well, that certainly deserves congratulations."

CHAPTER 29

B*ess*

I HUM ALONG with a Stevie Nicks tune on the radio as I drizzle some lemon icing on my coconut squares.

It was a real treat to come in early this morning and find the kitchen—which I never got around to cleaning up last night—in immaculate condition. I'm sure that was courtesy of Lola, who I insisted take the day off today. She's been working her butt off, and I'm excited for her to discover the raise I'm giving her on her next paycheck. Emmet gets a bump too, but Lola has really stepped up during construction, but also in getting the shop ready to open when I was still mostly focused on looking after Hugo. Hers will come with the brand-new job title of manager as well, and Emmet will be offered the option of going full time.

I'm happy to be doing the bulk of the baking, if that means I can be home at a reasonable hour. But Lola has already proven herself capable in the kitchen, able to follow a recipe and do the baking herself, so if I wanted to take a day, or a few days off, business would keep running as normal.

It's funny, I wouldn't have even considered taking a vacation before, but Hugo mentioned something about always having wanted to visit the East Coast, and now it's all I can think about. Maybe in September, after the height of the summer season, but when it's still nice out.

Grabbing the tray of pastries, I walk into the coffee shop, sliding the tray into the display case. This morning, we have jalapeño cheese scones, morning glory muffins, blueberry crumble muffins, apple Danish, and the lemon coconut squares I just finished. Next, I will tackle the sourdough bread, which has been rising in the proofing drawer.

I glance at the new painting Phil put up after the party last night to replace the triptych, which is now wrapped in brown paper, leaning against the wall in the back hallway, waiting to be picked up. I haven't turned on all the lights, but there's enough to see the new piece. It's a single, large painting featuring Angus, Brant Colter's goat, stealing colorful underwear off a clothesline, with a familiar view of the creek and mountains in the background. I smile remembering the funny story that signaled the start of Brant and Phil's unlikely pairing, which inspired this painting.

I turn to head back to the kitchen when I'm stopped with a knock on the front door. I see an older man wearing glasses and one of those *Peaky Blinders* caps. I have no doubt this is the buyer, Peter Abel. Lola mentioned the cap.

Dismissing a brief feeling of apprehension, I unlock the door, poking my head outside.

"Mr. Abel?"

I notice the man is alone. At the curb, a gray sedan is parked with its trunk already open.

"I'm sorry, I know I'm early," the man apologizes right off the bat.

"No, no, that's quite all right," I hurry to assure him, opening the door wide. "Please come in, your painting is packed and ready to go."

He enters, taking his cap off as he passes me. I quickly close the door and follow him inside.

"It's in the back hallway. Let me get it for you."

Slipping past him, I duck into the back hallway and grab the wrapped paintings off the floor, but when I turn I almost bump into him. He's followed me back here.

Unlike the coffee shop, the hallway is well-lit and it's the first time I get a good look at Peter Abel. He's balding, something I hadn't noticed earlier, and there is something familiar about him.

"You know, you look just like your mother."

Immediately the hair on the back of my neck stands up.

What the hell? Who is this man?

"My mother is dead."

He nods, a sober expression on his face.

"I know, and I'm so sorry."

I'm confused, and more than a little uneasy, but I'm also intrigued.

"How did you know my mother?"

"I knew her a long time ago, you wouldn't remember," he informs me with a kind smile. "But she spoke of Silence frequently. Described it in great detail." He coughs a little and blinks his eyes, as if fighting off emotion. "I never visited before, but it's every bit as beautiful as she mentioned. That's why I bought the painting, I'll take it with me as a reminder of this visit."

I'm still in the dark, hungry for more answers.

"If you'd never been here before, what brought you to Silence now?"

He looks down at the toes of his perfectly shined shoes, before lifting his eyes to me.

"You." Then he looks back down, shaking his head. "I've never been here before, but I've kept tabs. First on your mother, and then on you. I never intended to set foot in Silence, had sworn I would never intervene in any way, but then I received word you might be in danger."

I shake my head and start backing up into the kitchen, but he follows me at a generous distance.

"I don't understand."

"You don't have to. All you need to know is that you can breathe easy. That's the only reason I'm here now, to tell you you have nothing to fear. I was too late for the first one, but I made sure there is no one left to worry about."

I suck in a breath when he reaches into the inside pocket of his tweed jacket, but what he produces isn't some kind of weapon, but a simple blank white envelope.

"This is not for you to open. I ask that you pass it on to Chief Deputy Alexander. He will know what to do with it."

Then he places it on the counter.

The next instant he's gone, and for a moment I stand frozen, wondering what the hell just happened, but when I hear the front door of the coffee shop slam shut, I dart back out into the hallway. The three packages holding the triptych that were stacked against the wall are gone. When I poke my head into the coffee shop and glance out the front window, I'm just in time to see the vehicle that was parked outside take off down the road.

"I heard you talking."

I jump a foot in the air when I hear Lola's voice behind me.

"Who was that?" She wants to know.

I turn around, feeling like I've just escaped the twilight zone.

"I think that may have been my father."

HUGO

"THIS IS GREAT, man. I'm happy for you."

I clap Clem Tanek on the shoulder.

He's just given me a tour of the work he is doing on the old fire hall. Already the place is filling with mostly new equipment and tools, since nearly all of his inventory was lost in the fire.

"Yeah. It's coming together nicely, and I have you to thank for it."

I snicker. "I just reminded you this place was vacant. That's all."

"Yeah, well, let me be grateful for once. It doesn't happen often," he adds jokingly.

I'd seen Nate's work truck and a few other contractor vehicles back here since I came back to work, and was curious to see what was going on. Clem explained he'd needed to upgrade the electrical, make some minor modifications to the floor plan, and slap on some fresh paint.

"Anybody here?"

A woman's voice drifts up the stairs where Clem was just showing me his new office.

"Up here!" Clem hollers, and to me he explains, "Real estate agent. I had some final paperwork to sign."

"Hey, Rowan," I greet the woman who pokes her head around the door post.

"Hugo, are you following me? Didn't we just talk this morning?" she teases with a grin. "You're gonna have to be patient; your listing won't be up for another couple of days."

"I know."

I gesture for her to take the vacant visitor chair.

"What, are you selling?" Clem wants to know.

"Bess and I are buying Phil's place."

"For real? You're gonna live in old man Colter's backyard? Voluntarily?"

He's kidding. I happen to know he plays poker with Brant Colter just about every Thursday night at The Kerrigan. I was invited to play a time or two years ago but, at the time, I didn't want to be in a situation where I'd be taking my boss's money. Of course, a lot has changed since then, but I've never really been big on gambling with my money. I had a kid to pay for and then, of course, came the hospital bills for Emily's care and treatments.

"It's far enough away, and we like the peace and quiet," I respond, as I get to my feet. "Well, I'll leave you two to it. I'll catch both of you later."

I just come walking out of one of the big bay doors when I catch sight of Bess, her hair flying behind her as she comes running across the station's parking lot.

"Whoa, what's the matter?"

She doesn't stop and runs straight into my arms.

"Jesus, Twinkie, what's going on?"

"I was looking for you at the station but Brenda said you were over here."

"Why were you looking for me?"

Guilty Silence

She leans back and looks up at me.

"I couldn't get away from the coffee shop until now, but I had the strangest visitor this morning."

Flags go up immediately.

"What do you mean, visitor?"

"His name is Peter Abel—at least that's what he calls himself, I googled and can't find anything about that name —and he's the guy who bought Phil's painting yesterday."

"Right, he was supposed to pick it up today."

"Yes, but he showed up early, and he said he knew my mom and the painting reminded him of her. I have to admit, I was a little freaked out, especially when he said he'd been keeping tabs on me, and he knew about my brother and the Lotus Squad, but then—"

"He what?" I cut off her ramble. "He kept tabs on you?"

"Yes, but I think he was making sure I was safe."

She grabs my forearms and leans in, deep blushes on her cheekbones and her eyes shining with excitement.

"And guess what? I think he may be my father."

Her father?

I press the heels of my hands against my eyebrows to stop the headache I feel building.

"I think you need to slow down and tell me from the beginning," I calmly suggest. "Let's sit down in my office."

I grab her hand and we walk to the station, where I rush Bess through the lobby and into my office, closing the door behind us.

Then she gives me the whole story from the beginning, handing me a white envelope at the end.

"He told me to give this to you and not open it, but I've been dying to know what's inside."

I'm pretty curious myself, and use my finger to rip open

the envelope. Inside I find what looks like a Polaroid picture and a plain sheet of paper.

I pull out the paper first and read the single line written on it in black ink.

To kill a two-headed snake both heads have to roll.

THEN I START REMOVING the Polaroid from the envelope, but as soon as I get a glimpse of the gruesome picture, I quickly shove it back inside.

"What is it?"

"A picture you don't want to see. Stay here, I have to get this to Rick Althof."

I snag the sheet of paper off my desk and press a kiss to the crown of Bess's head.

"I'll be right back."

Althof is at his desk in the bullpen, and when I catch his eye, he immediately gets to his feet. I lead him into the conference room and close the door behind him. In a few sentences I get him up to speed before handing him the envelope.

First, he pulls a pair of latex gloves from his jacket pocket, before taking the envelope. Then he spreads open the piece of paper and extracts the Polaroid, laying them both down on the table in front of him as he hisses between his teeth.

The image shows a man, lying on his back with several bullet wounds in his body. He's obviously dead, because his head was removed and placed on a blackened tire jack by the man's elbow.

"I'm willing to bet that's Mike Lee," Rick observes.

"I think so too," I agree, before adding. "And I'm pretty sure I know where that is."

"Yes, so do I."

"But," I continue, "I have Bess in my office, wondering what the hell was in that envelope, and I don't want her exposed to any of this. Not until we know for sure. She's been through enough."

He nods, grabs what will be filed as evidence off the table, and walks out of the room ahead of me. When he walks into the bullpen, I hear him call out orders.

"Androtti, Brenner, and Torres. You're with me."

Tessa Androtti is the first on her feet.

"Where are we going?"

"Downtown. To Main Street Mechanics, and put the coroner on standby."

CHAPTER 30

Hugo

"Nothing?"

I throw a dirty look at the kid zigzagging his bike all over the road when I finally manage to pass him. It's that I'm running really late already, otherwise I'd pull the punk over and write him a damn ticket.

"Nothing," Mancuso returns on the other end. "Peter Abel does not exist. The license plate you pulled from the traffic camera was off a different vehicle that was stolen from Kirksville, Missouri, in 2011. And we have no match for the prints pulled off the envelope you guys handed over."

"If he doesn't exist, then who the hell was that?"

It feels like we've been chasing our tails all week, trying to get any kind of traction on who showed up at Strange Brew carrying the picture of a dead man. The dead man was Mike Lee, at least that much has been confirmed. When or how his body ended up in the ruins of Clem's old auto shop, who the hell knows? But I'm having a hard time seeing how the slight, rather nondescript older gentleman Bess described could possibly be responsible for that.

"I have no idea, but the man is one slick operator," the agent observes.

True, and if he did pull this off by himself, he has to be packing some amazing skill and impressive strength, which makes me wonder...

"You reckon he's a pro? Maybe a spook?" I suggest. "It would explain why the man stayed in the shadows all of those years, and how he would've been able to keep tabs on Bess and her mother."

"That makes sense, if he is a CIA agent, it would explain why we can't find him. I can put out a few feelers, but I'm pretty sure this is going to be a dead-end street."

To say I'm frustrated is an understatement, but at least it would appear there is no longer any possible threat to Bess, and for that I'm grateful.

Speak of the devil, the screen on my dashboard shows an incoming call from her.

"Mancuso, I've gotta go. We'll touch base later. I've got another call coming in."

"Wish the happy couple Godspeed from me."

"Will do."

I hang up and immediately answer the incoming call.

"Hey, honey."

"Where are you?"

Bess has a tell; when she is stressed or anxious, her voice rises in pitch.

"I'm about seven minutes out."

"Do you have the cakes?"

I glance over my shoulder where Lola has expertly stabilized the boxes with the three tiers of the wedding cake Bess worked on for two days straight.

"I do, and you'll be glad to know they're still in one piece."

"Oh my God, don't even joke about that."

"Relax. I'll get them there unharmed. I'll see you shortly."

"I'll be waiting."

As promised, she is standing in front of The Carriage House, directing me around the side of the main building. She's still in the casual clothes she left home in, but someone did her hair, piling it artfully on her head in a mass of curls and some flowers, and her beautiful features are enhanced with makeup.

"You look gorgeous," I tell her, getting out of the truck.

But when I reach for her, she sidesteps me.

"No kissing, or all of this..." She waves her hand around her face. "...will have to be redone, and there is no time for that. We're already running late."

That last comment comes with a pointed look for me.

"Hey, you told me to be here at one, and it's one on the dot."

Pulling open the back door, I carefully unwrap the towels and blankets Lola put around the cake boxes.

"Yeah, but I was expecting you to be here maybe ten minutes early," Bess returns, reaching past me into the truck to grab one of the boxes.

For sure that's what Bess would do; be five or ten minutes early to a scheduled appointment. Not me, when I have to be somewhere at a certain time, I'm there with barely a minute's margin on either side.

"Why would you expect me early? If you wanted me

here ten minutes early, you should've told me to come at twelve fifty," I suggest, grabbing the next box.

Then I follow her into a side door that leads to a large kitchen, about twice the size of the one at Strange Brew.

"Or..." Bess returns, as she slides her box on a long, stainless steel work station in the center of the space. "You could just come ten minutes early when you know that's what I mean."

I'm tempted to point out how irrational that is, but this is a silly argument that can go around in circles forever. As much as her point doesn't make any common sense to me, it doesn't cost me anything to mentally subtract ten minutes whenever she gives me a specific time. It will take less energy than perpetuating a recurring argument.

I slide my box next to hers and then crook my finger.

"Come here."

"I can't, I still have to get the third box and get this cake assembled."

"One kiss," I plead. "I'll grab the last cake from the truck, *and* I promise to try and be ten minutes early next time."

She capitulates, but does it with a little triumphant smile on her expertly painted lips. Minx.

Careful not to mess up her hair—I look forward to doing that later—I pull her close and curve my hand around the side of her neck as I drop a kiss on her shimmery mouth, my eyes locked on hers.

"I'm sorry if I'm snippy, I'm a little frazzled," she admits, when I let her go and head for the door.

"That's okay," I return over my shoulder. "I'm already looking forward to unfrazzling you tonight."

Her sweet laughter follows me out the door.

Bess

She's beautiful.

The simple cream-colored, satin sheath dress looks stunning on her, not quite hiding the swell of her belly, but not highlighting it either.

Savvy wanted her hair loose, mostly because she almost always has it up in a ponytail or tucked under a baseball cap, and for today she wanted to be as far from her normal tomboyish looks as possible. Her curls are flowing free, just brushing the tops of her bare shoulders.

I think she surprised even Nate, who can't seem to stop smiling at her like he can't believe his luck.

He's dressed in black dress pants and a black dress shirt, with the collar undone and the sleeves rolled halfway up his forearms.

They wanted it casual, but somehow, seeing them dance together under the twinkling lights out on the patio, they look like a movie star couple.

This whole day was perfect, and I'm glad now that my duties are over, I'm able to relax and reminisce.

I even ended up liking the dress Savvy forced on me to wear. It's also simple, but mine is a burgundy satin; the bodice is formfitting with little cap sleeves, and the slightly flared skirt stops just at my knees.

I was proud to stand beside her as they exchanged their vows. Unreservedly happy for them. Each time my eyes would drift the crowd to land on Hugo's blue ones, and I recognized the love in them, I felt happy for me too.

I guess it's true what they say, *happiness breeds happiness.*

Glancing around The Carriage House patio, I see evidence of that everywhere; Jim Turcotte, one of our EMTs, gently leading Mrs. Dixon around the floor; Tatum with her head on Carson's shoulder, swaying in place with their arms around each other; Phil laughing as she tries to coax her husband into dancing with her; and Buck Wilson showing off his skills as he twirls Bonnie Sadlowski around; and I even spot Tessa Androtti, the newest addition to the sheriff's department, dragging Clem Tanek from the man-huddle he was hiding in and onto the dance floor. Talk about an unlikely pairing, that'll be an interesting dynamic to watch.

But the moment I catch sight of Hugo, stepping out of the shadows and onto the patio, I only have eyes for him.

He stops in the middle of the dance floor—like a towering Viking, oblivious to anything or anyone but me—and simply holds out his hand.

Not that long ago, I might have wondered about that gesture, questioned if it was directed at me, scrutinized its possible meaning, or doubted its intention, but that's not me anymore.

Tonight, I get to my feet, smooth the wrinkles from my skirt, and move confidently to join the man I love on the dance floor.

"I may be a bit rusty," said man mumbles as I fold myself in his arms.

I beam a smile up at him in response, because I don't care if he tramples my feet. This is another one of my secret dreams fulfilled, and he doesn't even know he's decimating my list.

"Good day?" he asks, when we've found our rhythm.

Turns out he's not bad at all, quite limber on his feet for such a large man.

"The absolute best," I give him, settling my cheek against the lapel of his jacket.

"I'm glad to hear it, but I'm hoping I can make it even better."

I tilt my head back to look up at him.

"Better?"

Quite uncharacteristically, he bites his lip and does a quick glance around us. Almost as if he is nervous.

"Slip your hand in my inside pocket, Bess."

Confused, I tilt my head, but he urges me on with a nod. It takes me a moment to figure out the inside pocket is on his left, so my right, but as soon as my fingers slide in and encounter something, my feet stop moving.

Hugo's eyes are my anchor as my ears start ringing and my knees nearly buckle. But he stands firm, unwavering like a tree, and his voice is soft but strong.

"I have a question for you."

My heart starts beating in my throat, and I don't think I could swallow if I tried as he leans his forehead to mine before he continues.

"I could give you every reason under the sun, but I'd rather save them so I can remind you each day of the rest of our lives why I want you to share yours with me. Marry me, Bess."

I knew it the moment my fingers touched the delicate band of the ring he had tucked inside his pocket, but am still too afraid to believe it.

With our foreheads still touching, I can do little more than nod as I close my fingers around the ring, but it's enough for him. The moment I free my hand from his jacket, he reaches between us and takes the ring from me and, enveloped in our makeshift cocoon, we both look down as he slips it on my finger.

The next moment I'm back in his arms, swaying to the

music as if nothing at all just happened. Except it had, and it was momentous and absolutely perfect. In the presence of everyone we care about, yet just for us.

Except perhaps Savvy...she shoots me a wink when we dance by.

EPILOGUE

H*ugo*

"See?"

I nudge Tessa Androtti with an elbow.

We're standing at the edge of the new deck Nate helped me build out here over the summer. It's a party deck, as Bess calls it.

As it turns out, our house has become the hub for several cookouts already, and Bess loves it. It shouldn't be a surprise she loves entertaining and feeding friends, she built a business on it, and this place, out of the way of neighbors and busy streets, is perfect for it.

It's a great spot with lots of options for outdoor activities. In the spring and early summer, when the water was high, you could hop on an inner tube right out back, and float all the way down to town. All year round, there are plenty of trails to hike, and there are always fish in the creek.

Right now, the Chinook salmon are starting to run. It's not quite spawning season yet, that won't start until probably mid-October, but we've seen a good number come up the creek already. Of course, Carson is out there standing ankle-deep in the creek, tossing his line in the deepest part where the water still has some speed to it. With him are Tatum—she's rarely far from his side—and both Remi and Linc, Tessa's boys who have developed an interest in fishing the couple of times they've been here.

"Yeah, you told me," Tessa acknowledges with a grin. "I'd hoped and prayed I was making the right decision, but I was coming in blind."

"And now?" I probe.

"I'm good. It's all good. As far as they'll share with me, the boys seem to like the school—at least, I haven't heard any complaints on the subject yet—and I'm getting in a groove at work, and we all love our new house."

Ironically, my old house is Tessa's new one.

When she first came to town in the spring she was renting an apartment, but that got small in a real hurry with those two boys of hers. She started looking to buy, and happened upon my house, which had just been listed. Three bedrooms, open concept, rec room in the basement, a big garage for sports gear, bikes, and stuff, and a driveway that could handle two, even three vehicles in a pinch.

I had no idea she was the buyer until I signed off on the real estate paperwork and caught her name.

"I'm glad," I tell her truthfully.

Then I catch Clem waving me over to the barrel grill he made for me.

"Looks like I'm needed."

"Right," Tessa curtly responds as she tosses an angry glance in Clem's direction.

Not sure what that's all about, but I'm not about to wade in. Instead, I offer, "Can I send over another drink? Something stronger maybe?"

"I'm good with this." She holds up her bottle of iced tea. "Thanks though."

I flash her a smile and head over to the grill.

"What's up?" I ask Clem. "Burgers done?"

"Not yet, but you may wanna check on your boss."

I follow his line of sight to Savvy, who I can just see around the side of the house, leaning with her arm braced under her head against the brick. Her other arm looks to be holding up her substantial stomach.

Oh boy.

I look around to find Nate, only to remember he and his best man, Roy, went out on one of the trails where Carson had found some bear tracks last week to check them out.

Shit.

Ducking under the railing, I drop down from the deck and make my way over, hearing a worrisome groan when I close in on her.

"When did it start?"

She slightly turns her head to look at me.

"When my water broke five minutes ago. They're... ahhhh..."

She sags through her knees and I quickly take up position behind her, hooking my arms under hers so she doesn't hit the ground.

When the contraction passes, I ask, "And why are you standing here?"

"Because I look like I pissed my pants and I didn't want to draw attention. I'm just waiting here for Nate; he's not answering his phone—probably left it in the damn truck again—but I'm sure he'll be back soon. Ahhhh..."

She's immediately hit with another one, and I'm no doctor, but from the sounds she's making it sure looks like that baby is closer than she might think.

"There you are," Bess's voice sounds behind me. "What are you...Savvy? What's going on? Is she in labor?"

"She doesn't want to make a fuss," I quickly share, before Bess alerts a crowd. "Could you quietly alert Dana and then get my truck started? I'll bring her around the side."

I give Savvy a chance to field another contraction before I decidedly lift her up in my arms and start carrying her around to the front.

"I can walk, you know," she grumbles, hanging on to my neck.

"On those shaky legs? You'd drop that baby on the pavers before you even reached the front of the house."

To my relief, Dana is already waiting, with a medical kit I'm sure she got from her car slung around her shoulder.

I wince when Savvy's fingers almost pull out the small hairs at the back of my neck when another wave hits her.

Dana's eyes flash to mine when Savvy makes that low groaning sound.

"That's close. Bess and I will get in the back seat with her. You drive," she orders, taking charge immediately.

As soon as we start moving, I make a quick call to Clem, and explain what's happening.

"Call Carson over, tell him to go look for Nate immediately. Nate's gonna have to fucking hustle."

All I get in response is, "On it," and then the line goes dead.

"He'd better hurry!" Savvy yells from the back seat.

When I glance in my rearview mirror, all I see is Savvy's legs up in the air, and I quickly snap my eyes to the front, relieved I'm the one driving.

Bess

Hugo jumps to his feet when I walk out into the waiting area.

He reads the wide smile on my face correctly.

"Already?"

I can understand his surprise, it wasn't half an hour ago he hustled a frantic Nate into the room. Not a minute too soon either, since Savvy had been working hard all the way here to stop this baby from being born before its daddy got here, but had fast been losing the battle.

"Magnus Brant Gaines, eight pounds, four ounces, with all his fingers and toes."

"Wow, that baby was in a hurry. That's amazing."

What was amazing was Savvy begging me to stay, and having the privilege to witness that little miracle being born.

Suddenly overwhelmed with emotions I'd barely been able to keep in check as I watched Nate and Savvy greet their son, I do a face plant in Hugo's chest.

He rubs my back and kisses the top of my head, giving me a chance to pull myself together.

"Where are the kids?" I ask a few moments later.

Nate mentioned Tate came with him, and Carson had driven them.

"Carson went to pick up something to eat because, of course, he was hungry, and they missed out on the burgers at home, and Tate just went to the bathroom."

As if on cue, the girl emerges from the hallway on the far side of the lobby where the restrooms are.

"And?" she asks when she reaches us.

"Go look," I prompt her with a smile. "Someone's in there waiting to meet you."

Tate squeals and darts past me.

"What about Brant and Phil?" Hugo inquires.

I'd invited them to the cookout tonight, but Phil mentioned she was planning to surprise Brant with dinner and a drag show in Spokane today. I had to laugh so hard when Phil said she was simply helping him broaden his horizons. I would give anything to see the look on his face.

"Savvy's going to call them herself. I'm actually surprised the rest of the town isn't here waiting for news."

"I talked to Clem just now," Hugo enlightens me as he pulls me down in the chair beside him. "Once Nate tore out of there, everyone pretty much clued in to what was going on, so he kept them busy and turned it into a welcome baby party. They're drinking our booze and eating our food while placing bets on time, weight, and gender, and waiting to get the news."

That would explain why it's just us here.

"They were going to drink our booze and eat our food anyway," I point out.

"True enough."

Hugo pulls me closer, his arm around my shoulders as his hand rubs my biceps.

"How are *you*?"

I hear a touch of concern in his voice and I know what he's asking.

"I'm good. I'm so grateful I got to witness that. It's an experience I'll never forget. I feel blessed."

"Hmm," he hums, resting his cheek on top of my head. "I'm glad."

That's how Carson finds us five minutes later, when he

walks in with three paper bags from the Bread & Butter Diner.

"Geeze, Buddy. How hungry are you?" Hugo scoffs.

"Not just for me, I figured everyone would be hungry."

What a great kid he is.

He sets the food on the small coffee table and drops down in a chair on the other side, digging up a burger. Only after his first bite, he clues in his girlfriend isn't here.

"Where's Tate?"

I can't hold back a chuckle, it's so typical.

"In the room to greet her brother," Hugo informs him matter-of-factly.

"Shit, already? I'm glad it's a boy, that's what Tate was hoping for."

A seriously great kid.

I lean back and glance up at Hugo, who is also looking at his son, that little half smile showing his pride.

Yeah…I'm blessed beyond belief.

Tessa

"Mo-om! Remi's been in there for half an hour. I've gotta get ready!"

I swear I'm about to start drinking and it's not even eight in the morning.

Love my kids, but they sure wear me down.

"Use my bathroom, Linc," I yell up the stairs.

I'm not sure what's gotten into my youngest boy, Remi, recently. A few months ago, it would've been a chore to get him to brush his teeth or, God forbid, have the occasional shower, but lately he's been spending a lot of time in there.

Must be a girl. It was the same for his older brother, Lincoln, who went from looking like Pigpen and reeking like a gym locker most of the time, to clean-clothed and smelling fresh. Maybe a little heavy on the Axe, but definitely better than the scent of dirty socks.

Remi wasn't quite that bad—he's not into sports and athletics like his brother—but I was still relieved when he voluntarily took a shower a few weeks ago without me badgering him. I made the mistake of asking him what had prompted it—forgetting the unspoken parenting rule to never point out the desired behavior—and got my head bitten off in response.

Still, I'm focusing on the silver lining. For the first time since puberty hit our house years ago, I can breathe freely again. Offering up what I've come to treasure as my personal sanctuary for the sake of peace in the house is a small sacrifice.

Maybe now I can have five quiet minutes for my coffee to take effect. Grabbing my mug, I head out the back door to the deck.

It's a little chilly, but the cool air on my skin wakes me up and sharpens my senses. I love this time of day, everything smells fresh and full of promise, and this view is nothing to sneeze at. It's one of the things that sold me on this house. It's a much bigger place than we had in Spokane, and for less money, which is always a bonus. This is a quiet neighborhood on the edge of town, with mostly unspoiled nature at our back. I loved the idea of my boys having all this space with direct access to the outdoors. Heck, I'd even hoped it might spark some interest in Remi, who has been struggling to find his niche, but so far he's persisted in his displeasure to have been forced to move here.

I hate to label him as such, but Remi is my worry child. He seems so rudderless, compared to his older brother, who has always been so clear in his purpose. Linc is a typical jock, with a focus on athletic performance first, girls a close second, and last, but not least, his grades. Despite some of the family shit that went on in his younger years, before I divorced his father, he seems to skate his way through life.

It has to be tough for Remi to grow up in the shadow of his older brother, and I've tried to help him find his own light to shine in, but still my baby struggles.

"Ma!"

I tilt my head back to see my youngest poking his head out of his bedroom window.

"I need a ride."

"Why can't you go with Linc?"

Lincoln worked part-time jobs since he turned fifteen with the sole purpose of saving money to buy his own car. He is now the proud owner of an older Jeep Wrangler, rather beaten up, but running in good order.

"He's picking up Naomi."

Aha. These past few years, my eldest is never without

female companionship for long, and once school started last month, it didn't take more than a week for me to start hearing the name Naomi pop up.

Linc has picked her up for school a few times before, and I guess he told his brother to get in the back seat, so Naomi could sit in front beside him. Remi doesn't like to be a third wheel. I can see both their points, but I don't have the energy to try and negotiate a compromise this morning. I have a ton of work waiting for me back at the station and can't afford to be late.

Luckily the high school is just a few blocks from the office.

"You'd better hustle, because I'm leaving in—" I quickly check my watch. "Three minutes."

Once we are on our way into town, I look over at Remi, who is slumped in the passenger seat beside me, his head turned to the side window in a clear attempt to avoid any and all conversation. I'm his mom, so fat chance of that.

"Bud, happy as I am you're spending more time in the bathroom, you've gotta leave time for your brother to get ready."

A snort is my only answer.

"Hey," I voice a little sharper. "Don't give me attitude, when I'm doing you a favor by dropping you off at school. All I'm asking is for you to be considerate, that's all."

"Yeah, whatever."

I clench my jaw, resisting the urge to react to his disengaged response. I swear I can feel another gray hair sprouting every damn time we have one of these interactions.

Pushing him is only going to ramp up the tension in my vehicle, so I opt to let it go. Raising teenagers is like walking a minefield on a day-to-day basis.

I feel a little guilty at the relieved breath escaping me a few minutes later, when he darts out the passenger side door without a word, the moment I stop in front of his school.

Despite the coffee I had at home, I already feel like I need a damn nap. It's been another restless night, constant worry about Remi keeping me awake, so the moment I walk into the station, I make a beeline for the dark sludge passing for coffee in the kitchen. It doesn't taste great, but it sure packs the kind of punch I need this morning.

Brenda, the sheriff department's office manager, is just coming out.

"Mornin'," she returns my mumbled greeting as she cocks her thumb over her shoulder. "Fresh pot in there."

"Bless your heart."

I slip past her and inhale the fumes as I grab one of the department mugs off the shelf and fill it. I take my first sip before I turn around to find Brenda leaning against the doorway, her head tilted to one side as she scrutinizes me.

"Tough morning?"

Instantly my hand goes to my hair, which is already escaping the messy knot I turned it into after my shower.

"Is it that obvious?"

She grins. "You forget, I've got a couple of boys too; I recognize the look of exasperation on your face. Pretty sure I've worn that same expression from time to time."

That's right, I knew she had boys. I've been preoccupied getting us settled in, the boys ready for school, and myself up to speed at work, I haven't really had the time to connect with people on a more personal level. Maybe that's what I need for a better balance in my life.

"Exasperation, huh? Guess that describes my state pretty

accurately this morning," I return. "Any tips or suggestions are welcome; maybe over drinks some time?"

"Friday night my husband is taking the boys to Spokane to see the new Marvel movie on the big screen. Why don't you pop by? I've got a fully stocked bar," she adds with a wink.

"Sounds tempting," I admit. "Let me check in with my hoodlums to see what they have going on that night."

"Yeah, of course. See if it works."

She starts walking away before she stops and turns.

"Oh, before I forget, I sent a copy of the forensics report you were waiting for to your email. It must've come in late last night."

Finally.

About two weeks ago a local hunter stumbled onto what looked to be a brand-new Ford Mustang, abandoned on one of the old logging roads heading up Black Mountain. The vehicle had been intentionally covered with brush—clearly intended to hide it from view—and when the hunter peered inside the window and noticed the passenger seat covered in blood, he immediately contacted us.

Judging from the sheer volume of blood, it looked like someone bled out in that vehicle, but we found no evidence of a body, just a few smeared prints on the inside of the door. A VIN search on the Mustang came back to a stolen vehicle from the upscale Spokane neighborhood of Rockwood. A blood test confirmed the blood to be human, but who it might have belonged to, as well as the whereabouts of the victim, has remained a mystery.

Hoping the forensics report will give me some guidance on this damn case I've been spinning my wheels on these past weeks, I rush to my desk.

· · ·

*****

CLEM

"Go home, Kyle. I'll finish it up."

As glad as I am the new, young mechanic I hired on after reopening the garage does not seem averse to working longer hours, it's already been a long-ass day and I'm fucking starving.

"You sure?" the scrawny, redheaded kid asks, poking his head out from under the hood of the Infinity he's working on.

"Yep. Get out of here, it's Friday night. I'll see you in the morning."

Tomorrow will be a busy day, but Manuel should be back, so there will be three of us to tackle the work. Manuel had a rare few days off to visit his ailing mother. One of only a few times he asked for time off since he started working for me over ten years ago.

Anyway, we'll be at full strength tomorrow and should hopefully be able to clear out the back lot before next week.

I follow Kyle to the front and lower the massive bay door behind him, locking myself in for the night.

When fire leveled the old auto shop—which had been in the family for generations—I wasn't sure I'd have the heart or drive to rebuild Main Street Mechanics from the ground. It would've taken a year at least, during which time I wouldn't have had an income and I'd likely have lost most of my customers in the interim. Aside from that, the business had already outgrown the shop, and there wasn't a large enough real estate footprint to build anything bigger.

Repurposing the old fire hall had been at the suggestion of Hugo Alexander, Edwards County Deputy Sheriff, who is a buddy of mine. The place had sat vacant since they built the large new fire station on the outskirts of Silence. It had taken a bit of negotiating and working out a bit of creative financing, but I was able to buy it and set up shop here.

Turning the lights off in the shop—I'll come back down later to finish replacing the hoses on that Infinity—I head up the open stairway to the second level and aim straight for the spacious open kitchen and the cold beer in my fridge.

Originally, the upper level had housed the living and sleeping quarters for the fire crew but, with some minor renovations, I'd turned it into a comfortable apartment for myself.

The insurance check I'd received for the old place hadn't been enough to cover the cost of the fire hall, so I ended up selling the small house I'd called home for fifteen or so years to make up the difference. I didn't really have any emotional connection to the house anyway—the shop was my home and I spent the bulk of my time there—but it had been somewhere to lay my head at night.

With the extra money I was able to make a few adjustments to this upper floor, and already it feels more like a home than the house ever did. Although I suspect the smell of motor oil that follows me up here has a little something to do with that.

Along with a beer, I pull a block of cheese from the fridge, cutting off a chunk to tide me over until I can get some dinner together. I'm thinking I'll cut up some vegetables and a couple of those spicy sausages I picked up, and toss them on a baking tray in the oven. They can cook while I drink my beer and watch the news.

I've been trying to watch what I eat. I never took the time

to cook much before, just popped in a freezer meal in the microwave or stopped in at the diner for something greasy. It showed in the gut I'd been steadily growing since I hit my forties. Then right after the fire, I went in to see the new doc for a checkup. The guy warned me that with my high cholesterol and blood pressure, I was heading for a heart attack unless I started living healthier. Seeing as my father dropped dead from a heart attack when he was just a few years older, I took the warning and made some changes.

A lot has changed this past year and though I'm not normally a fan of changes, I feel I've landed in a pretty good place. My business is steady, my health is better, I've got my friends, my Thursday night poker game, and a kick-ass place that feels like a home to put my feet up at the end of the day. What else do you need?

After finishing up the dishes forty-five minutes later, I briefly consider leaving the Infinity until the morning, but end up heading back downstairs anyway.

The moment I flick on the bright overhead lights in the garage, I hear some noise out back. A metallic clang, like something bumping the lid of the garbage container out there. Maybe I startled something rummaging through the trash, it wouldn't be the first time. It's not unheard of for wildlife to venture into town, looking for an easy meal at this time of year.

Grabbing a large wrench from the tool bench—I'm not about to potentially face off with a hungry bear empty-handed—I head toward the regular back exit next to the large bay door. Unlocking it, I ease it open, poking my head out.

At first I don't see anything. Nothing seems out of place in the back lot where we park vehicles still to be worked on and those waiting for owners to pick them up. In the light escaping from the glass panes at the top of the large rolling door, I spot no bears, or any other creatures for that matter, hanging out by the dumpster.

But when I step outside, letting the door fall shut behind me, I can hear the sound of something scraping the gravel surface to my left. Swinging my head around, I just catch a glimpse of a red sneaker disappearing under the frame of the Jeep Patriot Tim Saunders dropped off for an oil change and fluid top up earlier this afternoon.

I slip my hand in my pocket to pull out my cell phone and turn on its flashlight as I duck down, shining it under the vehicle.

"Get your ass out from under there," I bark at the wide-eyed teenager looking back at me. "Trust me, kid, you don't want my fucking help."

Wisely, the boy crawls out and scrambles to his feet. It takes me only a second to realize who it is.

Well, shit.

Then I quickly scan the Jeep, noticing a hack saw as well as a familiar part lying on the ground beside the vehicle.

"Really, kid? Surely you can find better things to do than pulling catalytic converters from vehicles a stone's throw away from the sheriff's station."

"I wasn't...I didn't..." the punk stammers before snapping his mouth shut.

He realizes there is no denying with the evidence basically lying at his feet. I can see his eyes dart left and right, looking for the fastest escape route.

"I'm thinking your mom won't be too pleased when I call it in."

His mother being the sheriff's office most recent addition, Tessa Androtti. I recognize her boy from a cookout at

Bess and Hugo's place, at the end of the summer, they were at.

"Please don't," the kid pleads, and in that moment I see the vulnerable boy instead of the criminal teenager.

Fuck. Those big puppy dog eyes are getting to me, making me feel like a goddamn monster for even considering turning him in.

"How many?" I snap at him.

"What do you mean?" he returns, looking confused.

"Catalytic converters. How many did you drop?"

He indicates a white Ford F-150 a few spots down.

"That one too," he admits.

Dammit. It'll take up valuable time to install each of those again, adding to an already full workload for tomorrow.

"Do you know how much work it's gonna be to fix those?"

It's more of a rhetorical question, I don't actually expect an answer, but the kid gives me one anyway.

"With the right tools, probably a couple of hours each."

I regard him with a lifted eyebrow. "And you would know what the right tools are?"

This time he shrugs. "It's not that hard."

There's something about his casual arrogance that reminds me of myself, thirty years ago. I decide to call his bluff.

"Well, in that case, I want your ass back here tomorrow morning at eight on the dot, and you can put your money where your mouth is."

Now he looks shocked.

"You mean, I can go?"

I wag a finger in his face. "But if you're not here at eight, I will personally walk over to the sheriff's station and file charges. Right after I have a nice long talk with your mother," I threaten.

As I watch the kid take off on his red sneakers, I realize this may not have been the wisest move on my part. But the boy doesn't strike me as a hardcore criminal. If I'd venture a guess, he's—at worst—a misguided kid who is heading down the wrong path. I was that kid once, before my dad put me to work in the shop.

Who knows, maybe a little redirection of that energy, and some honing of what appears to be a passing interest in cars, will set the boy on the straight and narrow.

I'm just not sure how his mother will respond when she finds out.

I don't think she likes me much.

UP NEXT ARE TESSA AND CLEM IN COLD SILENCE.
GET YOUR COPY HERE.

ALSO BY FREYA BARKER

SILENCE
FINDING SILENCE
INSIDE SILENCE

HMT 2G:
HIGH FREQUENCY
HIGH INTENSITY
HIGH DENSITY
HIGH VELOCITY (2025)

High Mountain Trackers:
HIGH MEADOW
HIGH STAKES
HIGH GROUND
HIGH IMPACT

Arrow's Edge MC Series:
EDGE OF REASON
EDGE OF DARKNESS
EDGE OF TOMORROW
EDGE OF FEAR

EDGE OF REALITY

EDGE OF TRUST

EDGE OF NOWHERE

GEM Series:

OPAL

PEARL

ONYX

PASS Series:

HIT & RUN

LIFE & LIMB

LOCK & LOAD

LOST & FOUND

On Call Series:

BURNING FOR AUTUMN

COVERING OLLIE

TRACKING TAHLULA

ABSOLVING BLUE

REVEALING ANNIE

DISSECTING MEREDITH

WATCHING TRIN

IGNITING VIC

CAPTIVATING ANIKA

Rock Point Series:

KEEPING 6

CABIN 12

HWY 550

10-CODE

Northern Lights Collection:

A CHANGE OF TIDE

A CHANGE OF VIEW

A CHANGE OF PACE

SnapShot Series:

SHUTTER SPEED

FREEZE FRAME

IDEAL IMAGE

Portland, ME, Series:

FROM DUST

CRUEL WATER

THROUGH FIRE

STILL AIR

LuLLaY (a Christmas novella)

Cedar Tree Series:

SLIM TO NONE

HUNDRED TO ONE

AGAINST ME

CLEAN LINES

UPPER HAND

LIKE ARROWS

HEAD START

Standalones:

WHEN HOPE ENDS

VICTIM OF CIRCUMSTANCE

BONUS KISSES

SECONDS

SNOWBOUND

ABOUT THE AUTHOR

USA Today bestselling author Freya Barker loves writing about ordinary people with extraordinary stories. With 60+ titles to her name, Freya inspires with her stories about 'real' people, perhaps less than perfect, each struggling to find their own slice of happy.

Freya has her hands full with a retired husband, a needy pup, and a growing gaggle of grandbabies, but she continues to spin story after story with an endless supply of bruised and dented characters, vying for attention!

Recipient of the ReadFREE.ly 2019 Best Book We've Read All Year Award for "Covering Ollie, the 2015 RomCon "Reader's Choice" Award for Best First Book, "Slim To None", Finalist for the 2017 Kindle Book Award with "From Dust", and Finalist for the 2020 Kindle Book Award with "When Hope Ends", Freya spins story after story with an endless supply of bruised and dented characters, vying for attention!

www.freyabarker.com

www.ingramcontent.com/pod-product-compliance
Lightning Source LLC
Chambersburg PA
CBHW061029090226
39369CB00017B/202